Edge of

C000108673

H.L Day

Other books by H.L Day

Time for a Change

A Temporary Situation

Kept in the Dark

Refuge (Fight for Survival #1)

Taking Love's Lead

Copyright

Cover Art by H.L Day

Edited by Pam Ebeler at Undivided Editing
http://www.undividedediting.com/

Proofread by Judy Zweifel at Judy's Proofreading
http://www.judysproofreading.com/

Edge of Living © 2018 H.L Day

Warning

Intended for an 18+ audience. This book contains material that may
be offensive to some and is intended for a mature, adult audience. It
contains graphic language, explicit sexual content, and adult situations.

Blurb

Sometimes, death can feel like the only escape.

It's been a year since Alex stopped living. He exists. He breathes. He pretends to be like everyone else. But, he doesn't live. Burdened by memories, he dreams of the day when he can finally be free. Until that time comes, he keeps everybody at bay. It's been easy so far. But he never factored in, meeting a man like Austin.

Hard-working mechanic Austin has always gone for men as muscular as himself. So, it's a mystery why he's so bewitched by the slim, quiet man with the soulful brown eyes who works in the library. The magnetic attraction is one thing, but the protective instincts are harder to fathom. Austin's sure though, that if he can only earn Alex's trust then the two of them could be perfect together.

A tentative relationship begins. But Alex's secrets run deep. Far deeper than Austin could ever envisage. Time is ticking. Events are coming to a head, and love is never a magic cure. Oblivious to the extent of Alex's pain, can Austin discover the truth? Or is he destined to be left alone, only able to piece together the fragments of his boyfriend's history, once its already too late?

Trigger warning: Please be aware that this story deals with suicidal ideation. If this is a subject you find uncomfortable, then I would not recommend you reading this book.

CONTENTS

Prologue 1

Chapter One 4

Chapter Two...11

Chapter Three..19

Chapter Four 29

Chapter Five 36

Chapter Six..44

Chapter Seven 55

Chapter Eight 62

Chapter Nine 67

Chapter Ten 72

Chapter Eleven..80

Chapter Twelve..87

Chapter Thirteen 97

Chapter Fourteen 106

Chapter Fifteen...118

Chapter Sixteen 125

Chapter Seventeen 136

Chapter Eighteen 142

Chapter Nineteen..157

Chapter Twenty 164

Chapter Twenty-one..172

Chapter Twenty-two 179

Chapter Twenty-three 189

Chapter Twenty-four..201

Chapter Twenty-five 208

Chapter Twenty-six 220

Chapter Twenty-seven 226

Chapter Twenty-eight 235

Epilogue 244

Thanks, from H.L Day..253

About H.L Day 253

Finding H.L Day 254

More books from H.L Day..255

Acknowledgements

Thank you to the beta readers: Jill, Fiona, and Kayleigh. for their feedback on this book:

A special thank you to:

Barbara for spotting all of the places where the legal information needed tweaking.

Bryoney for carrying out a sensitivity read and giving feedback on the trauma aspects of the story.

Prologue

Sometimes it feels as if my body split into fragments a year ago. Large, jagged ones with bone-sharp edges. Those fragments joined back together, so that anyone looking at me wouldn't be able to see the difference. Not unless they looked too closely. Then they might be able to see the cracks. The ones that radiate out from my heart and cover every inch of my body. They get bigger with every month that passes. Deeper. More pronounced.

There's a simple solution: I don't let anybody get that close. I make sure to keep them at arm's length. Anything to stop them from seeing the emptiness that has filled up every atom of my body. If they see it, they'll ask questions. Questions I can't answer. Questions I won't answer. One of those questions might just be the thing that pushes me over the edge of the fine line of sanity I've been desperately clinging to.

How do I get through the day without people noticing I'm a mere shadow of a person? I copy people. Copy their normality because I can't remember what it feels like anymore; it's been way too long since I experienced it. I watch people. I borrow their mannerisms. I borrow their smiles and their laughter, and use them as emotional armor. I do what's expected of me. I say what's

1

expected of me. I'm sure my act's not perfect, but it's enough. Enough to make people leave me alone. Enough to convince them that I'm just like them. Maybe a bit quieter. Maybe a little less social. But, nothing more than an introvert. They have no idea what's going on inside my head.

I walk to the edge of the cliff and peer over it, down to the raging sea below. The tide's in so the sea's crashing against the base of the cliff, each wave throwing up a torrent of spray. There's nothing between me and the edge. No railing. No deterrent to stop me from throwing myself over. Hundreds of people have done just that in this very spot. A few every year. Sometimes more. It's what makes Beachy Head famous. Tourists come from all over the world to die here. It used to strike me as absurd. Now, I understand it.

Turning my face up to the rain, I close my eyes and allow myself the luxury of imagining what it will be like. I picture the fall through the air; the rush of the wind; the feeling of my limbs tumbling over and over out of control; the inability to stop it even if I did change my mind. But most of all, I imagine the release it will bring; the delicious feeling of numbness; the escape. I imagine how the fragments of my body will finally get the chance to break apart like they're nothing more than dust particles. They'll float away on the waves, carried away to the four corners of the earth. I think about the blessed feeling of nothingness that will follow, my soul completely given up to the sea. It will be beautiful. No more pain. No more fear. No more guilt. No more nightmares. No more nothing.

Reluctantly, I open my eyes, the driving rain running in rivulets down my face as my body automatically leans forward toward the cliff's edge, begging me to let go. I muster all my energy, or what little I have left anyway, and manage to stagger back a few steps. I check for observers, anyone who might report my behavior as unusual. But, there's no one. I'm all alone. Only an

2

idiot would venture out onto a clifftop in weather like this. The temptation to step forward again pulls at every atom of my being and I squash it down, burying it back inside as deeply as I can.

Not today.

I've made promises. Only to myself. But, I intend to keep them. There are things I need to do. Things I need to see. But, the time's growing closer. At least I have that to hold on to. My body is suddenly wracked by shivers. Away from the siren song of the sea, reality comes crashing back and I regain the ability to feel cold. It's not surprising. My clothes are soaked through. My teeth are chattering so loudly that if there were anyone else around, they'd be able to hear them.

I look down at my hands. They're almost blue; my fingers so numb, I can barely feel them. Stupid, really. I should have worn gloves. I knew today wasn't going to be the day. Sometimes, it's hard though, to remember what I need to do to keep myself alive when all I want to do is die. I force my freezing hands into the pockets of my thin jacket. It offers very little respite when my jacket's so wet.

I turn away and force my legs to move even farther from the cliff edge. I have a long walk back to the train station in Eastbourne, and an even longer train journey back to London. I sneeze, and pray it's not a sign I'm going to get ill. I don't need that on top of everything else.

With one last longing glance at the edge of the cliff, I walk away. My next visit here should be the last: the time when I can finally let go and be free. A smile crosses my face at the realization. Ironic really, that the thought of death is the only thing that can make me happy.

Chapter One

Austin

Libraries aren't my usual haunt. In fact, before this week I'd have been hard-pressed to recall when the last time I'd set foot in one might have been. Was it when I was at school? I had a vague memory of my entire class visiting when I must have been about five or six. Certainly, no older than seven or the memory would have been clearer. We'd all sat cross-legged on the floor, gathered in a circle around a woman who I remembered as very smiley with long blonde hair. I assumed she'd been the librarian. She'd demonstrated a haunted house pop-up book with lots of flaps and sliding bits which had had us all enraptured. Susan, with the pigtails and the missing front teeth, had cried when she wasn't allowed to touch it. I don't think she was used to anyone saying no to her.

Unfortunately, that was about as cultured as I'd ever gotten: never really graduating beyond picture books — unless car manuals counted — and I had a sneaky suspicion they didn't. If I'd set foot in a library since, then it hadn't been a visit worth recalling. In my mind, I stuck out like a sore thumb.

So, when my mum had asked me to return her library

books, telling me it would only take a few minutes during my lunch hour, it was for that reason I'd been reluctant. That was normally my older brother, Mark's, job. Mark was apparently too busy. Yeah, busy being a massive pain in the ass which seemed to be a full-time job for him. We'd never been close. Whether that was due to the five-year age gap between us, or the fact we were like chalk and cheese, I wasn't sure. He was my brother and under pain of death I might, and it was a big might, admit to loving him. I just didn't particularly like him that much and the feeling seemed to be mutual. He was academic in a way I'd never been or wanted to be. While I was tinkering in cars and learning all I could about the way different engines worked and what goes where, he'd had his nose firmly planted in textbooks. Even before he'd developed his passion for psychology, he'd been too much of a know-it-all. Now, he had letters to his name, he was even more insufferable, thinking he could tell what everyone was thinking just from the way they took their coffee or the way they sat.

Anyway, who still read *actual* books? It was nothing short of a miracle that the library was still there when numerous others in the area had already closed their doors for good. Yet it — just like my mum — seemed unable to embrace the age of technology. I'd bought her a Kindle for Christmas, assuming she'd jump at the chance for no more library visits and thousands of books available at the press of a key.

She'd made all the right noises, had even pretended to use it. That had lasted all of about five minutes, and then it had been stashed somewhere, never to be seen again. Something to do with, nothing comparing to the feeling of an actual book in your hands. I didn't really understand, and Mark standing next to my mum nodding sagely, like the dipshit had inside knowledge, hadn't helped matters either.

So, I'd agreed to return the books. I wasn't prepared to upset my mum. That idea was a non-starter. The effect of a look of disappointment in her eyes could linger for weeks. I'd entered the building feeling conspicuous, as if I was sneaking through the side door of a strip club rather than a place where people read and returned books. And bizarrely the place was busy: people either milling around or sat at tables reading. Didn't they know that there were a hundred better things going on outside its doors? But each to their own, I supposed. One man's good time was another man's nightmare. I didn't want to get too judgmental, or I might start turning into Mark.

The plan was simple: find the counter, hand the books over, and then get the hell out of there. Well, the counter was easy enough to find, located as it was right at the front of the library. An officious-looking woman took the books from me, raising her eyebrows at the sight of my oil-streaked T-shirt. I'd have liked to have seen how good she'd have looked if she'd spent the morning underneath a Ford Escort leaking copious amounts of oil. Did libraries have dress codes now? If so, that was another minus point against them. Job done, I'd been ready to implement the last part of my plan in getting the hell out of there when for some reason, I'd looked up, glanced across the library, and seen him.

He was obviously an employee. I don't know how I knew that, I just did. Like many people around him, he was studying one of the shelves. But, while they looked as if they were searching for something, or browsing, his face wore a look of slight displeasure. I found myself watching him, wondering what could be so upsetting about a shelf of books. Had someone put one back in the wrong place? Was that the kind of difficult problem librarians were faced with on a daily basis?

Then I looked at him—really looked at him. He was thin. Too thin. Almost to the point of appearing like he needed to eat more. Although, I had to admit it gave him amazing cheekbones. He was fairly short as well. I calculated no taller than five foot eight in comparison to my own six-foot-two frame. Although, it was difficult to tell for sure from this distance. Perhaps I was doing him a disservice. A mass of dark hair kept falling into his eyes and every now and again he'd pause to push it back, only for the same thing to happen again a few moments later.

He was about as far from my usual type as you could possibly get. My last boyfriend had been a huge, great muscly bloke with his own motorbike. The one before that was a bodybuilder. The bigger the muscles, the more my cock usually said yes, please. So, it was a complete mystery why I was finding it so difficult to drag my gaze away from him.

"Anything else I can help you with?"

The voice made me jump. I'd been so caught up in my scrutiny of the dark-haired man that I'd forgotten I was still stood at the counter. I shook my head, and left, glad that the man hadn't noticed me staring. I had no idea what the hell had gotten into me.

* * * *

It wasn't until I'd spent my next two lunch breaks sat at a table in the library surreptitiously watching him that I began to admit I had a problem. I didn't know what it was about him that drew me in, but it was as if I was a moth and he was my flame. At no point had he looked my way. In fact, he barely looked up at all, seemingly completely focused on whatever job he happened to be doing at the time. I didn't even know if he was gay. There was no wedding ring, but that didn't mean anything apart from the fact he wasn't married to either a man or a woman. All I knew was I needed to talk to him. I needed to ask him out on a date. He might say no. But there was always the tantalizing possibility that he could say yes.

I pulled the newspaper I'd borrowed from a trolley closer to me, my fingers drumming on the table while I tried to devise an excuse to talk to him. I'd never seen him check anyone's books out so that wouldn't work. Besides, I wasn't a member, and I wasn't

going to join a library just for the sake of one conversation. I
wasn't that desperate — yet. He seemed to spend most of his time
either in the back room doing whatever it was you did in the back
room of a library, returning books to the shelves, or answering
questions posed by members of the general public. Therefore, I
needed some sort of question to ask him. Only, I didn't know
what sorts of inquiries were normally made in libraries. I scanned
the shelves next to me, hoping for some sort of inspiration to hit.

There was no way I was going to leave — again — without
having said two words to him. I couldn't spend all my lunch
breaks skulking in a library hoping to be noticed. If the guys back
in the garage found out where I'd been secretly nipping off to, I'd
never hear the end of it. No doubt, I'd be accused of being a
pretentious wanker and it would give them enough verbal
ammunition to rip me to shreds for the next couple of weeks.
Definitely not worth it.

I'd even changed into a clean T-shirt in the car, figuring that
looking like the mechanic I was, wouldn't make the best first
impression. Checking my watch revealed that I had the grand
total of ten minutes to put my plan into action before I needed to
head back to the garage. It was now or never.

I reached across, grabbing the first book from the shelf that
my hand happened to land on and hurried in his direction before I
could lose my nerve. "Excuse me."

The trolley full of books he'd been pushing, as he returned
them to the shelves, squeaked to a halt and he turned to face me,
his soulful, brown eyes not quite meeting mine. "Yes?"

I held out the book so he could see the front cover. "Where
would I be able to find other books by this author?"

His gaze drifted down to the book, a slight look of either
surprise or confusion blossoming on his face. It was hard to tell
which. "You like Harry Potter?"

I turned the book around and took my first look at the cover.
It was indeed a Harry Potter book. One with a large phoenix

emblazoned on the cover. Maybe I should have been a little choosier about which shelf I chose my random book from. Avoiding the children's shelves would have been a good start. At least, I was familiar enough with the author to know that although it was primarily written for children, some adults read them too. It could have been worse. I could have been stood there clutching a copy of *The Velveteen Rabbit*. Anyway, it was the book in my hand so I had no choice but to go with it. "Sure. I mean, yes."

He kept his eyes trained on the book. "And you want to know where you would find other books by the same author?"

I nodded.

A small frown appeared on his forehead as if something didn't compute. "On the same shelf. Right next to it."

Shit! Shit! Shit! I was an idiot. "Really! Well, yes. I suppose that would make sense. Thank you."

He turned back to the trolley, obviously intending to continue on his way. I made a grab for the handle at the same time as jamming my foot in front of the wheel, meaning he either had to wait or run over my foot. "Actually, the book was just an excuse."

His body swiveled again, his gaze hovering somewhere around my chin. *Was he shy?* I found it hard to believe that somebody who looked like him could be timid. Up close, he was even more attractive: all creamy skin, doe eyes, and cheekbones. "An excuse for what?"

"To talk to you." *In for a penny, in for a pound. What was the worst that could happen?* "To ask if maybe you'd like to get coffee sometime? Or have dinner? Or go for a drink? Whatever it is you like doing in your spare time when you're not here. I'm up for anything really. Well, not anything...but..." I laughed at my own verbal diarrhea. I was normally much smoother than this.

His eyes darted to mine, the first time he'd made eye contact since our conversation started. My breath caught. Was that fear in his eyes? I knew I was taller than him and a damn sight wider, but I was stood a respectful distance away. I wasn't crowding him. I'd been polite. I hadn't been too pushy. Okay, I'd blocked the trolley which might have been a little over the top, but fear was surely a major overreaction. The look lasted mere milliseconds before it was gone, and I was left wondering whether I'd imagined it. He cleared his throat, his voice coming out quiet but firm. "I don't date."

I don't date. Not, I'm not gay. To my mind there was at least a tiny fragment of hope there before I gave up. "Why not?"

He took a step backward as if attempting to put more space between us. "I just don't. Thank you for asking but…" He didn't bother to finish the sentence, using the action of pushing the trolley away to terminate the conversation. Frustrated, I found myself watching him walk away, the buzz of attraction making my head swim despite his rejection. A no was a no, though. There wasn't much more I could do. I wasn't about to start stalking him. It was bad enough that it had taken several visits to the library to pluck up the courage to speak to him. But now I had, I had my answer. He wasn't interested. Therefore, it was time to stop. I regretted not asking his name. It would have been nice to put a name to the one that got away.

Chapter Two

Alexander

I quickened my pace at the distinct sound of footsteps echoing behind me, my heart beginning to pound. It couldn't be *him*. I knew it wasn't possible. But there were other threats out there. Just because it wasn't him, didn't mean I was safe. I wanted the oblivion of death, but I wanted it on my own terms at a place and time of my own choosing, not dictated to me by someone else. Sanctuary, in the form of my apartment, lay around the corner, less than two hundred meters away. I just needed to get there.

Rounding the corner, I resisted the urge to look back over my shoulder to see who was there. It would just waste time. I half ran down the path toward the door, my trembling fingers making difficult but hasty work of the lock on the communal door. Then it was open and I was inside the building, slamming the heavy door in my wake. I felt better, but I knew I wouldn't feel completely safe until I was locked away in my second-floor apartment. I took the stairs two at a time, desperate to be able to shut the whole world out for a few blessed hours. Inside my apartment, there was no one to judge. I didn't have to put on an act and pretend I was coping when I wasn't. There was just four walls and silence.

When I was halfway up the last flight of stairs with my apartment in sight, the door next to mine swung open; the man who'd appeared spotting me and leaning nonchalantly against the wall as he watched my approach with a smirk on his face. My heart sank. For the first six months, I'd lived next door to a young couple and their baby. While the crying of the baby had driven me crazy at times as well as reminding me of another crying baby that I never wanted to think about, the couple themselves had been nice. They were always friendly enough to say hello and apologize for their son's noise, but happy to leave me alone the rest of the time which suited me down to the ground. The month the apartment had sat empty after they'd moved out had been even better. Then, Richard Simpkins had moved in. I knew his name because he'd insisted on telling me the first time we'd met, his eyes raking me from head to toe and making his interest very clear.

It had been six weeks since our paths had last crossed. I worked days; his job at a security firm meant he worked evenings. Therefore, he shouldn't have been home at this time. Yet, there he was. Intending to ignore him, I kept my gaze fixed on the floor, studying the worn, dirty carpet under my feet as I climbed the rest of the stairs. If I was lucky, he wouldn't make any attempt to engage me in conversation. It was the last thing I needed after my scare outside. Just a few steps more and I'd be home free. A pair of shoes appeared in my eyeline as he stepped into my path, blocking my route. I forced myself to lift my head and look him straight in the eye. It wasn't easy to pretend I wasn't intimidated when I was quaking inside. "Excuse me."

He didn't move. His smirk grew wider, morphing into something akin to a leer, matched by the lascivious look in his eye. "Alexander! Why the hurry? We haven't seen each other for ages. Let's catch up."

I'd never told him my name. He must have looked at my

mail, delivering my name on the second occasion of meeting me as if it gave him sort of inside information and made us best buddies.

I made a move to side-step past him, the corridor not wide enough for the move to work unless he cooperated. "I'm busy. So..."

He remained firmly planted in my way. "Surely, you've got five minutes? It's been so long and I've got some good news for you."

Resigning myself to having to play along for a few minutes, I folded my arms and stared resolutely back at him. If it weren't for the fact that his every move and gesture gave me the creeps, I might have even thought he was good-looking. Maybe that was why he couldn't get it through his head that I wasn't remotely interested in him. Plenty of men probably responded enthusiastically to his brand of smarmy charm. I'd known another good-looking man once though; his attractive façade hiding a demon underneath. You couldn't always trust what was on the surface. I'd discovered that the hard way and I was never going to make the same mistake again, especially not for someone who thought it was funny to constantly try and assert his dominance over me. "What news?"

He smiled, but it didn't reach his eyes. "Someone left at my workplace. I'm back to working days so I'll be around in the evenings again. We can see a lot more of each other." He tapped on the plaster behind his head. "Just on the other side of the wall from you." His gaze trailed slowly down my body and it took all the willpower I had not to shiver. "Just knock if you need anything." He put extra emphasis on the word anything, making the sexual double meaning behind it quite clear.

Bile rose in my throat and I fought down the panic doing its best to bubble up inside. "That's not going to happen." I was impressed that my voice came out sounding so calm and

13

controlled when inside I was a mass of churning emotions. He laughed, finally stepping aside to let me pass. "Well, the offer's there, Alexander. Anytime."

I hated the way he said my name. He dragged out the middle of it, as if he was savoring the taste of it on his tongue. Getting my legs to work, I hurried past him. Knowing that he was still watching and determined to avoid giving him the satisfaction of knowing he'd rattled me, I forced my fingers to remain steady while I unlocked the door. After all, that's what I was good at: pretending. I'd spent all day doing it. This was just another thing to add to the list. The last thing. Then, I'd be inside my apartment where nothing and no one except memories and nightmares could touch me.

The door opened and I hurried inside, fastening the chain and the two bolts I'd added since moving in before crumpling to the floor against the wall and hugging my knees to my chest. Breathing deeply, I tried to stave off the panic attack threatening to send my body into overdrive. *You're safe now. You're inside. Nobody can get in. You're safe. Nobody can get in.* I repeated the mantra again and again until my pulse started to slow and I knew that I'd escaped the possibility of a panic attack.

I hadn't always been like this. There was a time when I would have brushed a man like Richard Simpkins aside like an unwanted fly and laughed about him afterward with my friends. But, those times were long gone and I was a mere shadow of the man I'd once been.

One year earlier

"Ally, can you babysit tonight?" The question had come from Victoria, my older sister. As a single parent, she'd made the decision to move back home so that my mum and dad could help her look after the baby. She was still there, showing no signs of moving out, five months later.

14

I gestured down at my clothes, dressed as I was in skintight jeans and an equally tight and sleeveless — not to mention see-through — top. "What do you think?"

She hoisted the baby further onto her shoulder, pulling a face when the motion made him burp. "You're going out?"

I grabbed my leather jacket from the chair, shrugging my arms into the sleeves. "You betcha I am." Peering into the mirror on the wall, I examined my hair which I'd spent at least twenty minutes styling to perfection. "Do you think I need eyeliner?"

My mum's face appeared in the mirror behind me. I hadn't even heard her approach. "With those eyes? You don't need anything extra." I smiled, meeting the almost identical pair in the mirror. "You would say that. I got them from you. It's just a shame I inherited your height as well."

My mum's eyes crinkled. "Good things come in small packages."

I rolled my eyes. "Yeah! Yeah! So you've been telling me for years. You also used to keep telling me I'd grow."

"Well, your dad's over six foot, so I thought you might."

As if summoned by the mention, he appeared from the basement, where he'd no doubt been working on some ingenious invention which would go terribly wrong and he'd give up on, only to start something else the following week. He bent to kiss my mum on the forehead and I dutifully pretended to be horrified by the show of affection. "Urgh, please! Can't you do that behind closed doors? Or wait till I'm at least forty and can handle it?" Secretly, I loved the fact that even after thirty years of marriage, they were still very much in love. Most of my friends' parents were either at the point of merely tolerating each other or had divorced years ago.

My dad tutted at my reaction before continuing on his way to the kitchen, my sister following him. I guessed he was going to be the next person hassled for babysitting.

A concerned expression settled on my mum's face. "You'll be careful tonight, right?"

Waggling my eyebrows, I patted the right pocket of my jeans.

"Condoms are in here."

She shook her head, a look of fond amusement on her face. "You know that's not what I meant. Although" — her eyebrows lifted — "it's good that you're prepared. I meant be careful who you talk to. Not everyone can be trusted you know...and ever since you were a little boy you've always been happy to talk to absolutely anyone."

I'd lost count of the number of times I'd heard this speech over the years. At least this time it didn't include the story of when five-year-old me had wandered off and after a major panic had been discovered safe and sound, chatting to a bemused busker and asking him to play nursery rhymes. "I don't know how you think I coped at university for the last three years without you there to look after me. I'm twenty-two now, you know. Big enough to look after myself."

"That was different." She leant forward, brushing a stray piece of hair back behind my ear. "When you were at university, I didn't know when you were out or not."

I smiled, knowing there was no point in arguing with the twisted mum logic. She cared and she'd always care. No matter how old I was and no matter where I was going. I'd always be her little boy in her eyes. "I'll be careful, Mum. I promise."

Her eyes softened and she leant forward to kiss me on the cheek. "Are you meeting Jack and David?"

I nodded. "Yep! The terrible trio are hitting the clubs." The three of us had been firm friends all through school before I'd gone away to university. I'd expected time and distance to have taken their toll and that it wouldn't be possible to pick things up where we'd left them. But to my surprise, it was as if I'd never been away. Even the fact the two of them were now a couple hadn't left me feeling like a third wheel. Maybe because I knew both of them equally well. I checked my watch. "Speaking of which, I better get going. I'm supposed to be meeting them in about half an hour."

She waved me away. "Watch out for Charlie. He's got this new thing where he keeps trying to escape whenever the front door is opened. He'll try and run through your legs if you're not careful."

"Got ya."

The Shih Tzu was right in front of the door. I bent down to pet him. "Charlie, mate. You need to work on your escape plan. Hide. Pretend you're not interested in the door and then make a run for it. You're kind of broadcasting to the world what you intend to do." I picked him up, carrying him into the front room and closing the door just enough to slow him down but not enough that he wouldn't be able to get out once I'd gone. Whistling, I made my own escape out of the front door, fantasizing about what delights the night might bring. It had been way too long since I'd pulled. At least a couple of weeks by my calculation. I had every intention of rectifying that tonight.

* * * *

"What about him? He's been eyeing you up since we arrived?" I followed Jack's gaze to where a blond-haired man leant against the bar. "Nah! Not my type."

Jack sighed. "You never used to be this fussy."

I gave him a long look. "I was eighteen, had a permanent erection, and was desperate to get my hands on a man. Any man. I'd like to think I've come a long way since then."

David smirked. "I'm sure you have COME a long way."

I was about to give the kind of response that such a smutty double entendre deserved when my eyes were drawn to the man that had just walked into the room. He was tall and broad-shouldered with dark hair swept back from his very handsome face and he was most certainly my type. His long legs ate up the meters between him and the bar until I was left staring at the back of his head, before my gaze dropped to take in the very pert backside. What I wouldn't give to get better acquainted with that ass. I wasn't sure where he'd been all night. He hadn't just arrived: the almost empty wine glass in his hand attesting to that fact. There was another room. Perhaps he'd been in there. Actually, who cared where he'd been. He was there now. That's all that mattered. "Now, he is definitely my type. Wish me luck. I'm going in."

Chapter Three

Austin

I ducked, narrowly managing to avoid the oily rag which had been chucked straight at my face. At least the distraction provided a bit more thinking time about the best way to answer the question that had just been aimed my way. "Huh, when?"

Wilko poked his head back out from the car he'd just slid under. "Yesterday lunchtime? Where d'ya go?"

Adrian — the thrower of the oily rag and technically my boss, although he didn't act like it most of the time — came to stand next to me. "Yeah, Aust. Where *did* you go? You seem to keep disappearing. What's the secret?"

I shrugged. "No secret." The fact they were questioning me meant I'd probably been seen either entering or leaving the library and this was a test to find out if I was going to tell the truth or not. The problem with the three of us being such good mates and working so closely together was you couldn't even go for a dump without one of them wanting to know how long you'd be gone for and whether it was your first of the day. "I had to take some library books back for my mum."

Wilko's face screwed up. "Again? You took books back for her on Monday. How fast does she read?"

18

Adrian bent over, looking down at Wilko. "Faster than you, I bet. Oh wait! That wouldn't be difficult...you can't read, can you?" He cackled loudly at his own joke while Wilko called him a dickhead and started throwing his own insults back.

Glad to have disappeared from their radar and escaped further questions, I took the opportunity to get out of there. "I'll nip out and grab coffee for us. See you in a bit."

* * * *

The coffee shop was a good ten-minute walk away. I could have taken the car, but it was nice sometimes to get a bit of fresh air and steal a bit of extra time out of the garage. It was close to empty when I arrived. But then I'd known it would be: one thing I'd learnt over the years was the times to avoid unless you liked queueing for ages and negotiating your way past crowds to have a chance at leaving.

About to head straight to the counter, I hesitated mid-stride when the person seated on the right-hand side close to the window suddenly caught my eye. Even with their head bent over a book, it was easy to recognize the man from the library. After a momentary tussle with my conscience about the best course of action when he'd already made his feelings perfectly clear, I headed for his table anyway. It had to be fate, right? I mean, what were the chances of our paths just happening to cross again so soon, in a place other than the library? I approached him slowly, as if he was a nervy wild animal at risk of bolting if I moved too quickly. Making sure he was aware of my presence first, I eased myself into the seat opposite him. "Hi."

He dragged his eyes away from the book, staring blankly at me. *Did he not recognize me?* That was a bit of a blow to the ego. "We met in the library yesterday. I was the idiot with the Harry Potter book. I saw you over here when I came in so I just thought I'd come and say hello. I'm just taking a break from work to get

19

coffee for the boys. When I say boys, I mean the guys in the garage, not kids. Although, sometimes they act like them so it can be pretty hard to tell the difference."

He continued to stare for a moment as if he was struggling to process why I was telling him all this. Finally, his lips parted. "You're a mechanic?"

I nodded. *Hadn't I already mentioned that?* Of course, I hadn't. We hadn't even gotten as far as names. At least, I could put that right. I cleared my throat. "Yeah, I'm a mechanic." I gestured down at my far from clean T-shirt with a cringe of embarrassment. I hadn't changed this time because I'd had no idea I'd bump into him again. "I'm Austin by the way. Austin Armstrong." I considered offering a hand to shake but decided against it. Along with my T-shirt, they weren't as clean as I'd have liked and then there was the fact that I didn't want to risk the possible awkwardness of him not taking it.

He shifted in his seat, giving the distinct impression of a reluctance to share the same information. When he finally spoke, the response was no louder than a whisper and I had to lean forward in order to be able to catch it. "Alexander."

Alexander. A beautiful name for a beautiful man. I found myself grinning at him, the simple knowledge of his name making me feel strangely elated. "Do you normally shorten that? Alex or Xander or —"

He cut me off. "Alex is fine."

I gestured toward the book he'd been reading. I didn't want to run out of small talk because then I'd be out of excuses to remain sitting there. While we were still talking, I could stay without feeling as if I was invading his privacy. "What are you reading? You looked like you were pretty engrossed."

He flipped the book so I could see the cover. The book was entitled *"Getting away with Murder"* I didn't even try and hide my surprise. "Wow! That sounds heavy. You're not planning one, are you?"

His eyes revealed his confusion at the question. He was obviously a man of few words, but at least I was getting eye contact today. "A murder? You're reading a book about how to get away with one, and you know what they say, it's always the quiet ones you have to watch. And you know, you're quite...quiet." Suddenly feeling as if I'd made a really bad joke, I sought to dig myself out of the hole I'd made. "Just a joke. I don't really think you're a murderer. You're not, right?"

Shaking his head, he pulled his mug toward him, taking a big gulp of the contents. It gave me another conversational opening. "What's the coffee of choice? Assuming it is coffee?"

"Hot chocolate."

"Ah, you're a hot chocolate man."

Another nod.

I cast around for another topic of conversation that would keep me there just that little bit longer. "You're not working today?"

"Late lunch break. If I stay in the library, they still ask me to do stuff. I have to head back there soon."

It was by far the most he'd ever said. I couldn't help feeling as if I'd won some sort of victory. Deciding it was better to leave on a high, I reluctantly stood up. "Well, it was nice seeing you again, but I'll leave you in peace to enjoy the rest of your lunch break." With that, I walked away toward the counter, joining the small queue of three people.

As I waited, I couldn't help sneaking the occasional glance in his direction. He'd gone back to reading his book, his dark hair falling over his face as he bent over it and his fingers sometimes tapping on the table as he read. On impulse, I added a hot chocolate and a chocolate muffin to my usual coffee order. If you liked hot chocolate, you had to like other chocolate things, right? And it wasn't as if he had to eat it.

I carried them over to the table, placing them next to him and wincing as he startled at the sound of the mug hitting the table. "Sorry. I…well, I got you these. I thought you might be hungry. You don't have to have them. Just…you know, in case you wanted them." I gestured at the items, as if he could have failed to notice them.

"Thank you."

I nodded, hurrying away before the slight flush on my cheeks ran the risk of developing into a full-blown blush. *What the hell was wrong with me?* If any of the guys in the garage could have seen me so flustered over a man I'd only met twice, they'd have an absolute field day with the wind-ups and I'd never hear the end of it.

Alexander

I stared at the muffin. It was a double chocolate one, the chocolate chips plentiful, the smell wafting across the table and teasing my nostrils. I finally gave in and broke off a lump, bringing it slowly to my mouth. It tasted good: moist and chocolatey, easily melting in my mouth as I contemplated the man that had bought it for me. I hadn't known what to think when he'd appeared from nowhere. Alarm bells had started ringing, questions racing through my head at lightning speed. *Was he stalking me? How did he know I was here? What did he want?*

It had taken every ounce of composure I had, to stay seated when my senses had been screaming at me to flee. His appearance alone should have been enough to trigger the urge to hide. The man was big. Really big, with bulging muscles barely contained inside his T-shirt. His physical presence hadn't seemed quite as oppressive back in the library when he'd approached me. Maybe because that was a place where I always felt safer.

But then as he'd talked, I'd gotten the impression that he

was somewhat of a gentle giant with his slow movements and carefully modulated voice. I'd found myself slowly relaxing, almost content in his presence and I'd had to remind myself not to let my guard down. It was easy to be wrong about a person. I'd been wrong before and look how that had turned out.

My confusion had grown even more when he'd brought the hot chocolate and muffin over. It wasn't the gesture. It was more the fact that he'd blushed, his tanned complexion not quite dark enough to hide it completely. All in all, I didn't know what to make of him.

All through the mostly one-sided conversation, I'd readied myself to turn him down again when the inevitable invitation came. Except, it hadn't. He'd handed the drink and muffin over and then left. I broke off another piece of muffin, hitting the gooey chocolate center. That bit tasted even better.

Sudden guilt burned through me. What right did I have to be enjoying myself? The remaining muffin in my mouth became suddenly tasteless and I swallowed it with great difficulty. Grabbing my book, I abandoned the rest of the muffin and left the hot chocolate on the table as I headed back to work early.

* * * *

"Alexander, do this. Alexander, get that. Alexander, have you finished yet?" The list of directives at work were never-ending. It hadn't taken long for the all-female staff to realize I'd obediently follow their instructions, and they usually capitalized on it, often passing over tasks they just didn't want to do themselves. What they didn't realize was, I needed it. While they were telling me what to do, I didn't need to think. I could just follow orders like some sort of well-trained robot. I could switch my brain off and simply exist, lost in whatever mundane task I'd been asked to do.

It was when they didn't tell me what to do, I struggled.

Then, in the space of the nothingness, the walls would start to close in and I'd forget how to breathe. Forget how to be Alexander Philips. The cracks on my skin would start to open up, revealing the emptiness inside, and the facade I'd built up would start to crumble.

This was one of those times. I fastened my gaze on a plant in the corner, barely aware of the voices in the library surrounding me. When I'd left university with a first-class honors degree in English with a specialism in journalism, I could never have envisioned a time where I'd ever feel useless in a library. I'd once had a brilliant mind. A mind capable of solving complex problems. Now, I couldn't even think for myself.

"Alexander, the phone's ringing. Can you get it? And then there's a pile of books in the back room that need labeling. Can you make a start?" The world snapped back into focus as I hastened to follow the order. I had purpose again. I had something to make the minutes go by faster. So I could tick another day off of the never-ending succession of time crawling slowly by.

The other good thing about working in the library was that my work colleagues didn't seem to mind that I didn't chat. I floated around in the background while they discussed favorite TV programs and talked about where they'd gotten their hair or their nails done. I barely said two words to them. I suspected that they thought I was mentally challenged. I didn't care. They could think what they wanted.

It meant I could save all my energy for necessary social interactions with members of the public, faking a happy persona that nobody seemed to see through. I thought of it as a social paint by numbers where each number represented something different: one, might be smile; two, a laugh; three, tell a joke; four, use their name as a means of bonding; five, recommend a book; six, use a natural mannerism such as running my hand through my hair or clasping my hands together in front of me. Each person I needed to speak to, I'd mentally swap the numbers around in my head. Person one: four, then one and six at the same time, five. End on two. Person two, I'd swap it around. Start with five, then one, then maybe six and so it went on. And nobody ever seemed to see through the act. They were all fooled. To them I was a real person, instead of a barely functioning shell of a human being.

* * * *

Richard Simpkins had taken to lying in wait for me every day now. I'd tried varying the time I came home. It didn't work. There were times I'd think I'd gotten away with it. I'd be almost to the top of the stairs, my apartment door mere meters away, sanctuary so close I could almost smell it and then his door would open and I'd find myself confronted with that same oily smile. He was careful never to touch, never to go so far I'd have something concrete to tell the police. All I could say to them at the moment was that he stood in my way, talked to me when I didn't want him to, and looked me over in a way that made me want to scrub myself with bleach. Not that I would ever go to the police anyway. I'd been there and done that and had learnt that in the long run, it didn't make the slightest bit of difference, but Richard didn't know that.

He was seated at the top of the stairs today, smoking a cigarette, his eyes fixed on me as my slow upward steps landed us on an inevitable collision course. He'd positioned himself diagonally, making sure he blocked the entire stairwell. That left me with only two options: attempt to step over him or ride out the usual comments and sexual innuendos until he saw fit to move. I halted in front of him, glad of the fact that his seated position meant I could at least look down on him. It made me feel slightly less vulnerable. "Can I get by?"

He squinted up at me, taking a long, slow drag of the

cigarette and exhaling the smoke slowly without offering any response. It was a deliberate delaying tactic, all part of his attempt to try and intimidate me. "What's the rush, Alexander? Don't you want to stay and chat a while? You look like a man who's in need of a bit of company."

Inside my head, I was screaming, but I kept my gaze fixed on his, careful not to give away how he made me feel. "I don't — sorry. I just want to get home. I've had a long day at work. So...if you don't mind?"

He cocked his head to one side, his mouth twisting into what I assumed was meant to be a charming smile. It reminded me of another man from a long time ago. A man who on the outside had been just as charming, right up to the point where he wasn't anymore. "I hate to think of you" — he brought the cigarette to his lips, releasing another plume of smoke — "all alone next door. You never have visitors. You never go out in the evening. You need a bit of fun in your life."

Surging panic flowed through my veins at the thought of him cataloguing my movements — or lack of. The urge to flee back the way I'd come was strong. My legs started to shake and I only kept myself in place through sheer force of will, praying he wouldn't be able to tell the effect he was having on me. "That's none of your business."

He stood, his arms reaching out to grasp the handrail on either side so that his body still remained an obstacle. His eyes trailed slowly down over my body, pausing for far too long at my crotch, his tongue darting out to lick his lower lip in a provocative gesture. "Pretty Alexander...all alone. Maybe I'll come around one evening, show you what you're missing out on by locking yourself away."

I couldn't help it. It was a step too far. I shoved my way past him, the momentary feel of his body pressing against mine making me feel sick to the stomach. The headlong rush down the corridor to get to my apartment door seemed to take forever, punctuated as it was by the sound of his mocking laughter. I'd shown him that he scared me. There was no chance of getting him to leave me alone now.

Chapter Four

Alexander

I strode up to the man at the bar. It was hard to miss the fact that there were several other interested glances being thrown his way. It didn't faze me. I didn't mind a bit of competition. I could usually hold my own. "Buy you a drink?"

He turned to study me, and I took the opportunity to do the same as the pretty blue eyes outlined by long dark lashes looked me over. The man was even more handsome up close. I waited patiently while he considered my offer. It was the age-old dance where one of two things would happen next: he'd decide he was interested, he'd say yes and I'd know that my night had just taken a turn for the better, or he'd turn me down. If it was the latter, I'd shrug, go back to my friends, and one of the other interested onlookers would move into my spot and take their turn. One thing was for sure, there was no way this beautiful man was going home alone tonight, unless he wanted to. I just hoped it was with me, rather than with someone else.

He smiled, the gesture revealing perfect white teeth, which accentuated his good looks even more. "Sure. Why not?"

I gave a mental fist pump, ignoring the disgusted look of someone to my right who'd been on their way over but just hadn't gotten there quick enough. I aimed a smug smirk his way, hoping it clearly conveyed the sentiments of, "Mine, bitch. Find your own." Gesturing for the barman to come over, I took the opportunity to introduce myself while I waited. "The name's Alexander. But, most people call me Al."

He leaned closer, a wolfish smile appearing on his face, his interest written all over it. "Oliver Calthorpe. Pleasure to meet you, Al."

Even the man's name was classy. "What do you want to drink? Or..." I let the sexual tension simmer between us. We both knew what we wanted. It was just a question of whether it was going to be now or later. "...did you want to skip the drink and just get out of here?"

He lifted his glass, swilling the remnants of red wine left in the bottom before bringing the glass to his mouth to drain the contents. It made me wonder what that wine was going to taste like on his tongue when I kissed him. "Let's get out of here." He slid gracefully from the stool and began to make his way toward the door. I turned back to the table where I'd left Jack and David, offering a wink and a wave while ignoring the eye rolls I received in return. Then, I followed Oliver's delectable ass out of the bar.

* * * *

Oliver's apartment turned out to be just as impressive as he was: all floor-length windows and art deco furniture. I stared out over the amazing view of the city, sipping the no doubt unbelievably expensive wine he'd handed to me on arrival, and trying my utmost to pretend like this was a position I found myself in every weekend. I smiled as he came up behind me, his breath teasing the sensitive skin at the back of my neck. "Do you like it?"

"The view? The wine? Or the apartment?"

He shifted, coming to stand alongside me. "All of them?"

I shrugged, determined to play it cool. "They're okay. I bet your bedroom's even better though. When do I get to see that?"

His mouth twisted, leaving me with the strangest feeling of having said something wrong. I had no idea why that would be the case though, it wasn't as if we'd made any secret of what our plans were after leaving the bar.

He stepped closer to the glass of the window, his gaze meeting mine in the reflection. "Tell me about yourself, Al. Let's get to know each other a bit before we move onto other stuff."

So, that was the problem. He thought I just wanted to use him for sex. I did. But I could make polite chit-chat for a few minutes if that's what was required to get him naked. "I'm not very exciting. Sorry. What do you want to know?"

The next fifteen minutes were spent exchanging conversational titbits which quite honestly, I could have lived without knowing. I discovered he was a banker, which explained the swanky lifestyle. I found out where he'd gone to university, where he shopped for his clothes and how he liked his steak cooked. He discovered, well, the little there was to know about me: straight out of university didn't leave an awful lot to talk about. I didn't think he'd be that interested in the last three years of campus life so I skipped over that. He did however seem interested in finding out about my family which killed some time as I detailed the ins and outs of family life while doing my best to gloss over the fact I'd had to move back there temporarily until I found a job and could afford my own place.

Finally, after what felt like an eternity, he took the now empty wine glass out of my hand and led me toward the bedroom; the space dominated by a huge king-size bed complete with black silk sheets. A part of me wanted to laugh. The man was a walking cliché: the handsome playboy living in the penthouse apartment with the huge bed and the silk sheets. Shame I wasn't a rent boy. We could have recreated Pretty Woman.

I stifled a yawn. It had taken so long to get to this point, the desire for sex had waned. If Oliver had suggested calling a cab instead, I would have leapt at the offer. Suddenly, being tucked up in my childhood bed felt like a much more attractive prospect. I shook the thought off. It was probably just the wine. Wine always made me tired which was one of the reasons I usually avoided it and stuck to beer. Oliver, didn't do beer. Probably not expensive enough for him. I bet if I searched the apartment

I'd find a horrifically expensive twenty-year-old bottle of Scotch hidden away somewhere, but definitely no beer.

"What's wrong?"

Shit! Something of what I was feeling must have shown on my face. I shook my head and lied. "Nothing's wrong. I just don't think I've ever actually seen silk sheets before. Not in real life. They surprised me, that's all."

"They'll feel fantastic against your skin." He rounded on me, his lips descending on mine while his hands moved to my hips to pull me closer. I made a concerted effort to get myself back in the mood as I returned the kiss. I could hardly be the tease that had picked him up at a bar, only to turn around and leave because he'd insisted on a bit of conversation first. Besides, he was really handsome. By far the most handsome man I'd ever been with. I should be thanking my lucky stars, not wishing I was somewhere else.

I just needed to work harder to get back those initial feelings from the bar when I'd first laid eyes on him. Something, though, and I had no idea what it was, was setting my teeth on edge. It was more than the silk sheets. Maybe it was the edge of arrogance I now recognized. The guy was rich and handsome though, it was ridiculous to expect that package to come without a touch of arrogance. I was being unfair. I was there now. I may as well enjoy it. I mean, I was staying at my parents' house. Who knew when the next opportunity for sex might be? It wasn't as if I could take anyone back there.

Decision made, I took charge, backing him toward the bed at the same time as stripping both of us out of our clothes. He lay back on the bed; a man who knew he had a perfect body. He probably paid a personal trainer to sculpt those abs and I would have bet anything that his personal waxing bills were higher than my family paid for groceries in a month. It suddenly seemed about as fake and artificial as the sheets. I dismissed the thought. The man liked to keep himself trim and he could afford to. Who was I to get all judgmental about it? Feeling guilty for the less than charitable thoughts, I traced those perfect abs with my tongue, enjoying the way he moaned and the way his erect cock twitched when *my mouth moved closer to it.*

His hand moved down, grabbing a handful of my ass, and using it to pull me toward him. "Come here! You're not hard, baby. Let me fix that."

Baby! I cringed. Endearments weren't really my thing at the best of times, but from someone I'd only just met, it came across as downright phony. He was right about one thing though: my dick wasn't hard, so I did as he'd asked, closing my eyes as he took me deep down his throat. I tried to clear my mind, concentrating only on the feel of his tongue and the firm suction as he expertly sucked my cock. It had the desired effect and within minutes I was good to go. Worried I'd lose it again, I wasted no time in rolling a condom on and pushing inside him. He groaned, his hips rising and his legs wrapping around my hips. "Yeah, Al. Fuck me, baby. Fuck me hard. Make me yours. Make me forget other men."

I did my best to zone him out; the porn dialogue doing nothing for me. It didn't work and I settled for kissing him instead. If his mouth was occupied, he couldn't talk. Wanting both of us to come fairly quickly, I fucked him harder than I normally would have done, doing my best to nail his prostate on every downstroke. Oliver apparently had a different idea. He pushed me off, wiggling his backside and arranging himself on his hands and knees before looking back at me over his shoulder. "Fuck me like this."

I did, quickly thrusting my cock back inside him. Only problem was that in this position I couldn't kiss him which meant the porn dialogue was back. "Baby, your cock's so huge!" It wasn't. I was under no illusions about that. It was average at best. "Make me feel you. Yeah! Like that! Baby, love your cock."

I closed my eyes again, my hips moving faster as I began to worry I wasn't going to be able to come. He had no such problems, his ass spasming around my cock and his body collapsing flat on the bed. I followed him down, sliding my cock back into him and taking the opportunity of the blessed silence to grind out an unsatisfying orgasm. Relieved I hadn't had to fake it — and if I was honest, that it was over — I pulled straight out and used the excuse of getting rid of the condom to head straight to the bathroom.

Alone in there, I took the opportunity to contemplate how soon I could make my escape. It was a one-night stand. What could he say? I'd go back in there, get dressed, call a cab, and I could be home before midnight.

Back in the bedroom, keen blue eyes followed my every movement as I retrieved my clothes from the floor and began to dress, my gaze deliberately averted from the man sprawled naked on the bed. "Why don't you stay?" He patted the other side of the bed. "Plenty of room. Give me half an hour and we can go for round two."

I flashed him a quick smile. "I can't. Sorry. Got to get home. I'm staying with my parents until I can get my own place. They'll worry. Especially my mum." It struck me as funny that the piece of information I'd been so keen for him not to find out earlier, was the one I was now using as an excuse. Finally dressed, I patted my pockets, checking everything I needed was there. My wallet and keys were, but my phone was missing. Frowning, I started to search around on the floor, thinking that maybe it had fallen out as I'd gotten undressed.

"Looking for this?"

Oliver held his hand up, my phone clasped in it. How had he gotten hold of it? It had definitely still been in my pocket when we'd walked into the bedroom. Had he taken it out of the pocket of my jeans when I was in the bathroom? If so, the question was why. I told myself to dial the paranoia down a notch. It was more likely that it had fallen on the floor, he'd noticed while I'd been in the bathroom and retrieved it for me. No big deal. No drama there worth getting myself worked up about.

Stepping over to the bed, I reached out to take it from him, but he snatched his hand back before I could make contact, a playful smile on his face. I wasn't in the mood for games. I just wanted to go home. "My phone, please."

Instead of giving it to me, he reached over to the nightstand, plucking his own phone from the surface. "Give me your number first."

I stared at him. What was this – emotional blackmail? I didn't want to give him my number, but to say no would look petty. I *reluctantly relayed it to him as he programmed the digits into his own phone. He still didn't return it, insisting on calling the number first. Did he think I'd given him a fake number? Or was he just making sure that I had his number as well? Whatever it was, I'd worry about it another day.*

* * * *

I woke from the nightmare with a start, my heart pounding and the sheets that were tangled around my waist soaked in sweat. It was the same most nights. There were usually no more than two or three a month where I managed to sleep through the night without waking up in a panic.

I attempted to breathe deeply and slowly, reminding myself that I was safe. As was the case at least fifty percent of the time, the reminder was useless and the darkness surrounding me became suffocating. I stumbled out of bed, almost tripping over the edge of the sheet, and made it over to the other side of the room and groped for the light switch. Hitting it, immediately bathing the room in bright light.

For a few moments, I just stood there, my eyes examining every corner of the room to reassure myself that I was alone. There was nothing there. It was just me. Me, the nightmares that were really memories, and my over-active imagination once I awoke. Then the nausea hit. I managed to make it to the toilet before the sandwich I'd consumed for dinner made its reappearance. Shaking, I sprawled across the toilet and gave in to the fully-fledged panic attack crawling its way to the surface. At least there was no one there to see it.

Chapter Five

Austin

It was my brother who answered the door in response to my knock, his nose wrinkling when he saw it was me. "You smell of oil."

I'd been hoping he'd be out. It was obviously my unlucky day. "You smell of books."

Mark's look said I was the most pathetic creature in the universe. I was used to it. He'd been looking at me that same way ever since we were kids. I suspected it had been the way he'd looked at me the day my mum had brought me home from the hospital. He'd just honed and perfected it over the years. "What does that even mean? Books don't smell."

I crossed my arms and prepared for battle. He never failed to bring out the worst in me, reducing me from a sensible mature adult, to an immature brat. And still, I couldn't stop myself from rising to it. "Alright. You smell of old, dusty books that have been sat in a garage for years because no one wants them, and a fox found a hole one night and wandered in and took a crap on them. Is that better?"

"You're a dick, Austin."

"You're a..." I didn't get the joy of coming up with a suitable insult to throw back at him before my mum's voice interrupted from down the hallway.

"Is that Austin?"

Mark quirked an eyebrow. "Unfortunately, yes."

With one last glare at Mark for his response, I made my way to the kitchen where the sound had come from. It was no surprise to find her elbows deep in flour. My mum was never happier than when she was baking something or other. If it wasn't for the family, it was for some cake sale somewhere. "Hi, Mum. Yeah, it's me. I was just trying to get past your unwanted lodger." Knowing there was no way I was going to shift her from the kitchen for the foreseeable future, I pulled out a chair and made myself comfortable at the kitchen table. Mark's entrance, him having followed me in, coincided nicely with my last comment.

It was my mum, though, who leapt to his defense. "Now, Austin. Don't talk like that about your brother. You know full well he's welcome to stay here as long as he needs to. As would you be, if you found yourself in the same situation."

The situation was that he was halfway through the PhD that would qualify him as a psychologist and had moved back home temporarily to save some money. I'd never understood why he'd started something that was going to take him ten years of his life to complete, in order to be qualified to sit there listening to people's problems, which I knew was a major over-simplification but that's what it boiled down to. Despite my mum's warning, I couldn't resist getting one last dig in. "I have a job. You don't need to worry about me having to return home. I can pay my own bills and everything."

My mum turned with a frown, waving a wooden spoon in my direction, her voice sharper this time which indicated she meant business. "Austin, lay off him. What's got into you today?"

I shrugged and did my best to ignore the smug expression on my brother's face as he sauntered out of the kitchen. Truth be told, I'd been antsy all day. I had no idea what was bothering me, but even the good-natured ribbing at the garage had irritated me—even when I wasn't the target.

A book in the middle of the table caught my attention. I reached out, curling my fingers around it, and turning it to face me so I could see the cover. It was some sort of bodice-ripping historical romance going by the picture of the bare-chested man and the hysterical-looking female draped across his chest on the front: my mum's preferred escapism when she wasn't baking. Dragging it closer, I opened it to confirm my suspicion that it was a library book. The sticker on the inside front cover did exactly that. Scooping it off the table, I held it up. "Have you finished reading this? Need me to take it back to the library?"

My mum lifted her head, pausing momentarily from the dough she was rolling out to see what I was looking at. "No, dear. I've only just started reading it."

Sighing, I gave it a shove, which sent it sliding back into the middle of the table. Was I that desperate to find an excuse to see the mysterious Alexander again? Is that what had been bothering me all day? If so, I needed to get a grip. I'd asked him out. He'd turned me down. That was the end of it. I knew nothing about him, other than his name and the fact he worked in the library. Unless you counted the fact that he liked to read about murder; a preference which really didn't fit with the rest of the persona.

Obviously picking up on my body language, my mum studied my face as she tucked a stray piece of hair back behind her ear, seemingly oblivious to the trail of flour it left behind on her cheek. "Are you staying for dinner?"

Was I? I wasn't sure why I'd stopped by if not. Sometimes, it was nice though—just to check in. But, dinner with a far too observant mother, not to mention having to spend more time fencing insults with Mark, was probably the last thing I needed right now. Maybe an intensive workout would go some way to ease the restlessness. I rose from the table, moving over to kiss the non-floury cheek of my mother. "Nah! Think I'm going to head to the gym. Thanks though. Tell Dad I stopped by."

"Sure." My mother smiled. "It was nice to see you — if only briefly. Come for dinner soon."

I nodded and then I was on my way out of the door less than ten minutes after arriving.

* * * *

Passing the coffee shop on the way to the gym, made me think about Alexander again. It was a long time since a man had gotten under my skin this way. Especially one that wasn't interested. But, I couldn't help feeling that there was far more to him than could be seen on the surface. I had no idea why I felt that. It was just a gut feeling and my gut feelings had rarely, if ever, been proved wrong.

I couldn't help glancing in through the window, my eyes drifting straight over to the table where I'd last seen him. Silly really. He'd been there because it was his lunch break. It was almost six. Long past the time where a regular routine would have him in the same place, and that's if it even was a regular routine. It might not have been. Except — there he was, seated at the exact same table, only one away from the window. I'd have recognized the top of that head anywhere, his hair spilling over his face as he bent forwards. I assumed he was reading again; the angle was too difficult for me to be able to tell.

On impulse, I raised my hand to the glass and knocked. His head shot up, his eyes darting in my direction with that same look of fear I'd glimpsed back in the library. I smiled and waved, wishing I could somehow make myself look smaller than the hulking brute I suddenly felt like. He stared at me for the longest time, his eyes wide, and then finally lifted his hand and returned the wave, a tremulous smile on his face.

Alexander had smiled at me. I wanted to jump for joy. I wanted a photograph of the historic moment. I wanted to...talk to him. Even if it was another two-minute conversation, it would probably still be the best two minutes of my day.

I changed direction, heading for the door. The gym could wait a few minutes. It wasn't as if it was going anywhere, and it was open till ten anyway. I had plenty of time. I grabbed a coffee, toying with the idea of getting another hot chocolate for Alex but deciding against it. I didn't want to come over as too pushy or too desperate. Rather than sitting with him straight away, I took a seat at the empty table next to his, instinct telling me that keeping a bit of distance was the best policy. My chair squeaked as I pulled it under and he raised his head in response to the noise. I offered him another smile. "Hi. Only me." I pointed down at my latte. "Having a coffee. Again."

Another smile, fainter this time, but he didn't offer any response to my scintillating conversation starter. I pointed to the book. "Murder again?"

He shook his head, lifting the book so I could see the cover. It was titled: *Justice, Crimes, Trials and Punishments.* He seemed to have a strange fascination with crime. I stood up, picking up my coffee and sliding into the seat opposite him, his soulful brown eyes following my every move, but not protesting. "Do you want to be a lawyer?"

Another headshake.

"You don't talk much." As soon as the words left my mouth, I regretted them. It was his prerogative. Besides, I was judging him based solely on his interactions with me. For all I knew he was an absolute chatterbox with other people. I doubted it though. My covert observations of him in the library when he hadn't realized I was watching would seem to suggest otherwise. "I mean, that's fine. I didn't mean to be rude...just, you know...making an observation...which I should probably have kept to myself. I can talk enough for both of us."

He continued to stare, his expression giving nothing away. "Look, just tell me to go away if I'm bothering you." There was a long pause while I braced myself for him to do exactly that. Then, he shrugged, as if he wasn't that bothered either way. Whether he'd meant it like that or not, I took it as an invitation to stay. "I didn't expect you to be here at this time. Not that I was looking for you. I don't want you to get the wrong idea. Only, I was passing by on my way to the gym and I just happened to look through the window and you were at the same table as you were the other day...so I thought I'd come over and say hi. And here I am."

"I come here a lot."

They were the first words out of his mouth since I'd joined him at the table and I seized on them like a hungry piranha which had just been offered a tasty piece of meat. "Yeah. Do you? I guess it's quiet at this time. Nobody to bother you. Except for me...and I did say you could tell me to go away...which I'm very grateful you haven't, but that offer still stands, so as soon as I start annoying you...don't be polite, just tell me to clear off." Was that a hint of amusement in his eyes? It was good to know that my verbal diarrhea had its uses. "I might not bother going to the gym actually."

His gaze dropped, drifting down over my arms, the form-fitting T-shirt doing nothing to hide the physique I'd worked damn hard to get. When your type was toned and muscular, it usually served you well to offer an equally good body in return. Also, my job was quite physical: lifting weights was good practice for lugging engines around. "It looks like you can afford to miss a gym session or two."

I smiled. "Yeah, probably. I might go and eat something instead." I rested my head on my hand while I contemplated nearby culinary choices. "Mexican maybe...or Italian. Or there's an American-style diner around the corner. Nothing fancy just burgers, fries, and milkshakes. Have you ever been?"

"No."

I gave further thought to the burger, my mouth watering at the thought. It definitely sounded more fun than the gym. "Yeah, there's a burger with my name on it, and you can eat in there on your own without people staring at you as if you're crazy." I scratched my chin, noticing for the first time that I'd forgotten to shave that morning. "Think I'll go there."

"You're eating on your own?"

I did a cursory scan of the coffee shop. It was in that winding down phase where it was preparing to close. Any customers that remained seemed to be getting drinks to go and only three of the tables were still occupied and that included the one we were sat at. "Yeah. Guess so. It's either that or go home and cook, but then I'll probably still end up having to order take-away anyway once I've burned whatever I've attempted. I'm not a very good cook. I could have eaten at my mum's, but my brother was there and he's a major dick, and I wasn't in the mood for his particular brand of dickery today."

A strange look passed over Alex's face, as if he wanted to say something but couldn't quite think how to phrase it. I cast my mind back over the last few things I'd said, trying to work out what might have triggered it. It couldn't have been the mention of my bad cooking. What had we been discussing before that? Me eating alone. Was he after an invitation? "Have you eaten? Do you want to come?"

His head dipped, his thick, dark hair falling forward to cover his eyes which made it difficult to read his expression. I finished my coffee while I waited. When he turned me down — again — I wouldn't be wanting to hang around. I mean, it wasn't quite the same. I wasn't making out as if it was a date this time, but still, it was going to sting nonetheless.

"Okay."

The word was said so quietly that for a moment I thought I'd imagined it. Then his head lifted and there was that tremulous smile again. Our eyes locked and my stomach did a little flip at the prospect of getting to spend more time with him.

Chapter Six

Alexander

I didn't know why I'd said yes to him. Or maybe I did, deep down. I was only in the coffee shop to avoid going home. The run-in with Richard Simpkins the previous day had left me emotionally drained. Add to that the panic attack in the middle of the night and the fact I hadn't managed to get back to sleep and I just didn't have the mental reserves to cope with seeing him again so soon. I was already living each day on a knife edge. So, rather than going home, I'd gone to the coffee shop.

I knew it had only ever been a temporary solution. It closed too early to be anything more than that. I'd been trying to come up with somewhere else I could go, but I'd drawn a blank. Most places were too busy for me to face on my own. There was too high a probability of running into another Richard Simpkins. I seemed to attract them and the more I withdrew, the more I tried to make myself invisible, the more they seemed to seek me out with their leering and their knowing smiles. I may as well have had victim written in capital letters across my forehead. The only solution seemed to be to go and sit in the park. At this time, it was usually empty, save for a few dog-walkers or runners. But then,

43

how long could I sit there for? I'd still have to go home eventually.

Then Austin had arrived and like an angel sent to give guidance, he'd provided an alternative, a possible place to go where I wouldn't be on my own and I could stave off the inevitability of facing my next-door neighbor that little bit longer. So, I'd silenced the little voice inside of my head screaming not to trust and I'd agreed to go with him.

So, there I was. Sat in an American diner with a man I didn't know, staring at the burger and fries on the plate in front of me that he'd insisted on paying for. In fact, like a perfect gentleman, Austin had insisted on finding seats and ensuring I was comfortable before going to the counter and ordering for both of us. He ate voraciously, but then I guessed that when you were as big as him and worked out as often as he seemed to, it took an awful lot of fuel to keep that body going.

I forced myself to pick up a fry, managing to put it in my mouth and chew methodically. I hadn't touched the burger. It sat there like Mount Everest, taunting me with my inability to tackle it when I normally lived on sandwiches and cereal. That's what dinner would have been, had I gone home: a bowl of cornflakes, and even then, it was doubtful I would have eaten the whole bowl.

Austin paused for a moment from describing the people he worked with at the garage to push the basket of onion rings in my direction. "Here, have one."

Reaching out, I dutifully plucked one from the basket, placing it on my plate next to the burger as Austin continued his story: something about a prank played on someone called Wilko. As far as I could tell from the little I'd been listening to, it involved a tire and a rubber chicken. I didn't mind though. It meant that apart from the odd grunt and nod, I wasn't expected to say anything. I chewed slowly on another fry, letting the wave of chattiness from the man opposite wash over me as I studied him.

He had a nice face, handsome without being so striking you'd constantly worry about other men throwing themselves at him, his hazel eyes crinkling with laughter lines as he spoke. If the lines were any indication, he laughed a lot. He was laughing now while he told the story, his full lips curling up at the edges. He talked a lot with his hands, seemingly oblivious to the tiny morsels of food that went flying off in various directions whenever his gesticulations were particularly animated. I wondered if he was aware he had a streak of something black just below his left ear. Probably not. He suddenly stopped mid-sentence. "Oh my God! I'm so sorry."

I startled, watching as he wiped a bit of stray ketchup from the corner of his mouth. "What?"

A guilty expression settled on his face and I found myself missing the laughter lines. "I'm just rambling on and on. I'm not giving you a chance to say anything."

"I don't mind. Honest." That was an understatement. I had nothing to talk about. Nothing I was prepared to talk about anyway. What was I going to do, tell him about my day in the library? Tell him I was terrified to go home because I couldn't deal with a man I'd once have been able to cut down to size with just a few carefully chosen words like he was a mere inconvenience? I remembered that man. Al had been his name. I just didn't feel as if I had any traces of him left inside me. They'd been extinguished as easily and as quickly as blowing out a flame.

Austin gestured at my burger, a frown on his face. "Aren't you going to eat that?"

I let my gaze drop, hoping that maybe I'd at least taken a bite and just didn't remember. But, there it was, completely untouched, the onion ring still lying next to it. "I'm not really hungry. Sorry."

The frown was replaced by a look of concern. I waited for him to pry further: ask what I'd had for lunch or point out that I was too thin. I'd once been accused of being anorexic. I wasn't anorexic. I just had little to no interest in food. I had no right to enjoy it when others who'd once been in my life didn't have that same luxury because of me.

Austin sat back in his chair, his broad shoulders rising in a shrug while his face expressed nothing but reassurance. "No worries. I do that all the time, think I'm hungry and then realize once I've started eating that I wasn't quite as hungry as I thought." He tapped the basket of onion rings, the two remaining onion rings jiggling with the movement. "I mean, look at that. I can't eat those." He rubbed a hand over his flat stomach, the six-pack of his abs showing through the thin T-shirt. "I'm stuffed! Anyway, I've spent ages talking about myself. What about you? What about your family? Do they live close?"

The fry I'd just bitten down on, turned to glue in my mouth. I schooled my face to give away nothing as I struggled to chew, trying to force the food to go down my throat by sheer force of will. "I don't have family."

His eyebrows shot up. "None at all?"

I suddenly wanted to be anywhere but there. This had been a huge mistake. I knew better than to think I was capable of doing normal things and having normal conversations. I felt trapped. Even facing Richard Simpkins was better than answering questions about my family. I managed a shake of my head, my gaze firmly fixed on the increasingly greasy-looking burger on my plate, my stomach beginning to heave, the six or seven fries I'd eaten feeling like they were trying to crawl back up my esophagus.

A loud crash nearby caused my head to jerk around. A stressed-looking woman was hovering by a table full of people, apologizing profusely. By the shattered glass scattered by her feet, it seemed like she'd knocked a glass off of their table. She bent down, still apologizing, and began to gather up some of the larger pieces of glass. She swore, snatching her hand back and cradling it to her chest as blood welled up from a cut and began to drip onto the table before she grabbed a napkin to stem the flow. I stared at the droplets of blood, my mind somersaulted back to another place and time. There hadn't just been droplets of blood there. It had been all over the floor, puddles of it, with bloody footprints and handprints leading all the way up the stairs.

"It's just a broken glass. Don't worry. They'll clear it up. Poor woman should have let the staff deal with it, rather than trying to pick up the pieces herself. I'm sure it just looks worse than it is though."

Austin's words barely permeated the fog of my brain. I felt dizzy. I felt both hot and cold at the same time, if that was even possible. The walls of the diner started to close in, the noise in there suddenly overwhelming. There were too many people. Too many smells. Too much of everything. I bolted, nearly tripping over the table leg in my haste to get out of there.

Out on the street, I gulped in oxygen as I kept walking. It was raining, but I didn't care. I barely felt it. I had no idea where I was going. Only that I needed to walk and I needed to put some distance between myself and the blood and the broken glass. The destination was nowhere near as important as the journey. Finally, I slowed, slumping back against a building, and only then becoming aware that someone was calling my name.

Austin came to a halt in front of me, his brow furrowed. He held his hand out and I tried to make sense of the object held in it. He smiled and I focused on the laughter lines that appeared. Something about them grounded me and I found myself able to think again, able to breathe; the fragments starting to knit back together and the noise in my head subsiding to a dull roar. "You forgot your book. It's a library book. I didn't want you getting into trouble for losing it. Especially when you work there."

I reached out, managing to get my fingers to curl around it

enough that I could take it from him. "Thank you." My voice came out raspy, as if it hadn't been used for quite some time.

"You don't need to be embarrassed, you know. It's quite common."

"What is?"

"Freaking out at the sight of blood. That's why you ran out of there, right?"

So, that's the conclusion he'd come to. Rather than assuming I was a freak, he'd tried to find a rational explanation. I wanted to laugh, but I was scared that if I started, I wouldn't be able to stop. Nodding, I seized on the excuse eagerly. "Makes me feel sick." Which was true, but not for the reasons he was assuming.

Suddenly, he stepped forward, wrapping his arms around me, and pulling me into his broad chest, the top of my head barely reaching his chin. I froze, unsure what I was supposed to do. It had been so long since I'd been hugged and he was a virtual stranger. I waited for the panic to hit. In my current state of heightened emotions, it should have come instantaneously. I should have been fighting him. I should have been struggling to free myself from his embrace. But, he was warm and solid, and more than that, for some reason he made me feel safe. It was ridiculous, but there was no denying it. Something about Austin Armstrong made me trust him. He was an oasis in the middle of the desert. He was a cool drink of water on a summer's day.

I relaxed and breathed him in; an earthy mixture of cologne and something else I couldn't identify that made me think of cars tickling my nostrils. Probably the same thing that had caused the streak on his neck. I not only didn't panic, I snuggled closer, feeling like I could have stayed there all night, listening to the solid thump of his heartbeat beneath my cheek.

He pulled back, his hand cupping my cheek, and the warm hazel gaze staring down into mine. Then he leaned forward, his lips brushing gently over mine. And I let him. I didn't protest. I didn't recoil. I let him. He jerked back, an epithet bursting from his lips. "I'm sorry. I didn't mean to do that. I mean...the hug, yes. You looked like you needed one, but the kiss...I shouldn't have done that. Forgive me?"

"I didn't mind." It was hard to tell who was more surprised by my words—Austin or myself. I was being honest, though. I hadn't minded. In fact, more than that, I'd liked it. His fingers, still pressed against my cheek, trembled ever so slightly before his head dipped again. This time I didn't just let him kiss me, I responded; my lips moving against his. It was still fairly chaste as kisses go, neither of us feeling the need to bring tongues into the equation, but even so, by the time our lips parted, we were both breathing as hard as if we'd run a marathon.

Austin looked around sheepishly, smiling and laughing, before his gaze swung back to mine, the smile still lingering on his lips. "Can I walk you home, Alex?"

Home! The word may as well have been a bucket of cold water. The thought of returning to my cold, dark apartment with the slimy Richard Simpkins lurking close by made the brief warmth I'd experienced in Austin's arms wither up and die. The words were out before I could stop them. "I don't want to go home!"

Austin frowned, his eyes scanning both sides of the street where we stood as if looking for a place we could go instead. "Okay. Well...I'd suggest a walk, but it's raining. We could go for a drink, maybe?"

I shook my head, immediate fear clawing at my insides at the thought of venturing into a crowded bar. Even with Austin there, I wouldn't be able to do it.

He thought for a while. "My place is only a few streets away. We could go there?"

The words were tentative, his face apologetic, giving the impression he felt it was a ridiculous suggestion to have made. It was for that reason that I considered it. That and the fact I was desperate. The rational side of my brain — a side that lay dormant all too often — argued what was the worst Richard Simpkins could do. But, the irrational side, the side that had taken precedence for the last year sent adrenaline coursing through my body at the mere thought of having to lay eyes on him, and at having to spend the night with him only a few feet away separated by a thin stretch of wall. But, there was no point if it was only going to buy me an extra hour or so of refuge. I may as well just get it over with and go home now. It was that side I listened to, the words tumbling out before I could even begin to consider how crazy they were. "Can I stay there tonight? With you?"

Austin's eyes widened, either in surprise or shock, I wasn't sure. Maybe it was a mixture of the two. I didn't know what I'd do if he turned me down, which was likely. After all, who invited themselves back after refusing to even go out on a date with the person. He chewed at his lip for a moment. Then the smile was back and he was holding his hand out, palm upwards. "Sure."

I took it and let him lead me in the right direction.

* * * *

Austin's house was smaller than I'd expected, his bulk barely seeming to fit in the tiny kitchen as he bustled about in there. I guessed that mechanics didn't earn that much and given house prices in London, it was unrealistic to expect him to be living in a mansion. Besides, it was still bigger and nicer than the apartment where I lived.

"Take a tour if you want."

I did, though more as an excuse to spend some time on my own than from a genuine desire to see the house. I started in the living room. We'd walked through it on our way to the kitchen but I hadn't really been paying attention. It was a typical bachelor's living room: low on decoration and high on a worn but comfortable-looking sofa and a large screen TV which dominated most of one wall. I could picture Austin sprawled across it, watching sport on the TV. He struck me as the type who'd follow a sport and a team with undying loyalty.

The only other room downstairs, apart from the kitchen was a small back room. Opening the door, revealed that it was virtually empty: just a few boxes stacked against one wall and a desk and computer. Backtracking down the hallway, I paused for a moment with my foot on the first stair. He'd said I could take a tour. Did that include upstairs? I guessed so, or he would have specified a tour of the downstairs. I ventured upward, finding a small unremarkable bathroom, a tiny box room which looked as if it was mainly used for storage, and lastly Austin's bedroom.

I stood in the doorway unable to tear my gaze away from the double bed in the middle of the room. It was hard not to consider the cost of having invited myself to spend the night. I had no idea whether that was a price I'd even be capable of paying. It was there that Austin found me, shoving a large mug of something hot into my hands. I took a cautious sniff: hot chocolate.

Austin crossed his arms. "I don't expect anything from you, Alex...if that's what's put that worried look on your face."

"What?"

He reached over, gently touching my brow as if smoothing away lines of worry. "You being here, doesn't mean anything has to happen. You can sleep here" — he inclined his head toward the bed — "with me. Or you can sleep downstairs on the sofa. Either way, you can just sleep. You don't owe me anything. You coming back here doesn't come with strings. I'm not that sort of guy. It's just nice to spend more time with you."

A huge wave of relief swept over me. "Are you sure?"

He nodded profusely, a small smile hovering on his lips.

"Quite sure. Now, come and drink your hot chocolate downstairs and then you can decide where you feel the most comfortable."

For the next ten minutes, I perched on the end of the sofa, sipping the drink Austin had made for me while he sat at the opposite end talking about nothing in particular. The sound of his voice proved almost as soothing as the milky drink. Every now and again, his words would slow, and he'd yawn loudly before picking his story back up at the point he'd left it. When I finally placed my empty mug on the small table at the side of the sofa, it was as if he'd been waiting for that exact eventuality, and he was already on his feet, taking hold of my hand and tugging me after him as he headed toward the stairs. "Where are we going?"

"Bed."

I fought down the small surge of panic. *Had he been lying before? Lulling me into a false sense of security?* Picking up on my hesitation, he paused halfway up the stairs, stifling another yawn. "I'm too tired to sort out bedding for the sofa. And to be honest, I'm not even sure I have any. I don't have many — actually any — sofa visitors. You'll be much more comfortable in the bed."

"Just to sleep?"

We'd reached the bedroom door. He flicked the light switch on and strode in, leaving me hovering nervously by the door, while he pulled the duvet cover back and patted that side of the bed. "Yes. Just to sleep. Get in." At least he wasn't expecting me to undress. I walked across the room and slid beneath the covers, turning away from the center of the bed, and lying there stiffly, listening to Austin's movements as he walked back across to the door, the room soon transitioning back into darkness. More footsteps and then the bed sagged under his weight. He shifted around and then I was being pulled back against his chest, his arm wrapping around me almost protectively. And just like when he'd hugged me in the street, that same strange feeling of safety returned. I closed my eyes, breathing out as my body relaxed, his voice a whisper in my ear. "Goodnight, Alexander."

"Goodnight, Austin."

Chapter Seven

Austin

I leaned back against the chest of drawers, my gaze fixed on the man still sleeping in my bed, his dark hair a perfect foil against the white pillow. His face looked younger in sleep, less guarded, the stubble on his face only serving to accentuate the delicate bone structure. It was hard to believe after spending so much time convincing myself to leave him alone, that we'd not only kissed last night, but he'd ended up in my bed.

It had felt so right when I'd woken up still holding him. The temptation to stay that way had been almost overpowering. I'd wanted to luxuriate in every single second, my nose buried in his coconut-scented hair. But I had an inkling that he wouldn't feel the same, that waking up in my arms in the cold light of day would produce very different emotions than it had for me.

So, reluctantly, I'd separated myself from the warmth of his body, showered, shaved, dressed, and made him a coffee—hot chocolate and early mornings didn't seem to fit together. He could always choose not to drink it. And now there I was, using the excuse of giving him a few more moments of peaceful sleep to admire the sleeping figure.

54

I couldn't leave it much longer because I had no idea what time he needed to be at work. A quick google search into the library's opening hours had revealed it opened at nine, but I assumed like most workplaces he was expected to turn up earlier than when the first member of public turned up at the door.

He stirred, his hand burrowing into the space between his cheek and the pillow and his lips slightly parting. The lips I'd kissed — twice. The first time had been a mistake: the result of my body reacting to the feel of his body pressed against mine as I'd hugged him. The second time, when he'd given permission was the sweetest kiss I'd ever had.

The attraction I could understand. I'd been attracted to him from the first moment that I'd seen him in the library. What was harder to get to grips with, was the feeling of protectiveness that I just couldn't shake. Something inside of me just couldn't help responding to the vulnerability I sensed. I wanted to wrap him up in cotton wool and protect him from the world, not let anyone get close enough to hurt him. It was stupid. I knew it was. I barely knew him, but I just couldn't help myself.

That over-protectiveness was the main reason I'd gone back on my word the previous night and taken the choice of where he was going to sleep away from him. I couldn't face knowing he was in my house, but out of reach on the sofa. If he'd argued, of course I would have let him sleep there, but he hadn't, and despite not looking entirely comfortable with the idea, he'd relaxed in my arms just like when I'd hugged him.

I checked my watch: seven thirty. I needed to be at the garage by eight thirty. That, and the rapidly cooling cup of coffee in my hands, meant I couldn't put off waking him any longer.

"Alexander." No response. I tried a little louder. "Alex! Time to wake up." He sat up with a start, his eyes darting all around the bedroom, no doubt trying to make sense of the unfamiliar surroundings. His gaze finally settled on me and I gave him what

I hoped was a reassuring smile. "Morning." I held the mug up in the air. "I brought you coffee. You don't have to drink it. I put sugar in it. I figured if you like hot chocolate, you probably like things sweet." Stepping forward, I held the mug out to him.

He stared at it for a moment before moving to take it from me, his hands wrapping around the mug as if seeking its warmth. "What time is it?"

"Just gone half past seven. I wasn't sure how early you needed to be up in order to get to work on time."

He rubbed his eye with the heel of one hand before bringing the mug held in the other one to his mouth and taking a sip. I had a feeling he'd force himself to drink it whether he liked it or not— just to be polite. "I can make you tea instead?"

He shook his head, sitting up straighter and bringing his legs around until his feet touched the floor. His shoes were the only thing he'd removed. The rest of him was still fully dressed. "I need to go home."

I'd already thought about that, assuming he'd need to change clothes. It wasn't as if I could offer him anything of mine to wear: my clothes would dwarf him. I hesitated, unsure how he was going to react to my suggestion. "I thought I could give you a lift home, wait while you do whatever you need to do, and then drive you to work."

He ducked his head, staring down at the mug as if the mysteries of the universe lay at the bottom. "I can get a bus."

"I know you can. But you don't need to, and it'll be much quicker my way. I'm just trying to help, Alex. I'm not trying to crowd you or force you into anything. I've got to drive to work anyway, so..." Aware I was starting to sound pushy, I backed off. "Sorry. It's your decision. There's a bus stop at the end of the road. I can point you in the right direction, if that's what you'd rather do?"

The hair was back covering Alex's face. He seemed to hide

behind it whenever he needed to think. I waited. Finally, he
pushed it back, his brown eyes finding mine. "Okay. A ride would
be good."

* * * *

Alex's building looked fairly run-down from the outside, the
colorful graffiti of what appeared to be a dragon eating a monkey
covered most of the front wall. It didn't look like it had been done
recently either, the paint fading away to almost nothing in several
places. The inside, at least, was graffiti-free, the walls looking like
they'd received the attention the outside was lacking with a
couple of coats of mass-produced, and presumably very cheap,
cream paint. It made me wonder what might have been lurking
beneath there prior to the paint job — maybe more dragons and
monkeys, or something equally imaginative that looked as if it
had been painted by someone high on drugs.

I followed Alex up the stairs, sensing his hesitation in the
way he slowed down as he drew near to what I assumed had to be
his apartment. I hung back, gesturing to the stairs before seating
myself on the top one. "I'll wait here."

He looked momentarily thrown, as if the thought I might
pass up the chance to nosy around his apartment had never even
occurred to him. I had to admit to being more than a little curious
about where he lived, but I was more interested in the long game:
earning his trust little by little than giving in to instant
gratification. Alex struck me as a man that needed his space, and
if I pushed too far or too fast, he'd run a mile. He chewed on his
lip for a moment, looking unsure. "You don't mind?"

"Not at all." I made a big deal out of pulling my phone out of
my pocket and unlocking the screen. "I've got to make a call
anyway." I didn't, but I could fake it: call Wilko or Adrian and
make up some question about the jobs we had lined up at the
garage today. Alex had unlocked the door but still hadn't gone

inside as if his good manners couldn't quite reconcile with leaving me there. I threw a smile in his direction before pressing the call button, Adrian's gruff voice answering with more of a grunt than a greeting.

I made myself sound as cheery as possible just to annoy him. "Hey, mate. Good morning!"

There was a stony silence before I got any response. Adrian wasn't a morning person. "What? I'm seeing your ugly mug in another half hour. What the hell couldn't wait until then?"

Alex opened the door and disappeared inside, the door closing firmly behind him. "Nothing. I pocket-called you. Sorry. See you in a bit." I hung up, laughing to myself as I imagined him turning the air blue while he stared at his phone, wondering why I'd wasted his time.

The wait was uneventful, the only incident of note being Alex's next-door neighbor leaving his apartment. He was a smarmy-looking man who might have been good-looking in the right light, and if he wasn't glaring. I seemed to upset him by not moving out of his way fast enough so he could get past. Either that or he was like that with everyone. I disliked him immediately, hoping that Alex had very little to do with him.

There'd been very little conversation on the way over, Alex seeming happy to sit and stare out of the window, which was fine by me: conversation first thing in the morning wasn't my strong point. I'd stopped off at a bakery, claiming I needed to grab breakfast for myself. Actually, I'd wanted to see if I could get Alex to eat something. I often went without breakfast. There was usually food hanging around the garage anyway, or one of us would go out for something mid-morning.

I'd casually handed a Danish pastry over and cheered inside when he'd eaten half of it. Sweet was obviously the way to go with him. The plan was to try and get him to eat the other half on the way over to the library. That's if he ever appeared. I checked my watch. If he didn't show his face soon, I'd be cutting it fine to drop him off at the library and make it to work on time myself.

As if summoned by thought alone, the door opened and a freshly shaved Alex in dark trousers and a plain blue shirt appeared, his hair still damp from the shower he must have taken. I smiled at the sight of him, carrying on smiling even when he turned his back to lock the door before sliding the key into his pocket. "I thought you might have gone."

I'd managed to stop smiling by the time he turned back around. Lucky, really, or he was going to start thinking I was crazy. "Nah! I've been enjoying the..." I cast my eye around the hallway, searching for inspiration, but it was plain: no paintings, nothing. Even the carpet was a plain dark gray. "No. I've got nothing." I inclined my head toward the stairs leading down. "Let's go. Your chariot awaits."

Back in the car, I passed the paper bag with the leftover half of the pastry back to him. "Eat that, would you? Or it'll attract flies or something. Maybe even a giant rat."

He looked less than convinced, but peeled the paper back and began to nibble on the corner anyway. By the time I'd parked in front of the library, it was nearly all gone. I chalked it up as a definite win. He didn't get out of the car immediately and an awkward silence hung between us. I glanced over at him. There was no way I was letting him just walk away. "Can I have your number?"

"I don't have a phone."

Huh! I considered that for a moment. Was that just an excuse? But then surely, he'd have come up with a more believable one. I couldn't help asking the question. "Why not?" He shrugged, disappearing behind his hair again. My fingers itched to reach over and brush it back, but I forced myself to hold still. "Then, how am I going to see you again?" I held my breath, worried the next words out of his mouth would be a rejection, and

I'd discover that a night with him in my bed — platonic as it had been — would be all I was going to get. I didn't mind a slow courtship. I didn't mind waiting for him. He was worth it, but I needed him to be on the same page.

He lifted his head without looking my way, staring out through the windshield and seemingly fixated on something in the distance. Finally, his head slowly turned my way. "You could meet me after work?"

"Today?"

He nodded.

I did my best to stop my face from breaking out into a huge grin. "From here?"

"From the coffee shop. I'll go there after work. I'll be there from about five."

Taking encouragement from the fact he wanted to see me again, I reached over palming his cheek. When he didn't draw back, I took the liberty of pulling his head around and dropping a lingering kiss onto his lips. Lips that tasted of sugar from the pastry. I reluctantly let him go, sitting back in the seat and feeling as if I'd won the lottery. "You'd better go or you'll be late."

I watched him walk away until he disappeared through the front door of the library. He might have gotten there on time, but I was going to be late for work myself. Sad thing was, I didn't care. Adrian could moan and grumble all he wanted. There was no way he was going to be able to shake me from my good mood today.

Chapter Eight

Alexander

My phone beeped for about the fifth time in the space of an hour. I glanced at it, reading the message before placing it back on the table.

"What the fuck, man! What's with the being so popular today?" Jack rolled his eyes at the same time as wiping beer away from his mouth with his sleeve, David frowning at his boyfriend for his lack of manners. "Or is it your mum? Awww...is mummy making sure her little boy is safe and sound and not up to any mischief?"

I gave him the finger. "Fuck off, moron! It's not my mum."

Jack batted the finger away. "If you're not going to stick that somewhere interesting, then don't tease me with it."

I made a retching sound. "You wish."

David's voice cut across our teasing. "Whoever it is, they seem pretty keen to get hold of you, and I can't help noticing you're ignoring them. Everything alright?"

I sighed. I should have put my phone on silent. "Remember that guy I picked up the other night?" They both nodded. "It's him. Wants to take me out on a date."

Jack looked bemused. "And that's a problem...because..."

"I don't particularly want to see him again."

He snorted. *"Then you shouldn't have given him your number, dipshit."*

I shot Jack a dirty look. *"I didn't. Well, I did...but I didn't really have a lot of choice."* I was reluctant to share the rest of the story. Something still didn't sit right about Oliver's actions. Maybe I was reluctant to share those doubts because my friends would laugh and tell me I was being an idiot. I probably was.

David looked thoughtful. *"I thought you said he was horrifically rich and lived in a swanky penthouse."*

I shrugged. *"So?"*

Jack perked up a little bit. *"Really? Gorgeous AND rich. Pass your phone over."*

I raised an eyebrow but did as he asked. I wasn't worried about him seeing the messages. They were all pretty similar, just variations on the theme of Oliver asking when he could see me again. I certainly couldn't fault the guy's effort. It was confusing though, given my lack of interest in the sex. Had he really not been able to tell? And maybe it had been due to the wine, or the fact it was getting late, or a combination of the two, but it seemed strange for him to be quite so oblivious. I mean, it wasn't as if I was that much of a catch in comparison to him. I guessed it was flattering, really. It wasn't until Jack started typing that I realized his intention and began to protest. *"Hey."* I reached out, attempting to snatch my phone back, but Jack was quicker, moving his arm out of reach with a huge grin on his face as he pressed send. *"What did you type?"*

He passed the phone back, the grin showing no signs of fading. *"Not much. I just figured we'd find out how serious he is."* Frowning, I read the message he'd sent. *"How about you take me for dinner in Paris?"* The response came through instantaneously. *"Sure. When are you free?"*

I tilted the phone so Jack could read the response to his meddling, David leaning in so that he could see it too, his eyebrows shooting up. *"Wow! He really likes you, Al. Maybe you should give him another chance. Where are you going to find another man willing to wine and dine you in Paris?"*

I pulled a face, sending my own message to try and alleviate some of the damage Jack had done. It was the first time I'd responded to any of his messages. "That was a joke. Paris not necessary."

The cursor started flashing immediately. "Dinner at Nobu then as a compromise? My treat." I looked over at my friends. Jack shrugged. "What's the worst that could happen? He buys you an expensive dinner, and then if you decide you can't stand him, you give him the brush-off. My parents —"

I cut him off. I'd heard the story a thousand times. Everyone knew it. His parents' first date hadn't gone well. It had taken his dad two weeks to convince his mum to give it another go. That was twenty-five years ago and they'd been together ever since and were just as much in love as they'd ever been. It did make you think, though. Maybe I was being a little too hasty, dismissing Oliver so quickly without giving things a second try. What was the worst that could happen?

* * * *

When things got a little too much for me in the library, I retreated to the staff toilet. That's where I was now, staring at my pale reflection in the small mirror attached to the wall. I usually had about fifteen minutes before anyone would notice I was missing. I put the lid down on the toilet and sat down, my thoughts returning to the previous evening and night and desperately trying to make some sense out of it. I'd been so careful over the last year to keep everyone at bay. Yet, somehow Austin had managed to worm beneath my defenses, to the point where I'd even agreed to see him again. What was I agreeing to anyway? Dating him? Sleeping with him? All I knew was that in his presence, the raging noise in my head died down to a dull roar. It didn't go away. There was nothing in the world that could eradicate it entirely. And I'd slept last night. The whole night. No nightmares. No constantly waking up every hour and watching the clock tick its way toward dawn. I couldn't even remember the last time I'd slept that well. Yet somehow, wrapped in a virtual stranger's arms, I had. Maybe it was just a coincidence, but I didn't think it was.

What did I know about him though, besides the fact he was a mechanic? He might seem safe and unthreatening, but what if it was all an act? What if underneath that gentle giant exterior, there was a psychopath fighting to get out, just waiting for the right, gullible victim to come along. I closed my eyes, recalling the kisses we'd shared. They'd both been fairly chaste. What would it be like to kiss him properly or maybe even go further than that? Would he still be gentle? Al had liked it rough, but Alex, well, he may as well be a virgin. It had been so long since I'd let anyone touch me, I wasn't even sure how I'd react. But then, I'd have said the same about kissing yesterday, and that had come as naturally as breathing with Austin.

I forced my eyes open as a knock at the door sounded. "Alexander, are you in there? We need you out front. Maureen's waiting to take her break."

I took a deep breath. It figured that it would be one of those days where my absence was noted well before the fifteen minutes was up. It had barely been five. "Coming!"

The rest of the day passed the same as any other. Life in the library was uneventful. Books were predictable, the words in them staying the same and the page count never changing. Customers were the same ones, with only the occasional new face. No one came into a library to do anything but read, take books out, or do research. I needed that predictability. Craved it. Relied on it. The time of the day when the library launched into its closing down routine, always came as an emotional wrench. The knowledge I had to leave and head into the outside world, no matter how briefly, always weighed heavy. If I could have gotten away with sleeping in the back room and never leaving the library, I probably would have.

On a day where I hadn't even left the library for lunch, it seemed far worse. The pastry I'd consumed this morning when I wasn't used to eating anything at all for breakfast meant I hadn't eaten a thing since. Maureen rattled the keys in my direction as I dragged my feet. That meant she was waiting to lock up. I made my way reluctantly toward the door, the added pressure of my upcoming meeting with Austin made me wish I could ask her to lock me in.

I thought about him on the walk to the coffee shop. If he was everything he seemed at face value to be, and if I was honest, there was nothing I'd seen so far to indicate he wasn't, then he deserved better than having someone like me in his life. All I'd do is drag him down. And I had plans. Plans I could never share with him. Plans that meant there could never be anything long-term between us. I hesitated by the door of the coffee shop, my hand hovering in mid-air while temptation, and common-sense warred inside me. Common sense won. I dropped my hand and walked in the opposite direction, away from the coffee shop and toward my apartment.

The mailboxes for the whole building were by the front door. Mine usually lay empty. Today, however, it held an official-looking brown envelope. I pulled it out, my fingers trembling as I turned it over to see if it was what I thought it was. The courthouse address stamped on one side was confirmation.

I took the stairs two at a time, relieved to discover a distinct absence of sleazy next-door neighbors. Perhaps my no-show the night before had made him think I'd gone away or something. Once inside my apartment, I wasted no time in tearing the envelope open, my fingers still shaking. If I was right about the news it held, then this was what I'd been waiting for. I pulled the single sheet of paper out and stared at the trial date typed on it. It was only a few weeks away. The beginning of the end was in sight.

Chapter Nine

Austin

I poured all my frustration into lifting the dumbbell high above my head, my muscles straining under the heavy weight, and sweat running down my torso in rivulets. He hadn't shown. I'd sat in that coffee shop for over an hour yesterday coming up with a long list of possible excuses for him. Maybe some sort of problem at the library? Or he was just running late? Or he'd had to go home first? Deep down, I'd known they were all bullshit. He'd changed his mind. It was as simple as that. He'd agreed to meet me and then regretted it, and I'd sat there waiting and waiting like a lovelorn idiot, only leaving when the staff had quite literally thrown me out to lock up.

I knew where he worked. Hell, I even knew where he lived. And as it was my day off, the temptation to go and find him at one of those places had been almost overwhelming. But, I hadn't. It would have been too much like an invasion. He'd made his decision. Again. And I needed to respect that. So, I'd gone to the gym instead, determined to take my frustration out on a set of inanimate objects. I put the dumbbell down and moved over to the weight bench.

A man appeared in my line of vision, his muscular physique giving away the fact that he was no stranger to heavy weights either. "Want me to spot you?"

I let my gaze run over him. He was my usual type: dark short hair, a ready smile, and muscles you could use to crack walnuts. I'd seen him in there before. We'd exchanged glances but never spoken. I wondered why it had to be today of all days that he'd decided to make his move, because it was obvious that his offer was about more than just buddying up. The way he was looking at me made that all too clear. It was incredibly tempting to say yes. We'd flirt. We'd end up back at whoever's house was closest and we'd fuck. It would probably be mine, seeing as I only lived a few streets away. It would be good to lose myself for a couple of hours and have some no-strings fun without any messy attachments.

I imagined him laid in my bed, his head on the same pillow Alex's had been only two nights ago. Immediately, I felt sick. I needed soulful brown eyes and kisses that tasted like sugar, not a quick fuck that would prove satisfying for two seconds and then leave me feeling empty. I shook my head. "Nah, mate. I'm fine. Thanks for the offer though." Disappointment and a hint of surprise registered on his face before he backed off. I managed two sets of weights before grabbing my towel and hitting the showers.

* * * *

It was beyond stupid that I was in the coffee shop. If he hadn't showed up yesterday, I was living in cloud cuckoo land if I thought there was a chance in hell of him turning up today. Even if by some miracle he did, he'd probably head in the opposite direction as soon as he spotted me. I was even sat at what I thought of as Alex's usual table. A newspaper had been left behind on the next table, I grabbed it, and began leafing through it, just to give myself something to do. If nothing else, it would

67

give me a rest from dwelling on what an idiot I was.

Lost in an article about Audi's new crash detecting sensors which altered the suspension on impact, I barely noticed the shadow that fell across the table.

"I'm sorry about yesterday." My head shot up at the sound of the familiar voice. Alex hovered on the other side of the table, his hands gripping onto the back of the chair like it was the only thing holding him up. Seeing him right in front of me, I forgot I was meant to be annoyed at him. He was there now. That's all that mattered. And he was apologizing. Realizing I'd done nothing but stare at him, I forced words into my mouth. "That's okay."

He shook his head. "No, it's not." His brow furrowed. "You deserved...you *deserve* better than that."

I gestured to the chair that he still had a death-grip on. "Will you sit down?" Despite it being my suggestion, I was still surprised when he did, pessimism telling me he'd make an excuse, that it was only guilt that had forced him into apologizing. He laid his hands flat on the table, palms down, staring down at the back of them. "I'm not a good person to be with, Austin. If that's what you wanted, then it's not a good idea. I was trying to do you a favor."

"Okay." My head was spinning, both at the words that made no sense, and the fact he was talking. It was just a shame that it was with the intention of warning me off. "Why's that?"

His fingers curled reflexively, his hands transforming momentarily into fists, until he seemed to make a conscious decision to relax them again. His gaze still didn't lift from the table. "I can't explain."

"Maybe you're wrong?"

He finally looked up then, his gaze holding mine for less than a second before returning to the continued scrutiny of his hands. I wanted to reach across and take hold of them, but I stopped myself, scared I'd frighten him off. "I'm not."

I studied the top of his head, his hair catching glints of sunlight. I needed to come up with the right thing to say. I could figure out any type of car engine, but the man in front of me was a complete and utter mystery. "Maybe I don't care. Maybe I want to take the risk. Maybe I think you're worth more than you obviously think you are."

He sighed. Just the tiniest exhalation of breath that I wouldn't have noticed, had I not been so attuned to him. "It won't be a long-term thing."

I frowned, chewing the strange words over, and trying to work out how he could be so sure. I did reach across then, curling my hands around his. His eyes lifted slowly to mine and I found myself staring into the gorgeous brown eyes that I was already completely addicted to. "You can't guarantee that anything's going to be forever. All I know is...I like you, Alex, and I want to spend more time with you and see what happens. No pressure. No promises. Just you and me seeing what might develop between us. Together." I watched his face closely, trying to discern the effect, if any, that my words were having. But as usual, Alex gave nothing away, his face remaining blank. He was a master at hiding his emotions, but he had to feel something or he wouldn't be here, right? I still had hold of his hands. I squeezed gently, trying to back my words up with action.

There was no reaction. But he didn't try and pull his hands away either. "I don't understand what you could possibly like about me?"

Coming from anyone else, I would have thought they were fishing for compliments. But from Alex, and with everything else he'd already said, I knew the question was genuine. He'd obviously been burned by someone in the past. Badly. I thought about my answer. I really thought about it, not just because I wanted to get it right, but because it wasn't an easy question to answer. Hadn't I been struggling to work out the same thing, ever since the first time I'd caught sight of him in the library? If I couldn't even fathom it myself, how was I meant to be able to explain it to him?

I'd never been someone who was into the thrill of the chase so it wasn't that, even though I'd have been hard-pressed to find anyone playing harder to get than Alex had so far. The magnetism I felt toward him almost defied description, but I needed to try because he needed to hear it. "My soul likes your soul."

He ducked his head, his hair sliding back into the familiar position. This time I took the liberty of reaching across, my hand pushing his hair back behind his ear before coming to rest on his cheek. "What's wrong? Don't hide from me."

He took a shaky breath. "What you said. It's...it's..." He seemed at a loss for words. Even more so than usual.

"A bit too poetic for a grease monkey?"

He smiled. "Something like that." His next words were spoken more quietly, but for the impact they had on me, he may as well have shouted them to the rooftops. "I like you too, Austin."

I took a moment to bask in our mutual liking of each other, everything else in the coffee shop ceasing to exist. "Now that we've got that sorted, can we go somewhere else?"

He nodded, and I stood up from the table unable to keep the grin off my face. The day was really looking up.

Chapter Ten

Alexander

I watched Austin move around his kitchen, his shoulders almost too broad for the small space. He paused from chopping to wave a carrot at me. "You're going to love my spaghetti Bolognese. It's got chili in it. Most people make it without but wait till you taste it."

I nodded and he carried on talking about the ingredients that were going to go into the meal he'd insisted on making for me. I don't know what my intentions had been when I'd gone to the coffee shop, only that I'd felt irresistibly drawn there, my guilt at standing him up the previous day without an explanation eating away at me. I doubted he'd even be there. Except he was, and an apology had somehow turned into a conversation.

I didn't know whether it was the sincerity that virtually shone from him, or the way he'd looked at me which had made me stay and listen to him. Then, he'd had to go and say that crazily romantic thing about his soul and mine, and I was lost — unable to fight it any longer. I couldn't explain it, but I just knew I needed to spend more time with and find out more about him. It was a compulsion I didn't have the strength to battle. He soothed me. He gave me some sort of purpose. It was selfish. I knew it was. But, I couldn't stop myself, and he'd looked so damned happy. Still looked so damned happy, just because I was here with him and letting him cook a meal.

He glanced over at me, and I smiled. One thing was for sure. If I was going to let him into my life, I needed to up my pretending game. He'd already witnessed enough cracks in the facade I showed to the world. I couldn't allow him to see more, or he was likely to start digging and asking questions. That meant if I wanted to convince him I was a fully rounded human instead of an empty shell, I needed to talk more. I guessed there was no time like the present. I opened my mouth and nothing came out. Luckily, Austin was too caught up in stirring the bolognaise sauce to notice. I tried again. "I thought you said you couldn't cook?"

He winked. "You haven't tasted it yet."

"Yeah, but it looks good." I took a deep sniff. "And it smells good."

He grinned. "Well two out of three ain't bad."

"What else can you cook?"

He screwed his face up while he thought about the question. "Am I allowed to lie?"

Why not? I'm going to have to lie to you. "Is that your way of admitting that this is your one and only dish?"

"Pretty much." He laughed at his own admission, the sound deep and throaty. I could get used to hearing it. "But, if you've got a car that needs fixing, I'm your man" — he patted the toaster — "and I'm pretty good with fixing most household appliances as well. Am I selling myself enough yet?"

"You don't need to sell yourself." The words were true. He didn't. Not to me anyway.

Smiling, he reached over, pulling spaghetti out of a cupboard, and dropping it into a pan of boiling water. "Thank God for that! Because, that was pretty much it. I'd have had to start making things up."

* * * *

There hadn't been any discussion about whether I'd stay the night, or where I'd sleep if I did. After the last time, there was an inevitability to the fact I'd end up in Austin's bed so I didn't say a word as he led me up the stairs. It was only when he started to undress as I sat on the edge of the bed that something akin to panic started to grab a hold of me. He paused, both hands gripping the bottom of his T-shirt, but making no move to pull it over his head. "I get hot if I go to bed with clothes on. Do you mind?"

I shook my head. It was his house. His bedroom. His bed. To say he couldn't undress would be ridiculous and unfair. Still, he hesitated, his hands hovering before finally tugging it over his head and turning to drop it over the back of a chair. I got my first look at his chest, the sight impressive as my gaze trailed slowly over the defined muscles of his abdomen. When his hands drifted to the button on his jeans, I looked away, a strange feeling I hadn't felt for over a year fluttering in my stomach. Again, he paused. "Aren't you going to..."

"Undress?"

He nodded. "You'd probably be a lot more comfortable."

I wriggled myself back on the bed and managed to maneuver myself beneath the covers, pulling them right up to my chin as if clothes weren't already enough of a barrier. "I'm fine." I continued to watch through my lashes as the jeans were unbuttoned. Austin stepped out of them, leaving him in tight boxer briefs only, which left very little to the imagination. The jeans joined the T-shirt on the chair and I held my breath, wondering if I was about to be confronted with a naked Austin.

The briefs stayed on, Austin switching the light off so the only thing I could see was darkness. I listened as he made his way

73

across the room, in that way that only a person who was completely familiar with the layout could manage. The bed gave under his weight and then we were lying side by side in silence. I stared up at where the ceiling would be if my eyes had grown accustomed enough to the darkness to be able to see it. I searched for something to say, but my head was empty of anything save my awareness of the man lying next to me. Was Austin going to sleep? Or was he lying there trying to think of something to say as well?

"I want to kiss you?"

Despite the fact Austin's words were instilled with a strong sense of longing, it was still phrased as a question. I knew if I said no, or just didn't answer, he wouldn't protest, wouldn't even ask why. He'd just accept it. "Yes." My voice came out husky, my heart rate already increasing before he'd even touched me.

Strong fingers reached across, turning my head gently to the side before lips closed over mine. This time Austin's tongue probed at the seam of my lips. I didn't hesitate, my lips parting and my tongue meeting his in an exploratory caress. Our bodies gravitated toward each other as we learned the taste of each other. Desire sizzled through me, the feeling so alien I almost didn't recognize it. It had been a long time since I'd felt it. I hadn't even touched myself since... No, there was no way I was thinking about that. Now wasn't the time. Not when Austin was kissing me.

He rose up over me, his obvious intent being to cover my body with his. At the last moment, he stilled, his elbows taking the strain as he seemed to reconsider the action. He moved back, his shoulders flat on the bed, pulling me over so that I was on top of him instead, our lips still glued together.

Grateful for his thoughtfulness, I broke the kiss, reveling for a moment in the feel of all that muscle beneath my hands, my palms spread over his chest with his heartbeat thudding beneath my fingertips. Austin's hands skimmed over my back, dipping briefly under the hem of my shirt to touch bare skin before darting away again like a nervous butterfly as if he were afraid he wasn't allowed to touch. I readjusted my weight, the new position meaning I could feel the hardness of his cock pressed against my thigh, separated only by two thin layers of fabric.

Austin's voice was a mere whisper in the darkness. "Are you okay? We can stop whenever you want. You just need to say the word."

There was that flutter of desire again, my own cock beginning to strain at the zipper of my trousers. What was shocking was, I didn't want to stop. I wanted to feel his hands on me. I wanted to get lost in him. For the first time in as long as I could remember—I not only wanted, I needed. I felt dizzy. I felt hot. But, it was down to arousal rather than fear. It was like Austin had reignited something in me that I thought was gone forever. I could run from it, or I could embrace it.

Reaching down, I tugged my shirt over my head in one swift move, pulling Austin's hands onto my bare skin and delighting in the shuddering breath that ran through his body. For a moment, they remained immobile like he was giving me time to change my mind. Then slowly—so slowly, it was torturous—they began to explore, his rough callused fingers tracing over every prominent rib one by one. Satisfied he'd mapped them all, he moved upward, gentle fingers seeking out my nipples before brushing my collarbone. Finally, his touch moved back down, fingers almost dancing across my abdominal muscles and flat stomach before coming to rest at the waistband of my trousers. I arched up, grinding my swollen cock over his, my fingers digging into his chest as I gave permission. "Yes."

Like all his actions so far, the movements were slow and careful, his fingers barely brushing the zipper of my trousers. I shifted forward, pushing my crotch into him until he took the hint, his hand making more prolonged contact, cupping and squeezing my cock before pulling the zipper down, the sound obscenely loud in the silent room. Then he was pulling at them, and between us we managed to wriggle, pull, and push until I was back astride him, gloriously naked, having removed my underwear along with my trousers.

Austin returned to his exploration, his hands tracing patterns over the muscles of my back. When his fingers dipped below my waist, the gasp of surprise at encountering bare skin was music to my ears. My bare ass fitted perfectly in his hands, almost as if the two things had been made for each other. He paused there for a moment, his fingers tracing lazy circles on both cheeks of my ass, moving closer to the cleft without dipping between. "You're so beautiful!"

Even if they were said in the heat of passion, the words still rocked me to the core. "You can't see me."

"I don't need to see you. I can feel you. You're perfect."

My head dipped, my hair sliding forward to cover my face. It was a ridiculous reaction given the fact the room was pitch-black and as I'd just pointed out, he couldn't see me. Somehow, he knew anyway, one hand coming up to push the hair back. On impulse, I turned into his hand, delivering a kiss to the center of his palm, his throaty laugh revealing his joy at the simple gesture.

I could feel the tension in his muscles, the way he was holding himself still. I knew he was trying to follow my lead. But, I didn't want that. I was more than rusty. It was like being a virgin all over again. I needed him to take over. "Austin..." The words lodged in my throat and all I managed was his name.

"You can tell me anything, Alex. Say anything."

I shook my head, unable to communicate what it was I wanted. With his hand still resting against my cheek, he felt the movement.

"Do you want me to stop?"

I placed my hand over his, holding it pressed more firmly

against my face as I gave another shake of the head.

"You want to carry on? You want this?"

I gave a nod.

There was a long silence as he desperately searched for the right questions to ask. I wanted to help. I really did. But, I just couldn't. All I could do was wait.

"When I said I wanted to kiss you, I didn't think we'd get this far, but I figured if we did, you'd want to set the pace?"

My head shake this time was much more frantic.

"No!" The surprise in his voice was clearly evident. "You want me to be in charge?"

"Yes." I managed to squeeze the one word out.

"Okay." Although he said it, he didn't sound too sure. "But, you have to promise me something, Alex. At any point...if I'm doing something you don't like...or you want to stop, you" — he took my hand, placing it against his temple and moving the fingers in a tapping motion — "just tap. You don't even need to use words then. Can you promise me that?"

"Yes."

Then he was tipping me off him, and I was on my back, a wall of muscle pressing me down into the mattress as his lips devoured mine much more urgently. I wrapped my arms around him and held on tight, our groins automatically notching together and starting a slow grind. I pressed myself more firmly against him, feeling tiny in comparison to his bulk, but without feeling threatened. How could I, when he was exhibiting such gentleness and care.

The next few minutes were a blur, my desire rising to such a degree that I barely registered the point at which he stopped to reach for a condom. When he finally pushed his cock inside me, I cried out, the mixture of pleasure and pain so alien and intense, I could do nothing but clutch onto his biceps, my fingers digging into the muscle as he slowly pushed deeper. He kissed my forehead, my cheeks, every inch of skin that he could reach, his hips held in check until he was convinced I was ready.

At the first deep thrust, I was already lost, the pleasure quickly building in my stomach until I felt like I was about to burst. We moved together, my legs wrapped tightly around his waist, his shallow pants sounding increasingly ragged in my ear as he picked up the pace. I didn't even recognize the noises that were coming from me. They were midway between a moan and whimper. All I knew was that right now, Austin and his cock moving deep inside me were all that existed in the world.

When his hand fisted my cock, I couldn't hold on any longer. My first orgasm in over a year almost ripped me apart in its intensity as I screamed my release into Austin's neck, feeling the spasms of his body as he followed suit within seconds. A gentleman to the end, he didn't collapse on top of me, instead rolling us both and gathering me against his chest as we breathed together, the sweat drying on both of our bodies.

Chapter Eleven

Austin

"Seven thirty."

I pushed back with my feet, the trolley gliding out from under the car to leave me looking up at Wilko in confusion. "Huh?"

He crossed his arms over his chest and regarded me as if I was deliberately yanking his chain. "Tonight."

I frowned, clambering to my feet, and leaning against the side of the Peugeot I'd been working on. "I have no idea what you're talking about."

A gruffer voice came from the other side of the garage. "You promised, Austin."

"Promised what?" There was a loud crash as Adrian threw his wrench into the box of tools before walking across to join us. I looked between him and Wilko, racking my brain to try and work out what they were going on about.

The genuine look of confusion on my face filtered through to Wilko first. He made a sound of disgust. "Man! You never used to be this flaky. What's with you? Fine. I'll refresh your shitty memory. Remember when you were meant to meet us at the

79

Kings Head and didn't show?" I did remember. It was the day Alex had stood me up at the coffee shop. I'd been more interested in meeting him than them, figuring they'd understand when I explained later. When Alex hadn't shown, meaning I could have gone after all, it had been the last thing I'd felt like doing. I'd made some sort of weak excuse. Probably something to do with having a headache or needing to visit my mum.

"Yeah! So?"

Adrian shook his head, the two ganging up on me. "You said you'd definitely be there next time and that you'd get two rounds in to make it up to us." He lifted a finger, pointing it in my direction. "So...don't even think about trying to get out of it. Suze has the kids tonight. I have to grab my opportunities for serious drinking while I can."

I had a vague recollection of making some sort of promise just to get them off my back. I'd been so bummed about Alex's no-show I'd probably have promised them the world. Also, I'd felt guilty for lying to them. I sighed. "Guys, I don't think I can make it tonight."

Wilko's eyebrows shot up as if he couldn't believe I was going to try and wriggle out of it for a second time. I bit down on the urge to point out that the three of us spent all day together...and we weren't married. But then, I hadn't had a problem with it before Alex. It was just that my priorities had changed. He raised his chin, challenge in his eyes. "Why the fuck not?"

Adrian smirked. "I'd say it's pretty obvious. Austin's found himself another muscle-bound hunk who needs help adding up and tying his shoelaces."

I shot a glare his way. "Fuck off. My boyfriends are not that bad. And he's not muscle-bound. Far from it." My subconscious immediately summoned an image of Alex's slender limbs wrapped around me while we fucked. It had happened every night since the first time. Seven glorious nights of having Alex in my bed. It was almost like he'd moved in, and I couldn't care less. As long as he wanted to be there, I was happy to take as much of him as I could get. He was still quiet, still reticent to open up, but he talked more and smiled more so I took that as a win. The rest would come in time. I just needed to be patient.

"So, you are seeing someone then?"

I nodded in the direction of Adrian who'd asked the question.

Wilko looked like I'd stabbed him in the back. For a man who was even bigger than I was, he could be surprisingly oversensitive at times. "Why's it such a huge, fucking secret?"

Massaging the back of my neck to try and relieve some of the tension, I regarded them both steadily. "It's not a secret. I just..." I hesitated. I could see their point. Usually, I was quite happy to regale them with stories of the men I was seeing. For two straight guys, they were amazingly cool with the gay sex parts as well. In fact, I'd sometimes suspected Wilko was just that little bit too cool with it; his inquisitive questions often making me wonder if he wasn't veering toward the bi-curious side. As for Adrian, he was just a happily married man who didn't give a damn what anyone else did as long as it didn't affect him.

But, Alex was different. Alex wasn't just a casual fling. I had feelings for him I'd never had for anyone before. I wouldn't say it was love...yet, but I could see it heading that way. Therefore, it had felt right to keep him to myself for the time-being, with the added bonus of guaranteeing that Wilko couldn't ruin it with his blunt and oafish questions."...it's different this time."

Adrian waved a dismissive hand, seemingly bored with the conversation already. "Whatever! Bring him along tonight."

"I can't. It's..." But, Adrian was already walking away, heading toward a customer, impatient to pick up their car and get the hell out of there. Wilko raised an eyebrow. "Have you fucked yet?"

I sighed, turning away, and pretending a great interest in the appointments book. We were still old-school, preferring to write them down rather than log them on a computer. I hadn't had lunch yet. I could go to the library and let Alex know I couldn't see him tonight, or see if there was any remote chance I could get him to come along. I hated the thought of not being able to see him, even if it was only for one night, but I guessed I couldn't spend the whole time wrapped up in him. They were my friends after all.

"Is that a no?"

Trust Wilko not to take a subtle hint. The man didn't know the meaning of the word. You had to pretty much hit him with a sledgehammer to get a point across. I turned around, my patience wearing thin. "None of your business. And I swear that if he does come tonight, and you even think about asking him anything like that, I will punch you in the face."

Wilko looked taken aback. "Jeez! A bit sensitive, aren't you?"

I ignored him, using the excuse of wheeling myself back under the car to pretend I hadn't heard him.

* * * *

The library was busy. Well, busier than I'd ever seen it before. I was nervous how Alex would take me just turning up there. It wasn't as if I could call him though, what with the whole lack of phone thing. That was another thing I needed to try and get to the bottom of. Who in this day and age didn't have a phone? There had to be a story there. Could he not afford one? Was that it? It only occurred to me as I stepped through the door of the library that I could have gotten their number and asked to speak to Alex. But, it was too late now. I was already there.

There was no sign of him near the counter, so I went

searching, wending my way in and around the rows of shelves and hoping that he hadn't gone out for lunch or I was going to have to extend my search to the coffee shop. Then I spotted him, right at the back of the library, stood facing a bare wall. "Busy?"

He jumped, then spun around, looking dazed, his gaze taking a moment to focus and show recognition.

I looked back at the wall. There was nothing there except for bare paintwork. No marks. No spider. Nothing I could see that was worth the scrutiny he'd been giving it before my arrival. "What were you looking at?"

He shrugged, the usual curtain of hair sliding into place. I resisted the temptation to do what I usually did and brush it back. He was at work. I didn't want to embarrass him in front of his colleagues. He might not even be out to them.

He squared his chin, his gaze finally meeting mine. "What are you doing here, Austin?"

He didn't sound annoyed, just perplexed. "I needed to speak to you. Nothing major." I didn't want him getting the wrong idea and panicking. "I promised some friends of mine that I'd see them at the pub tonight." I grinned sheepishly. "Only I'd forgotten I'd promised."

"You can't see me tonight?"

The words were soft and delivered with zero emotion. As usual with Alex, I had to try and decipher the true meaning behind them with very little to go on. I wished I could tell whether the thought bothered him.

"I was kind of hoping you'd come?"

"To the pub?"

"Yeah. There'll only be Adrian and Wilko there. It's not like it's going to be a huge crowd of people. And they're alright. Well, Adrian is. Wilko's a bit of a dick sometimes. He speaks without engaging his brain. But, his heart's in the right place. He—"

"Okay."

"You will?" I couldn't hold back my surprise at him agreeing so readily. "We don't have to stay there long. I apparently owe them two drinks. Although I'm not entirely convinced they didn't make that up. So, if you want to leave after we've had a couple, then just let me know, and we can. Shall, I pick you up from here?"

He nodded.

"Great!" I took a few steps backward with a smile on my face. "I better let you get back to work then. I don't want to get you into any trouble." I gave the blank wall one last puzzled glance before turning on my heel and heading back to the garage, relieved beyond belief that I wasn't going to have to spend an evening without seeing Alex. I definitely had it bad.

* * * *

"He's not what I expected."

I slid Adrian's pint along the bar so he could grab it, glancing over to the corner table where I'd left Alex with Wilko. They were sat in silence, Alex studying the beer mat on the table while Wilko looked at something on his phone. "Yeah! I could see that." I wished I'd gotten a picture of the expressions on their faces when they'd first laid eyes on Alex. Wilko, for once, had kept his thoughts to himself. Maybe he'd taken my earlier threats of violence seriously.

"You could have warned us he doesn't talk."

I immediately bristled on Alex's behalf, not caring how defensive I came across. "He does talk!" Adrian raised an eyebrow, taking a sip out of his pint of lager. His lack of reaction making me feel like I needed to say more. "He's only just met you. He's quiet. Give him a bit of time to get used to you and he'll be fine."

I looked back over at Alex, wondering whether it was wise to have left him alone for so long. Just at that moment, it was like a switch had been tripped; the blankness on his face suddenly giving way to animation. He turned to Wilko, suddenly launching into conversation, his hands gesturing to make a point. Catching Adrian's eye, I inclined my head back toward the table. "See! He talks." He turned in the direction I was indicating, giving a grunt of recognition to confirm he'd seen. He was a fine one to be pointing out someone else being quiet. He wasn't exactly Mr. Wordy himself. I picked up the drinks to take over to the table. The only thing worse than Alex *not* talking to Wilko, was him *talking* to Wilko. I estimated I had about thirty seconds before Wilko managed to put his foot in it.

Chapter Twelve

Alexander

The very second Oliver announced his intention to visit the bathroom and left the table, Jack and David pounced, matching expressions of annoyance showing on their faces. Jack, always the most forthright of the two, was the first to verbalize what was bothering them. "I thought we agreed it was just going to be the three of us tonight?"

I sighed. I'd known this conversation was imminent, the minute Oliver turned up. I had a choice: admit he hadn't been invited and I had no idea how he'd gotten wind of where I was going to be, or act affronted. Not ready to admit how frustratingly clingy Oliver had become in such a short time, I went for the latter. "Oh, so you two get to hang out with your boyfriend, but I can't?"

Playing his usual role of peacemaker, David jumped in before Jack could respond. "It's not that, Al. It's just that we haven't seen you on your own for the last three weeks. And it's just when you're with him, you're..." A muscle twitched in his cheek, a surefire sign that he was doubting whether he should release the words on the tip of his tongue out into the wild.

"I'm what?"

"Different. You're different when you're with him."

Jack snorted. "Understatement of the day."

Now I was confused. "What do you mean?" I directed my question at Jack, knowing I was more likely to get the truth.

His gaze drifted away, his hand wrapping firmly around the bottle of beer. "Do you even like him?"

Now, wasn't that an excellent question? Reluctantly agreeing to have dinner with him had somehow turned into more dates, and then in the space of a couple of weeks, he was calling me his boyfriend and talking about our future together. For some reason it had seemed easier to go along with it. The sex was better. Still not great, but better, and I supposed I hoped that it would continue to improve. Besides, sex wasn't everything. Jack's gaze dropped to the new watch I wore. The very expensive watch. I was pretty sure it was a Rolex which meant it had cost somewhere in the thousands. I'd tried to turn it down. I really had.

Oliver had a way of overriding my objections though. He'd grabbed my wrist, unfastening the cheap Timex on it, and throwing it straight into the river before I could object. Then, he'd smirked while fastening his present around my wrist, claiming I had no option now. I stared down at it. Jack and David weren't stupid. They knew I couldn't afford a watch like that. "I..."

Realization blossomed on Jack's face. "Oh my God! You don't. You're a gold digger! I'm friends with a gold digger."

"Jack!" David's voice held a note of warning. His face softening with concern as he looked my way. "We're worried about you, Al. You didn't even want to see this guy again after the first time. Now, it's like the two of you are inseparable. Which would be fine...if you seemed happy, but you don't. You're more guarded when he's around. And, dude, he's really, really possessive. What's with that? I put my hand on your shoulder last week and...my God...if looks could kill, I would have died right there on the spot. What's going on?"

I turned my head, checking there was no sign of Oliver's imminent return yet. David and Jack were both staring at me expectantly, waiting for an explanation. What David had said about me not seeming happy had struck a nerve. The truth quite often did. Maybe *it was time to start being a bit more honest, both with myself and with my friends. They might have given me a lot of flak over the years, but at the end of the day, they had my back. The same as I had theirs. I lowered my voice to a whisper. "I didn't invite him tonight. I don't even know how he knew where we were going." I gestured around the bar. It wasn't the one we normally frequented. "I've never even mentioned this place to him."*

Jack's brow furrowed. "That's a bit fucking weird, isn't it? What did he do? Put a tracking app on your phone?" He laughed heartily at his own joke, missing the fact that my face paled, an immediate image jumping into my head of Oliver's outstretched hand holding my phone back on the night I'd met him. Could he have done that? No, it wasn't possible, surely? You'd have to be able to unlock it and he hadn't known my password.

David leaned closer across the table. "Listen, mate. If you're not happy, end it with him. You don't need the stress."

I laughed bitterly. "I've tried." I cast another glance over my shoulder. He was taking a long time in there. What the hell was he doing? "It just seems to go over his head. And then he does stuff like this." I held up the wrist the Rolex was wrapped around. "And I feel guilty. Yeah, he's a bit on the possessive side, but you know he's a nice guy. I should..."

An arm wrapped around my waist seconds before lips descended on my cheek, the kiss long and lingering. So much for keeping my eyes peeled for him. "Did you miss me, babe? You should what?"

"Get more drinks for us. That's what I was saying." Using the excuse to slide out from his embrace, I forced a smile before heading to the bar and praying he wouldn't follow. I needed some time on my own, the conversation with Jack and David bothering me more than it should. Something about saying the words out loud, made it seem all the more pathetic. And now they knew it too. I was stuck in a relationship I didn't want to be in, because for some reason I was allowing myself to be manipulated. I needed to grow some balls and decide what it was I really wanted.

"Hi."

I turned my head to look at the man who'd joined me at the bar. He was cute in a kind of disheveled way, his blond hair looking like it had fought with a comb and lost. His broad smile was infectious and I found myself smiling back. He looked like he'd parachuted in from the country for the weekend, his appearance so at odds with the men who normally frequented the bar that it was endearing. "Hello."

His smile grew wider. "I was thinking of offering to buy you a drink? But, then I started thinking about how badly I'd react if you rejected me, so I decided not to."

I laughed. "So, you've come over here to tell me that you're not going to buy me a drink?"

He shrugged. "Yeah. Guess so. You could offer to buy me one though. You're probably a lot more thick-skinned than I am. Then of course, there's the fact you already know I won't say no."

The conversation was the most fun I'd had all evening. A bit of banter was exactly what I needed. Arms wrapped around me from behind, pulling me back against his chest. Oliver. For one glorious moment I'd managed to forget he was even there. "Is this man bothering you?"

He directed his next words at the blond guy. The guy whose name I hadn't even got as far as learning, who unsurprisingly was looking supremely uncomfortable while Oliver staked his claim. "He's taken. Fuck off and chat someone up who's single."

The blond guy held up both hands, reacting to the unfriendly tone in Oliver's voice by backing off. One minute he was there and the next he was gone. I didn't even get a chance to apologize. Wriggling out of Oliver's grasp, I shot him the most venomous look I could muster, my blood boiling. It was tempting to tear a strip off him right there and then, but there had to be at least a hundred people present in the bar. Did I really want them as witnesses? I took a deep breath. "Outside."

Despite looking confused, he nevertheless followed as I made my way through the throngs of people until we were out in the fresh air. I kept walking, putting space between us and the people outside the bar smoking. When I couldn't hold it back any longer, I rounded on him. "What. The. Fuck. Was. That?"

He stared calmly back, the blank expression ratcheting my fury up another notch. "What was what?"

I huffed, shaking my head in utter disbelief, my fingers curling into fists. "That...that ridiculous display of...I don't even know what that was...jealousy, I guess? You can't act like that just because I happen to be talking to a guy. We were having a friendly conversation. It's not a crime."

"You're my boyfriend. You shouldn't be talking to other men."

I started to pace. "Three weeks, Oliver. We've only been seeing each other for three weeks. You can't be that possessive already. That's not..." I hesitated before I used the word which seemed the most apt, and then said it anyway. "...normal." After all, there was no way back for us when I took into consideration my own doubts, Jack and David's concerns, and now Oliver's out-of-order behavior. It was time to rectify this huge mistake once and for all. "It's not normal."

Something sparked in Oliver's eyes. Whatever it was, I didn't like the look of it. He took a step forward, and I automatically took a step back. He cocked his head to one side, his blue eyes turning cold. "What are you trying to say, Al?"

"That...this isn't working...for me. I never agreed to be your boyfriend. You just railroaded me into it. I certainly never agreed to never talk to anyone again, just in case you get upset! I can't live with that sort of jealousy or possessiveness, or whatever the fuck it is. I don't want to see you again, Oliver. We're done." I fumbled at my wrist, pulling the expensive watch off and holding it out to him. "Here. Give this to your next boyfriend. I never wanted it anyway. You forced it on me."

He stared at the watch, his lips squeezing into a tight line. Together with the look in his eyes, it turned his handsome good looks into something much darker. He reached out, taking the watch, but then planted the same hand in the middle of my chest and shoved me back against the wall. I staggered back, shock rendering me temporarily *immobile before I came to my senses and tried to push him off. He proved surprisingly strong, his fingers splaying as he applied more pressure, the hard edges of the watch digging into my chest. He leaned in, his face only inches from mine. "Are you sure about this, Al?"*

The question sounded almost like a threat. I met his gaze, refusing to show weakness. There were people around. It wasn't like he could do anything. I'd dented his male pride by dumping him. He was just trying to scrape some of it back by proving he could dominate me. That was all. I'd let him, and then we could go our separate ways. "Very sure."

He turned his head to the side as if he was contemplating my words. I held my breath, my gaze fixed on the small crowd of people outside the bar, hoping one of them might happen to look over and notice he had me trapped against the wall. I could shout for help, but that would be like letting Oliver win, showing him that he'd succeeded in scaring me. "Let me go, Oliver."

His head swiveled back to center. "You're going to regret this."

Wow! No mistaking that as anything other than a threat. "I don't think so." I gave another exploratory shove back, and this time Oliver let go. I was away from the wall and free, putting distance between myself and the man who'd just scared the shit out of me. "Have a nice life, Oliver." I forced myself to walk back to the bar, rather than run. I refused to look back, but I could feel Oliver's gaze burning into my back for each and every step I took.

The noise and bustle back in the bar was incredibly welcome and I immediately felt safer. I made a beeline for the table where I'd left Jack and David, sinking into the chair, and willing my hand not to shake as I picked up a beer bottle — I wasn't even sure whose it was — and downed the contents in a matter of a few swallows.

"Are you alright?"

I took more time than I needed to placing the empty beer bottle back on the table before meeting David's question with a forced smile. "I am now. Now, I'm back to being single."

Jack raised his beer bottle in a salute. "Thank fuck for that! Let's get wrecked to celebrate." He nudged David in the ribs. "Get more drinks. Al came back without them."

* * * *

I hid in Austin's bathroom, taking slow, deep breaths in an effort to force the panic attack hovering at the edge of my subconscious back into the realms of darkness where I liked to imagine they came from. I gripped onto the edge of the sink willing the coolness of the ceramic to spread through my body and calm the fires of panic. It didn't help that I knew I only had a limited amount of time to gather all the parts of myself back together before Austin would come looking. There was no way I could allow him to see me like this. I imagined the scenario. He'd start asking questions. I'd refuse to answer them. He'd get annoyed and then I'd have no choice but to leave. I'd have to spend the rest of the night back in my own apartment rather than wrapped in Austin's arms soaking up the warmth and safety.

It was always like this after I forced myself to do something I didn't really want to do. It was the price I had to pay. Meeting Austin's friends had been difficult. More than difficult. I don't know why I'd agreed to go in the first place. All I'd had to do was say no. Austin would never have tried to force me. He would have given me one of those patient understanding smiles and gone on his own while I went home. Was that it? Had my apartment become such a cold, dark, lonely place that I'd rather subject myself to social situations than end up there? Or was it my irrational fear of Richard Simpkins? I'd seen him once since I'd met Austin, and on that occasion, I'd been lucky: he'd been deep in conversation on his phone, meaning I'd been able to sneak past him with nothing but a leer thrown in my direction.

But, whatever the reason was, I'd gone, finding myself alone with a man who was even bigger than Austin while he'd gone to the bar with his other friend. He'd tried to make conversation, but my brain had frozen, managing nothing more than the occasional nod and one-word answers. He'd quickly given up and we'd sat in silence. I would have been fine with that, if it weren't for the fact I'd noticed Austin looking over. My brain had screamed at me to act normal.

Al had been the life and soul of a party; his confidence and easy-going nature meaning he could, and would, talk to anyone. I'd dragged him out from somewhere, kicking and screaming, and managed to engage Wilko in a conversation about cars. When Adrian and Austin came back, I'd done my best to keep it going, joining in with the conversation wherever I could and refusing to let myself sink back into that safe world of silence. I'd laughed. I'd joked. I'd drank; the taste of alcohol alien on my tongue after so long of being teetotal. I'd been too worried about developing a reliance on alcohol as a means to get through the day to drink. I'd figured it was safer never to drink at all.

When Austin had suggested leaving after the third drink, I'd readily agreed. And now I was completely and utterly emotionally and physically drained; clutching a sink for support and desperately trying to hold it together. I should have insisted on going home. At least there I could have allowed myself to go to pieces.

I jumped at the gentle rap on the door. "Alex, are you okay?"

"Yeah!" My voice came out in a croak, sounding less than convincing. I cleared my throat and tried again. "I'm absolutely fine. I'll be out in a minute."

"I was worried. You've been in there ages."

"Have I? Sorry. I didn't mean to worry you."

There was a long pause while I examined my pale and clammy-looking reflection in the mirror over the sink. I waited, praying Austin wouldn't demand that I open the door. One look at me and he'd know something was wrong and everything would start to unravel. He'd ask questions. I'd panic even more at the prospect of having to talk about things I didn't want to talk about and being forced to recall things I didn't want to have to remember. I couldn't do it. Being able to keep seeing him was dependent on being able to successfully pull the wool over his eyes. He deserved better. I knew he did. But, I had nothing better to offer him and that was the selfish decision I'd made back in the coffee shop when I'd agreed to give a relationship a go. And even worse, I'd let myself need him. If I had to let him go now, then I had no idea how I'd manage to get through the next few weeks.

"Okay. I'll be in bed. Don't be long."

"I won't." I breathed a sigh of relief as the footsteps moved away from the bathroom door. Turning the tap on, I quickly brushed my teeth before splashing cold water on my face. At least the threat of a panic attack seemed to have receded. I just needed to make it to the bedroom. I could do that. I scrubbed at my face with the towel, forcing some artificial color back into my cheeks. Satisfied, I'd done as good a job as possible, I stripped down to my boxers in the bathroom, leaving my clothes there in a pile for the next morning. The quicker I could get into bed and hide underneath the covers, the less chance I had of Austin noticing there was something amiss. I took a deep breath before opening the door and walking silently toward the bedroom.

Ever considerate, he'd left the light on. I kept my face turned away from the bed in case he was looking over as I took the few steps to the switch. Then I navigated the now familiar path over to the bed and slid beneath the covers. Austin reached over, feeling blindly in the darkness until his hand rested against my neck. I brought my own hand up, wrapping my fingers around his. I loved his hands, the rough calluses telling a story of a man used to manual labor.

"Are you too tired?"

I knew what he was asking. Apart from the very first night I'd ever spent there, when we'd both lain there fully dressed, we'd never spent a night together which hadn't involved sex of some kind. Even if it was only mutual hand jobs. "No."

I pulled him over to me, the weight of his body settling on top of mine as our lips met hungrily. I lost myself in his body. In the dark with him, I wasn't Al. I wasn't Alex. I was just a man allowing himself to feel passion, and refusing to feel guilty for snatching a few precious moments of happiness from life.

Chapter Thirteen

Austin

It had been a bit of a wake-up call to watch Alex come alive in front of my friends at the pub. I'd always assumed he didn't want to spend time with people, but maybe that was what he needed. Perhaps I'd been doing the wrong thing by keeping him to myself night after night, when what I needed to do was persuade him to get out more. Nothing major. It wasn't like I was intending on forcing him into spending time with large groups, not that my social circle was that wide that I could muster a large group if I needed one.

With that in mind, as well as the rapidly developing feelings I had for him, it had seemed like a natural progression to bring him home to meet my parents. Looking at his face as we sat in the car outside the house, I wasn't so sure it had been a good idea. "It's only my mum and dad. And probably my brother as well...who granted is an idiot, but he's bearable in short doses...or so I hear, from other people. To be honest, even short doses is a struggle for me." Alex continued to stare out of the window in the direction of the house I'd already pointed out as belonging to my parents. The way he was looking at it, you'd have thought I'd brought him to a

96

creepy-looking castle in the middle of nowhere with bats fluttering around the turrets, rather than a semi-detached suburban house nestled in the middle of an ordinary street. "They'll like you. My mum likes everyone, and my dad is really easy-going."

"Is he like you?"

I considered my dad. I'd certainly inherited my bulk from him. Physically, I was more like him whereas my shorter, thinner brother seemed to have a lot more traits from my mum's side. "I think so."

Something in my answer seemed to pacify him. At least enough that he got out of the car. I gave him a reassuring smile. I supposed it was natural for him to be nervous about meeting my parents. Thank God I hadn't told him that I'd never introduced one of my boyfriends to them before. Not officially anyway, not in a "bringing them to the family home for dinner" kind of way. More in an "I happen to be out on a Sunday morning post-drinking-hungover-greasy-breakfast session, and oh look that's my parents over there" way. I grabbed Alex's hand. "Come on. Stop looking like I'm taking you to an execution and let's get the tricky first introductions out of the way."

* * * *

If I'd been hoping for the return of the more outgoing Alex, I was sorely disappointed. There were moments where he sparked to life, but they were few and far between. My parents didn't seem to mind; they could chat enough to fill any two-second silence. As for Mark, he seemed to be trying to match Alex in the silent stakes. At least when his mouth wasn't moving, he couldn't annoy me. Much.

Intent on getting beers out of the fridge in the kitchen, I didn't hear my mum's approach until she spoke. "Hi, darling."

I spun around, snatching my hand out of the fridge as if I'd been caught doing something I shouldn't. It must have been a strange hang-up from childhood when she'd often catch me eating leftovers that were meant to be for the next day's meal. "Hi, Mum."

"Have you had enough to eat?"

I patted my very full stomach. "Definitely."

"What about Alex?"

I laughed. "Are you joking? Have you seen the size of him? He's just eaten more in that meal than he's eaten in the last week." I didn't know whether it had been fueled out of a need to be polite, but for once, he hadn't picked at his food. He'd eaten everything that was put in front of him, including dessert. It was a wonder he hadn't collapsed into a food coma.

"He is very thin."

I shrugged. I could hardly dispute it. The evidence was right there in front of them and I wasn't about to start making excuses for him.

She smiled. "I like him though. He's very sweet."

"Yeah. He is."

"Carol!"

We both turned our heads as the loud summons came from the living room in my dad's booming voice. My mum pulled a face. "I better go and see what his lordship wants. Help yourself to anything you want, sweetheart. You may have moved out, but this is still your house."

"Thanks, Mum. I will." I turned my attention back to the fridge, pulling two beers out, one for my dad and one for me, before deciding to take a third as well. Alex had been nursing the same one ever since we'd arrived. It had to be nearly empty by now, or warm. Whichever one it was, there was no harm in offering him a fresh one.

I closed the fridge door, intending to head straight back to the living room, only to be startled when I turned to find Mark leaning casually against the kitchen table, watching me. "Dick!

You did that deliberately."

He smirked. "Maybe. I wanted to talk to you."

"About what?"

"Your boyfriend."

All my defensive mechanisms went straight onto red alert. That rush of protectiveness only grew stronger the longer I spent with Alex. At this rate I'd be spoiling for a fight the moment anyone dared mention his name. "What about him?"

Mark scratched his head. "What's his story?"

I reached over, grabbing the bottle opener on the kitchen counter, and popping the top off one of the beers while I tried to work out what Mark's angle was. There was a bottle opener in the living room, but it looked like I had to get past the inquisitive troll guarding the kitchen door in order to get there. "None of your business."

"But, you do know?"

I took a long swig of the beer, eyeing my brother suspiciously over the rim of the bottle. "Listen. Why don't you just spit out whatever it is you've come to say so that I can get back to him."

Mark nodded in a knowing fashion. "You're worried about leaving him on his own for too long?"

"No! I'm..." I gathered together the shreds of my rapidly disappearing patience. "Don't put words in my mouth! He's a guest. My guest. Of course, I'm not going to leave him alone for too long. That would be rude. Plus, he's my boyfriend. I want to be with him. Now, if you've quite finished."

I went to step away, but didn't get far before Mark grabbed my arm, swinging me around to face him. "Hang on. Wait! Perhaps I didn't start this conversation in the right way."

I arched an eyebrow. "You think? But then, when do you ever?"

Mark gave a slight tilt of his head as if acknowledging the

truth in that statement. *Well, that was a goddamn first.* "Give me two minutes."

I put the other two beer bottles back on the kitchen counter and sighed. "Go on."

"His behavior is concerning."

"Alex's?"

He nodded.

I frowned. "What do you mean?"

Mark hesitated. "I've been watching him. He disguises his body language a lot, and at other times he displays body language which is expected of him, but doesn't come naturally. And he detaches frequently."

"Detaches?"

Mark's brow furrowed as if he was struggling to come up with a word simple enough for his poor uneducated brother to understand. "He zones out. Chooses to blank things out, rather than face them. It's a coping mechanism."

"So?"

He looked uncomfortable. "They're psychological red flags for some sort of personality disorder. Or if not that, some sort of deep-seated psychological disturbance. I'd have to spend more time studying him to be sure, but—"

I finally understood what this conversation was meant to be about. I shook my head vigorously. "For fuck's sake, Mark! Can't you give it a rest for even one day? I invite him around for dinner and you want to run a full psychological profile on him. What are you going to tell me next? That he's a serial killer?"

"Of course not. But, he clearly has some deeply repressed issues. I'm only telling you because I'm worried about him."

My sigh of exasperation filled the whole kitchen. "We *all* have issues. Name one person who doesn't. For example, I have issues with my brother because he never switches off the goddamn psychology bullshit."

"It's not like that." Mark's teeth chewed at his bottom lip. It was a sign he was thinking. He'd done it ever since he was a kid. "Has he spoken to you...about anything? I don't need to know the details. I'm not digging for information here. I'm not even speaking to you as your brother. I'm talking to you as a professional. I've studied —"

I cut him off. There was only so much I could take. "I'm not disputing that somethings happened in the past that's affected Alex. I don't need to have a psychology degree to recognize that. He has trust issues. He...well, you don't need to know the rest. He obviously has...secrets. But, he's getting better. You should have seen him when I first met him. He's eating now. He's sleeping better. You should have seen the bags under his eyes when I first met him. So, whatever those secrets are, he'll tell me when he's ready."

"Are you sure?"

Was I? I gave myself a reality check. It had only been a few weeks. Of course, he wasn't ready to bare his soul to me. It didn't work like that. And if I pushed, I'd just end up driving him away. I looked my brother straight in the eye. "Yes."

He still didn't look convinced. "Only...sometimes things can be even worse than they look on the surface. The fact that he's hiding emotions and body language and he does it so well is really worrying. When patients do this, it's —"

His choice of word was the last straw. "He's not a fucking patient! He's my boyfriend who I brought around for a nice meal and to meet Mum and Dad. *He's* fine. *We're* fine. Stay out of it, Mark!" Grabbing the other two beer bottles, I pushed past him and left the kitchen before I did something I'd regret like hit him with a beer bottle.

* * * *

"They were nice, right?"

The leather car seat squeaked as Alex shifted his body

weight. "Yeah, they were. Your brother was a bit odd though. He kept staring at me."

I slowed for the turnoff. "Ignore him. He's got some sort of personality disorder." I smirked at being able to use the exact same term he'd used himself earlier, even if he wasn't there to appreciate it.

Whether it was my brother's words still ringing in my ears, or the fact I'd just spent the evening with my own parents that made me ask the question, I didn't know. Or maybe it was neither, and curiosity had simply gotten the better of me. "So...your family? Did you never have one? I mean...you must have done, right? You weren't an immaculate conception. So...at some point, you had to have had a mum and dad. Were you in foster care or something? Is that why you don't like to talk about it?"

There was no response. I glanced over, hoping to gauge whether Alex was deliberately ignoring me or just thinking about his answer. I did a double take at the sight of his face. It was as if all the color had drained from it and he looked like he was struggling to breathe. "Alex?"

His eyes were glazed. He was looking in my direction, but it was like he couldn't see me. I pulled over at the next available place, turning the engine off and quickly undoing my seatbelt so I could swivel around in my seat to face him. He looked even worse than he had before: a fine sheen of sweat coated his forehead and he was shaking, his breaths even more ragged. His hand had come up to grip his chest like he was suffering from chest pain. *Oh God! Was he having a heart attack?* I fumbled for my phone on the dashboard, nearly dropping it in my haste. "Hang on. I'll call an ambulance."

Alex's hand shot across the space between us, gripping onto my arm as a means of getting my attention. He shook his head and opened his mouth as if he wanted to say something, but no words came out. "You don't want me to call an ambulance? But, this could be something serious!"

He shook his head again, holding his free hand in the air as a signal I should wait. Then, he closed his eyes and started to take slower and deeper breaths. I felt powerless. There was nothing I could do but watch, his fingernails still digging into my skin as he concentrated on breathing in and out. What felt like hours later, he finally seemed to have his breathing back under control. His eyes, though, remained shut. "Alex, are you okay?"

His eyelids flickered before finally lifting and he stared at me as if he couldn't recall who I was. When he realized he still had a hold of my arm, he let it drop and I was left rubbing the crescent-shaped indentations his fingernails had left in my skin. He sank back into the car seat, looking better than he had, but still looking like whatever had just happened had left him completely wrung out. I toyed with my phone, fighting the urge to go against his wishes and call someone anyway.

"Pan...ic att...ack." The words seemed to come out with some difficulty, his tongue struggling over them like he had a mouthful of boulders.

"Oh." I'd heard of panic attacks. Of course, I had. I'd just never witnessed anyone having one. "You scared me. You looked like you were dying."

"Feels like it."

"You've had them before?"

He nodded.

Now he was facing forward again, he seemed to be avoiding looking my way. Was he embarrassed? I needed to convince him that it wasn't a big deal. It had been scary to witness. But, now I understood what had been happening, I was less worried. "Lots of people have them, right?"

He shrugged.

"And how do you feel now?"

"Tired. I never feel good after them. I just want to go home."

"Sure." I turned the key, the engine roaring back to life. "And once we get there, I'll make you a hot chocolate...and if you want to go straight to bed, then—"

"No. I want to go *home*."

It took a moment for my brain to work through the correction and figure out what Alex meant. Since the first night we'd slept together, we'd always stayed at mine, even though I'd made it perfectly clear that I was fine with the idea of the occasional night at his apartment. He'd always fobbed me off, saying my place was far more comfortable. Now all of a sudden, he had a burning desire to go there. Was this his way of trying to get rid of me? If so, he was going to have a battle on his hands. There was no way I was going to leave him on his own after watching him suffer through that much physical distress. He'd have to bodily throw me out in order to get me to leave.

Chapter Fourteen

Alexander

It was mortifying that I'd had a panic attack in front of Austin, and all because he'd asked one damn question. Maybe it wasn't just that. Perhaps it was the combination of holding myself together in front of his family and then being interrogated. *Not interrogated,* I reminded myself. He'd asked a perfectly normal question. It was just that my freak brain had decided to react like it was the end of the world. When my mind had wanted to say that I didn't want to talk about it, my body had gone into meltdown. I was ashamed of my lack of control. Is that what it had come to now? I couldn't even take a simple ride in a car or have a normal conversation without dissolving into a puddle of anxiety.

Austin's discrete cough from right beside me served as a reminder that we'd been stationary outside my building for the last minute. I climbed out, wondering what he'd do. If I was him, I'd probably wave and drive off, glad of some time away from the needy freak. But of course, he didn't. This was Austin—the most patient and considerate man in the universe who instead joined me on the pavement and locked the car, making it clear that he was coming in.

I led the way, hesitating outside my apartment door and thinking how strange it was that Austin had still never seen it despite the number of nights we'd spent together. Whenever he'd brought me to pick up clothes, he'd patiently waited outside, just like the first time, never pushing for more. It was stupid really. There was nothing in there he couldn't see. It was just an apartment.

I unlocked the door and stepped inside, watching Austin's curious gaze flit around the hallway and the part of the living room he could see from this angle. I tried to see it from his point of view. The walls were painted a generic cream color; the carpet a kind of patterned beige. There were no pictures on the walls. No rugs. No cushions. No decorative touches. I didn't even have a TV. It looked like what it was, nothing more than a place to sleep. "Do you want a drink?"

"Do you have beer?"

I took him through to the kitchen. It was just as unexciting as the rest of my apartment: kitchen units, oven, refrigerator, kettle, and a toaster. The only addition I'd made was a microwave and that was only because when I forced myself to eat something other than sandwiches and cereal, microwave meals were quicker. I opened the fridge despite knowing what I'd see: gone off milk, moldy cheese, a lettuce that was slowly turning into green slime, and a bottle of water. That was it. "No beer. Sorry. I could make you a cup of tea, as long as you can drink it without milk?"

"Sure."

Austin hovered nearby while I gathered two mugs and stuck the kettle on to boil, the unusual silence from him putting me somewhat on edge. "You don't have to stay."

He picked up the half loaf of bread from the kitchen counter, turning it slowly so he could stare through the cellophane. "You like things moldy."

106

I stuck tea bags in the mugs and poured boiling hot water on the top. "Not really. I just haven't been here." I shoved Austin's mug toward him, along with a teaspoon, motioning that he should work out how strong he wanted it and take the tea bag out himself. It wasn't until he'd fished it out and thrown it in the bin that he responded to my earlier statement. "Unless you throw me out, I'm staying."

My body seemed to heat from the inside, the words meaning an awful lot after the humiliation of having a panic attack in front of him. "I'm not going to kick you out."

He smiled but it came over as strained; more an attempt to cover his relief than anything else. It was obvious that despite turning it into a joke, he'd considered it a possibility. We went through to the living room. It was another bare room, containing only a sofa, a small table, and curtains. My one concession to luxury was the small radio in the corner. It was useful when I couldn't bear the silence any longer or needed a break from the noise in my own head. I'd spent many a night, unable to sleep, listening to talk shows or music. Austin looked around for a moment before lowering himself on to the sofa, his hands cradling the mug. That's when the noise from next door started.

It was something Richard had started a while back when he knew I was home. The walls throughout the building were incredibly thin, meaning noises traveled easily. He liked to stand on the other side of our adjoining wall and make lewd noises knowing I'd be able to hear him. The noises were a mixture of grunts and groans, designed to emulate the sounds of fucking. In case I was in any doubt they were artificial and aimed at me, he'd throw in my name every now and again just for good measure. After everything else that had already happened today, it was the last thing I needed when I was still trying to piece myself back together after the panic attack.

Austin turned toward the sound, his brow scrunching in

confusion. "What the hell is that?"

"My next-door neighbor. Just ignore him. He'll stop eventually."

"Is he...why is it so loud?"

Just then, Richard let out a particularly loud, "Oh yeah, Alex, bend over for me. Show me that ass. That's it, you slut."

I cringed as enlightenment dawned on Austin's face. "That performance is for your benefit? What is he? Some sort of sick pervert?"

I shrugged, ducking my head, and staring at the carpet. "He'll get bored and stop in a few minutes."

"He's done this before?" Austin couldn't have sounded more pissed if he tried.

I nodded, still unable to make eye contact with Austin. It was just another layer of pathetic to add to all the other layers that made up pathetic Alex: panic attacks and a next-door neighbor who got off on taunting him because I was too weak to stop him.

"How many times?"

I gave a tiny shake of my head, hoping he'd change the subject. All the time, Richard kept up his background soundtrack of noises straight out of a bad porn film.

"How many, Alex. Tell me."

"A few."

"What else has he done?"

I did raise my eyes to his then. I don't know what I was expecting to see, but it wasn't the sheer amount of anger burning in his eyes. *Was he angry at me for letting someone do this to me?* "Not much."

"Alex?"

"He waits for me sometimes to come home from work. He stands in my way and doesn't let me get past. He says...stuff...and undresses me with his eyes. But, that's it. He's never touched me." Austin was already on his feet and striding toward the door. I placed the mug I was still holding down on the table and hurried after him, catching him up just as he wrenched my apartment door open. "Are you leaving?"

He turned back toward me, the anger morphing into tenderness. "No, I'm not leaving. I'm going to go next door and have a word with that piece-of-shit neighbor of yours and explain to him in words he might understand that his behavior needs to stop."

I made a grab for his arm which he easily side-stepped. "Don't! Just leave it. I don't want you getting hurt."

Austin continued walking, his steps taking him down the hallway and right up to Richard's door. I didn't know what else to do but follow. "Don't worry. It's not me who's going to get hurt." He raised his fist and hammered on the door. When there was no response within five seconds, he repeated the action. The door opened a crack, Austin wasting no time at all in using the considerable bulk of his shoulder to force it open wider and barge his way inside. He used the element of surprise to hustle a startled-looking Richard back against the wall, his hand wrapping around his throat. I pushed the memories away that immediately sprang to mind: a time when I'd been the one on the receiving end of such an action. I reminded myself that this was Austin and he was nothing like that other man.

I stayed in the doorway, preventing the door from closing but not wanting to set foot in his apartment. While it was great to see Richard having to pay for his actions, I just hoped that Austin wouldn't take it too far.

Richard's eyes bugged. "I...I can't...breathe."

"Good!" Despite his words, Austin relaxed his grip slightly, allowing Richard to take in a good few lungfuls of air. "You and I need a little chat."

"Who...who...are you?" It was like Richard had reduced in size next to Austin. Out in the corridor, he'd always seemed to tower over me, but with Austin pinning him in place, and obvious fear on his face that made it look like he was only one step away from pissing himself, it was hard to remember why I'd ever been scared of him. His eyes flitted around, dawning comprehension blossoming on his face when he finally spotted me in the background. "You know Alex? Listen, man. It was just a joke...just a wind-up. I didn't mean anything by it. Me and Alex, we're — "

Austin's grip tightened again producing a strangled noise from the other man. "I'd suggest not telling any lies." He pulled him away from the wall, only to bang him back against it. It wasn't done with any real force, but it was enough to stop Richard from talking. Austin leaned in, putting his face close to Richard's. "Here's what's going to happen, nod if you understand. Are you with me so far?" Austin paused and Richard nodded obediently, his eyes wide. "You're going to leave Alex alone. You're not going to stand by his wall like a fucking pervert making disgusting sounds again. Agree?" Another nod. "You're not going to block his path so that he can't even get into his own apartment." Richard was getting into the nodding now, not even waiting until Austin had gotten to the end of his sentence before doing it. "In fact, you're not even going to so much as look at Alex again. Do you know what will happen if you do?" Richard's nod turned into a shake of his head. "He's going to tell me and just like any concerned boyfriend would, I'm going to be coming back here...and well, I probably don't need to tell you what will happen, do I? Because from what I've just heard, you've got an incredibly vivid imagination. Do we understand each other?" Another vigorous nod. Austin let go and stepped back, Richard remaining firmly against the wall, like he was still being held in place. "Just one more thing. I haven't heard an apology yet."

Richard rubbed at his neck, the fingermarks standing out starkly against his pale skin. He lifted his gaze to Austin's. "I'm sorry."

Austin gave him a look like he was stupid. "Not to me. To Alex. He's the one you've been harassing."

Richard's head slowly turned, his gaze hovering somewhere above my right shoulder. "I'm sorry, Alex."

Austin crossed his arms over his chest, the action making him look even more imposing than he already did. "For what?"

"For..."

Austin cracked his knuckles.

The rest of Richard's words came out in a rush, "I'm sorry for talking to you outside in the corridor."

Austin made a sound, halfway between a cough and a splutter. "Talking! Is that really the right word?"

"Harassing you...and I'm sorry for making noises. I won't do it again."

I wasn't sure what response I was meant to give. It wasn't as if I was going to accept his apology, forced as it was. I looked toward Austin, searching for guidance. He shook his head before turning his attention back to Richard. "Well, lovely as this chat has been, Alex and I have got better things to do than spend any more time with you." He took a step back toward the door, his gaze still fixed on the man quivering against the wall. I held the door open wider so he could get through it. "Hopefully, we won't have any reason to ever meet again." The door closed behind him, drowning out any possible response Richard might have given.

A few moments later and we were back inside my own apartment, Austin pacing the living room while I watched silently. He was obviously still rattled from the altercation and I had no idea what I was supposed to say to make it better. He paused by the window, opening the curtain so that he could stare out onto the street. The silence stretched between us until he eventually spoke. "I'm going to get you a cheap pay-as-you-go phone."

"You don't—"

He turned away from the window, his steady stare signaling that the subject wasn't up for discussion. "You need to be able to call me, if that..." His face twisted as he gestured toward the wall separating my apartment from Richard's. "...perverted idiot does anything else. I'm serious. If he so much as speaks to you...or looks at you...I want to know. You don't have to use the phone for anything else. I won't even call you on it, if that makes you uncomfortable. But, I need you to have one for my peace of mind. Don't fight me on this, please."

There was no arguing with the plaintive expression on his face. His face softened as I nodded my agreement. I hadn't had a phone for the last year. I didn't want anyone to contact me. Contact meant talking and questions. Contact meant people getting close to me and being able to see that I wasn't whole. But, I supposed that if only Austin had the number, it would be safe. He turned back to the window. "Are you sure you want to stay here tonight?"

I looked around the living room, the sheer emptiness seeming even more pronounced. It had never been a home. It was always just a resting place between what had come before and an impending meeting with the edge of a cliff. I had no idea why I'd demanded to come back there. I didn't need multiple locks on the door when I had Austin. "Not really. Can we go back to yours?"

A half smile appeared on Austin's face and he held out his hand. I took it without either of us feeling the need to say more. He led me out of the door and back down the stairs to where he'd left the car. I paused for a moment before climbing into the passenger seat, my paranoia insisting I scan the street. My stomach lurched at the sight of a red car parked opposite my apartment. It was a stupid reaction. It wasn't the same car. It wasn't even the same shade of red, but even so, I couldn't help the avalanche of memories it released.

* * * *

I rounded the corner, turning onto the street where my parents'
house lay while listening to Jack's voice through the phone pressed to my
ear. He'd been rambling on for about the last fifteen minutes about an
argument he'd had with David."...and he leaves his pants on the
bedroom floor. How annoying is that?"

I rolled my eyes. He'd called me in a foul mood, annoyed because
David refused to cancel the plans he'd made with his parents to attend a
festival with Jack the following weekend. That had turned him into
listing all of David's supposedly many faults. The thing is, I knew by
this time tomorrow, they'd have made up and David would be back to
seeming practically perfect in Jack's eyes. Therefore, I needed to navigate
a fine line between lending a sympathetic ear and not agreeing so readily
that it could be thrown back in my face at a later date. Christ! Friends
could be such hard work sometimes. Or at least mine were. I made a
noise which signified nothing more than the fact I was still listening.

"And do you know what else he does?"

"Nope." Having reached my parents' gate, I paused, wanting to
finish the conversation before going inside so I could give my family my
full attention.

"He's never learned to separate the coloreds from the whites in the
washing machine. He dyed my shirt!"

"The devil!"

"Are you taking this seriously?"

Grinning, and grateful he couldn't see it, I lied through my teeth.
"Of course, I am. I was just agreeing with you. I mean, who does that?
Poor shirt. Poor you."

Jack let out a snort of disbelief. I stopped mid-silent laugh as I
caught sight of the red car parked over on the other side of the street. I
kept seeing that same car. It had been there the previous evening, parked
in exactly the same place. I might have assumed it was a new purchase
by a neighbor, if it weren't for the fact I'd also seen it parked outside the
building where I'd gone for an interview two days ago. I'd ignored it, but
the coincidences were starting to pile up to the point where they could no

longer just be coincidences. I squinted in its direction, the man behind the steering wheel suddenly turning to one side and giving me a perfect view of the very familiar profile. "Fuck!"

"What?"

I'd almost forgotten that I was still on the phone with Jack. "Oliver's sat outside my house. I think he's been following me."

Jack's laughter was extremely loud and prolonged.

"I'm serious!"

Something in my tone must have gotten through to him as the laughter died away. "What's he doing?"

I risked a glance in that direction. He stared right back at me. He didn't even seem to care that I knew he was there. What the hell did he think he was playing at? "Just sitting there, looking at me."

"Creepy fucker!"

I took another glance. He was still staring. "You're telling me. Do you think I should speak to him? Tell him to fuck off?" I didn't really want to go over there, the memory of the look in his eyes and the way he'd pinned me against the wall when I'd dumped him was still far too fresh in my mind. But I couldn't have him thinking that I was going to put up with him sitting outside my house like some sort of stalker.

Jack made clicking noises while he considered it. It was an old habit of his. "Nah! He's probably just after attention. If you go over there, you'll be giving it to him. Best to just ignore him and he'll get bored." He paused. "Or you could call the police?"

"And tell them what? There's a man sat in a car, who's made no attempt to speak to me and hasn't even gotten out of the car. They'd laugh me out of the station."

"Probably."

An engine started up and I watched from the corner of my eye as the red car pulled away from the curb and disappeared up the road. I exhaled slowly. "He's just left."

"And I was just on my way to rescue you."

"Were you?"

"Nah! I have holes to cut in David's clothes."

I laughed, and said goodbye, before going inside. I was still waiting to hear if I'd gotten the job at the local newspaper. If I had, at least it would give me the money to find my own place. But, until that happened, I was going to make the most of living at home again. They were all holed up together in the kitchen. Baby Kieran was in his high chair, waving his pudgy arms around as my sister tried to spoon baby food into his mouth without the majority escaping or ending up all over his face.

Charlie the Shih tzu was having the time of his life hovering by the bottom of the high chair and eagerly hoovering up any stray morsels of baby food that came his way. My mum was over by the stove stirring something which smelt like stew while my dad frowned down at the newspaper he was reading at the kitchen table. My mum was the first to notice my entrance. "Al, sweetheart. You're home. Are you staying for dinner?" I walked over to her, kissing her on the cheek as I leaned over her shoulder to peer into the pan. Yep. Beef stew. I'd been right. "Definitely. It smells great. Is there enough?"

"There's enough for the whole street." I glanced over at my dad, his head rising from the newspaper just long enough to make the acerbic comment before he returned his attention to it. My mum aimed a mock glare his way.

My sister grabbed my arm, resisting my attempts to shake her off. "Al, can you take over here, please? Just for a minute? I am absolutely desperate to go to the toilet."

I sighed, taking the spoon from her, and regarding my nephew with suspicion. He grinned and slapped his hand straight down into a large splodge of baby food, sending droplets flying over the side of the chair. Charlie gobbled them up in record time. "Just to clarify, am I feeding the baby or the dog?"

My dad closed the newspaper. "Good question." I exchanged a grin with him, both of us shaking our heads in unison as Kieran's response to me shoving the spoonful of baby food into his mouth was to shake his head vigorously from side to side. I stared balefully down at my once clean T-shirt, all thoughts of Oliver and his strange behavior forgotten and replaced by the normality of family life.

Chapter Fifteen

Austin

I smiled down at Alex, his head pillowed against my right biceps muscle. We were both naked, our bodies covered only by a thin sheet, the fabric fluttering in the cool breeze coming through the open bedroom window. It was Saturday evening, the sun just starting to set and the shadows were slowly beginning to fade and give way to dusk. These were my favorite moments with Alex. It was at times like these, that he actually seemed to relax and let little snippets of information about himself escape. Nothing major. Just things like songs he'd once enjoyed, places he'd visited, dishes he'd eaten or the name of a TV program he'd once watched. Nevertheless, I squirreled them away as if they were precious jewels. They were all pieces of the puzzle that I hoped one day to be able to fit together to form the whole picture of Alex. I shifted slightly, his head lolling to one side in response to the movement.

His brow furrowed. "Do you want me to move? Is your arm going numb?"

"No, it's fine." I craned my neck, dropping a kiss on his

117

temple before relaxing back onto the pillow. "Stay where you are."
I plucked his hand from where it lay on top of the cover, placing it
on my chest as I examined each and every finger, noticing for the
first time, a thin white scar on the side of his hand. "How did you
get this?"

He turned his head to see what I was looking at, his face
taking on a look I recognized. It signified that there was very little
chance of getting an answer to my question. Therefore, it came as
a surprise when he did.

"Broken glass."

It was only two words, but it was something. I traced the
thin white scar with my index finger, hating the thought of him
being hurt. I debated for a moment whether I should push for
information. I didn't want to ruin the relaxed atmosphere but
curiosity won in the end. "How?"

"In a bar."

I let his hand go and slid mine beneath the sheet, letting my
fingers trail gently over his rib cage. I could never get my fill of
touching him, especially now that I'd coaxed him out of the
darkness and into the light. He was getting better in so many
ways. He was eating and talking more and he was a lot less self-
conscious than he'd been a few weeks ago. I said a silent fuck you
to my brother and all of his psychological clap-trap. He hadn't
mentioned it again, but every now and again he gave me a look
which I knew meant he wanted to. "I didn't think you were much
of a bar person?"

"I used to be." Alex's words sounded almost wistful, his gaze
never leaving the window. I held my breath as I waited for him to
say more. But, I should have known better. "Tell me about the
day Wilko saved you from the bully at school again."

And there it was, the subject change. Alex pushing me away
from discovering anything meaningful about his past. I bit down
on the sigh that wanted to escape, always doing my best to avoid

letting any frustration show on the outside. Sometimes he got a certain look in his eye. The look said he *wanted* to tell me what was going on behind those beautiful eyes. But his lips, well, they told a different story. Or no story at all. "You've heard me tell that at least three times. You should be able to tell it to me by now."

His lips curled into a half smile. That was the Alex I liked to see, not the one who carried sadness around like a blanket wrapped around him. I knew he thought he hid it a lot of the time, but I saw more than he thought. How could I not, when I spent all of my free time with him? I was slowly learning ways though to shake him out of it. I leaned in, tracing the delicate outside of his ear with my lips before dipping my tongue inside.

He squirmed away with a laugh, which was exactly the reaction I'd been going for. "Stop! You know my ears are sensitive."

I removed my arm from beneath his head, taking care to ensure that his head slid onto the pillow as gently as possible. I turned sideways and came up onto one elbow, tugging the sheet down at the same time so it pooled around his waist. I let my eyes devour every dip and hollow of his chest, the lean muscles starkly defined under the skin only accentuated by the lack of body fat. If you'd asked me a few weeks ago what really turned me on, I would have said the complete opposite to the sight that was already causing my cock to swell with arousal. I traced my finger lazily around one nipple, watching the pale flesh goose-bump beneath my touch. "You're sensitive everywhere."

He didn't deny it. It would have been pointless when his own cock was already beginning to tent the sheet. I let my hand skim down over his stomach, the back of it briefly brushing the still covered mound of his cock before I returned my fingers to his chest and continued to stroke every plane and hollow. Sex was always long and slow between the two of us, like he was a wild animal whose trust I needed to regain before I could move closer.

It didn't make it any less satisfying. It just took longer to get to the same point. Did I wish that sometimes I could throw him on the bed and let the extreme lust I felt for him take over without having to worry about scaring him or hurting him? Maybe. But, Alex was different, so it fitted that our physical relationship would also be different. I'd trade every single quickie I'd ever had for just one night with Alex. Hell, not even a night — an hour.

"Why are you smiling?"

I lifted my head at the question. I'd been so busy watching my hands move over his skin that I hadn't even been aware he'd been watching. "Just thinking."

"About what?"

I didn't even consider lying to him. I was always honest with Alex. There was no point in trying to hide my feelings when I was convinced that they shone out of me every time I so much as looked at him. "How happy I am to be here with you. How, I wouldn't want to be anywhere else with anyone else rather than being here with you."

He smiled. "You say the sweetest things."

I moved closer, my nose tickling his cheek as I inhaled his unique scent. "Sweet? Or nauseating?"

His smile grew. "Definitely sweet."

I kissed my way slowly down his jaw. "Good. Because they can get worse. So, it's good that I haven't quite reached nauseating levels yet. Just let me know when I do and I'll try and dial it back a notch."

His head turned, our lips meeting in a long, slow kiss. He tasted of the orange juice he'd drunk earlier and a taste that was pure Alex; a taste I hungered for more and more with each passing day. Still kissing him, I reached down, curling my hand around Alex's cock, still covered by the sheet, and breathing in the predictable hitch in his breathing when I gave a gentle squeeze.

There was no point in asking what he wanted. Even though

we'd made great strides since the first time, he still didn't seem able to put his needs into words. Instead, I'd learnt to read his body. I liked to think of it as being able to speak fluent Alex, using the way his breathing changed, the look on his face, and the way his fists clenched when he really enjoyed something, to give me guidance. *"He has a tendency to disguise his body language."* Well, here in bed he didn't. So, my bloody brother could just get the hell out of my head as it really wasn't the time or place to be thinking about him when I was about to make love to my boyfriend.

Gaze locked on his, I slid down Alex's body, removing the sheet altogether and eyeing the beautiful cock I'd revealed like the prize it was. To me anyway. Moving slowly enough to allow him to stop me if he wanted to, I crouched over him, lowering my lips down the length of his cock until the head nudged the back of my throat. The next few minutes were spent giving it all the attention it deserved. I delighted in the quiver of his abdominal muscles beneath my hands and the way his silence gradually gave way to a series of soft cries and pants, the noise growing even louder as he grew closer to orgasm, his fingers tangling in my hair.

At the point I could taste the slight sweetness of pre-cum, I forced myself to stop, raising my head to look into his flushed face. "Want me to finish you this way?" He shook his head, spreading his thighs and bringing his knees up in a gesture that told me what he wanted far more than words ever could. "Are you sure?" I studied his face searching for any signs of indecision. When there were none, I wasted no time in grabbing a condom and adding extra lube. I positioned myself between those gorgeous thighs, my lips finding his again.

"Austin..."

I knew what that meant, the urgency in his tone meaning get on with it: the slow dance transitioning into a desperate need for Alex to come. I sat back on my haunches, lining my cock up with his hole and pulling his hips forward when the angle wasn't quite

right, my fingers dark against his skin. I savored the moment as
his body took the head of my cock in, his lips parting in a
strangled gasp of what I hoped was pleasure. That sliver of doubt
was enough to make me hesitate.

Alex's hands came down, gripping onto my thighs and
encouraging me to move deeper. It was all the encouragement I
needed to sink the rest of my cock into him, his body accepting me
eagerly. I came down on top of him, bracing myself on my elbows
as our lips found each other again as my hips started to move.

I started slow, not only because it was Alex, but because I
wanted it to last. It felt way too good to rush. But when arms and
legs wrapped firmly around me, the body underneath me
squirming as small gasps of pleasure came from Alex's mouth, I
was lost to anything but the need to watch him come apart.

I sat back again, resuming my grip on his hips, and almost
pulling him onto my lap as I concentrated on giving him long,
deep strokes while he stroked his cock, his hand moving faster as
his eyelids closed.

Finally, Alex came, his body spasming around my buried
cock as my name burst from his lips. Still, I held back, wanting to
enjoy the sight that little bit longer before I became lost to my own
pleasure. I lasted as long as it took him to open his eyes, a small
smile of satisfaction still on his lips. Then, my hands were sliding
on his sweat-slicked skin as I bucked forward, my own body
shaking as my muscles strained and waves of pleasure shot
through me as I filled the condom.

I rolled sideways, just enough presence of mind left, to
avoid crushing him. Needing the contact though, I scooped him
up, pulling him across me so that he sprawled across my chest,
my arms holding him close. We lay there for a moment, both
breathing hard, and neither of us speaking. Not that there was
anything unusual about that for Alex. He was probably glad that
for once I was giving him a bit of peace and quiet.

It was dusk now; the shadows having disappeared completely, swallowed up by the darkness. I wished there was a way of pressing pause on the world, so that Alex and I could stay like that forever. Just the two of us with no outside influences. There'd be nothing to ruin our steady-growing relationship and Alex's underlying sadness would slowly drip away like water trickling between the cracks of a pavement. It was a ridiculous thought and there was no way I was going to share it with Alex, but it was enough to cause a lump in my throat and a strange feeling of disquiet to bubble beneath the surface.

Alex's head shifted, his neck twisting to look into my face. "Are you okay?"

I pushed the feeling down and forced a smile, my arms tightening even more around him, our naked bodies plastered together from head to toe. "Yeah, I'm fine. You?"

He nodded into my chest, his eyes closing as his body relaxed. "Going to take a nap."

I continued to hold him, trying to work out what had caused that peculiar feeling of foreboding. I still hadn't figured it out when I joined Alex in sleep.

Chapter Sixteen

Alexander

I gazed at the group of children excitedly taking it in turns to climb the steps to the slide before disappearing over the edge in a flurry of limbs and graceless landings before picking themselves up and doing the whole thing over again. They couldn't have been any older than six or seven, and as I watched them, I was jealous of their innocence and their love of life. They had no idea yet how cruel the world could be. I instantly felt guilty. I'd been the same at their age. It wasn't until much later that life had shit on me.

I shifted on the park bench, my eyes drifting over to the building I could see in the distance: the library. I should have been there twenty minutes ago, Austin dropping me off, with a kiss, a smile, and a wave, the same as every morning. I'd waited until he was out of sight and then I'd come to the park instead.

I had no intention of going to work. That possibility had disappeared along with the arrival of the official letter bearing today's date. There was somewhere far more important I needed to be. This was the day I'd been waiting for, for a year. It was the beginning of the end and a huge feeling of peace settled over me at the thought. *What about Austin?* I closed my eyes, refusing to

124

give him any space in my thoughts. I couldn't. There was no room for more guilt in my life. I was already full to the brim with it. Besides, hadn't I always told him that we were never going to be long-term? Just because he hadn't understood what I meant, or realized just how short a time we'd have together, didn't negate the fact that I'd warned him. I'd considered telling him the truth, or at least part of it. Of course, I had; he was my boyfriend. I'd even opened my mouth a couple of times, the words hovering on my tongue. In the end, I'd said nothing. I couldn't bear for the way he looked at me to change: to see pity, or even worse accusation when he realized it was all my fault in his face. And what if he somehow guessed what I was planning to do? What if he tried to stop me? No. It was easier all around for him to stay in the dark.

I needed to decide what I was going to do about the library. Whether I was going to say something to them or just not turn up and let them make their own assumptions. I reached into my pocket, curling my hand around the pay-as-you-go phone that Austin had insisted I have after the run-in with Richard Simpkins. I'd only seen him once since, and he'd hurried past me so fast that there may as well have been a fire. Fear of Austin had obviously done the trick. I could call the library. I knew the number. But, it seemed ridiculous to waste money — Austin's money at that as he'd insisted on adding the credit to the phone — when I was so close to it.

Decision made, I heaved myself off the bench, feeling like I was at least a hundred years old, and crossed back over the road to walk through the doors of the library a few minutes later. My arrival was met with a steely stare from the colleague of mine who happened to be manning the front desk. She grabbed my arm, tugging me after her into the back room, and not even trying to hide her displeasure. "Alexander, you're nearly an hour late. What the hell has gotten into you?"

I took a moment to recall her name. It was something

beginning with R—Rebecca or Ruth, or maybe even Rachel. I'd worked there for eleven months. She'd been there less than five. She wasn't my boss. If anything, we were on an equal footing, yet there she was lording it over me. In those eleven months, I'd never been late once. In fact, I often arrived early and left late. I checked my watch again. "Thirty minutes."

She placed her hands on her hips. "What?"

I raised my head, looking her straight in the eye. It was the first time I'd ever really studied her. Mutton dressed as lamb came to mind, with make-up plastered on her face that might suit a twenty-year-old, but on a fifty-year-old, it just looked all kinds of ridiculous. "I'm only thirty minutes late. You said I was almost an hour late."

Her lips pursed. "Well, I suppose you're here now. It just better not happen again. That's all I'm saying. You're lucky that Mrs. Walters isn't here today to notice your tardiness. Now, there's a big pile of books over there that need sorting, and then once you've done that, you can make a start on returning books to the shelves. Then you can—"

I cut her off. "I just came in to tell you that I'm not working today."

She frowned. "What do you mean? Are you ill?"

I shook my head. "I quit. From today. I'm not going to be working here anymore."

She looked stunned. "You can't do that! You have to work a notice period of at least two weeks, and that's only if Mrs. Walters agrees. If not, it's a month."

"Sorry." I wasn't, but it seemed like the right thing to say. I turned to leave.

"You won't get a reference."

I shrugged, continuing my walk to the door. I had enough money saved to get me through the next couple of weeks and then I wouldn't have any more need of money, or a job, or anything really.

* * * *

The courthouse made for an impressive-looking building as I approached it, what with its white stone facade and the roof which culminated in a spire. It didn't matter because I wasn't going inside. Not today anyway. I wasn't allowed. I found a spot on the opposite side of the street, close enough that I could see, but far enough away that I was hopefully out of sight. I checked my watch. It was two hours before the trial was due to start. If my calculations and research were accurate, then I was here in plenty of time for what I needed to see.

While I waited, I studied the scene in front of me. The steps leading up to the courthouse were crowded. The majority of the people present were easily recognizable as having some sort of media coverage role. There were even a couple of local TV news anchors doing a piece to camera. I stepped back into the shadows as one of them finished their piece and looked my way. I didn't know if they'd recognize me, but it paid to be careful. They'd probably seen photographs of me, and it wasn't as if I'd changed that much in the last year, apart from losing weight and my hair being considerably longer than it had been before. It would be unavoidable later in the week, but for now I planned to stay out of the spotlight. It was lucky that in all the time I'd been with Austin, I'd never seen him watch the news and the only time I'd seen him with a newspaper had been that once back in the coffee shop. If he'd been a news addict, there's no way I'd have been able to keep him from discovering the truth.

With every vehicle that slowed or pulled up in front of the courthouse, my heart leapt into my throat. It was stupid. Half of them were cabs or family-owned vehicles. I knew it would be a police van. There was always the possibility I'd missed it, that they'd arrived earlier at the courthouse than all the literature I'd devoured had stated. If that was the case, then I didn't know what I'd do. I needed to see him before I had to stand in front of him and give evidence. I needed to prove that I could at least bring myself to look at his face.

Then a police van drew up and I held my breath. It had to be him. Two uniformed officers got out and walked to the back of the van. My stomach churned. I hadn't eaten anything that morning, even the piece of toast Austin had made for me had gone in the bin once his back was turned. They unlocked the back of the van and one reached in, shepherding the cuffed man out of it and onto the street. The media assembled on the courthouse steps surged forward as one, the excited murmur of voices audible even from the other side of the street. Flashbulbs lit up the street as they all competed to get the best photo.

I didn't care about them. I couldn't tear my eyes away from the man stood calmly on the street waiting for the officers to accompany him into the building. There he was. Oliver Calthorpe in the flesh. I took the opportunity to study him. I'd hoped to see evidence that the year in prison hadn't been particularly kind to him, but he looked the same: the same handsome face and the same toned body underneath the suit. I guessed what prisons were lacking in personal trainers, they made up for in free access to a gym and plenty of time to work out.

Oliver Calthorpe's head turned, his keen blue eyes scanning the street. Despite the fact that there was no way he could possibly know I was there, I stepped further back into the shop doorway, my heart beating even faster and sweat puddling under my armpits. His eyes swept over the place I stood. And then he was being turned around by the accompanying officers and marched up the stairs. I wondered what his approach to the media would be. Would he ignore them? Smile and pretend to be charming? The thought made me want to be sick. I leaned against the wall, not trusting my shaky legs to hold me up until my heart rate calmed down a bit.

I already knew he was pleading not guilty. That particular piece of news had come in an email months ago and had hit me like a physical blow. It had seemed ridiculous, given the circumstances, but according to the numerous legal texts I'd read, it was standard procedure. Even if their guilt was beyond doubt, the thorough investigation that a criminal trial ensured could lead to a lesser sentence if extenuating circumstances were proven. I just had to pray that in this case, that wouldn't happen.

I stayed there for another twenty minutes, replaying the brief moment I'd seen him over and over again in my head. After all, it wasn't as if I had anywhere else I needed to be.

* * * *

It was a stroke of luck to have bumped into the blond guy again; the same one that Oliver had so comprehensively scared off less than a week ago. Once I'd assured him that Oliver was no longer my boyfriend, and in point of fact never really had been, he'd relaxed. His name was Harry. He was nice, uncomplicated, easy to talk to, and a damn good kisser, which was exactly what I needed.

I backed him against the railing of the dance floor, our kisses growing more heated with every passing moment, and quickly reaching that point where it was only a matter of time before one of us would suggest taking it to somewhere more private than a crowded nightclub. I smiled at the thought, hoping that he had a place to go back to. And then suddenly, I was wrenched away. I barely had time to witness my own feelings of surprise and confusion mirrored on Harry's face before my momentum sent me careening face-first into a table full of people.

Glass broke. People started screaming abuse, prompted by my sudden and unexpected interruption. A girl, pulling at her top now soaked in beer started crying. I stumbled, my hand coming down on the table as I tried to right myself. There was no time to even think about apologizing to all the people I'd upset before I was pulled in another direction, my back hitting a wall, moments before my head did too, hard enough to make me see stars.

A hand in the center of my chest pinned me in place; the sick familiarity of the gesture filling in the blanks seconds before Oliver's face floated into view, his normally handsome features twisted in rage. What the hell was I supposed to have done? Right, I'd been kissing Harry. But, even with that recollection, this reaction still made no sense. We were done. I'd made that blatantly clear and he'd accepted it.

The hand on my chest moved upward, fingers curling around my neck and squeezing. As I stared into his face, I was completely and utterly filled with fear. There was nothing of the Oliver Calthorpe I'd known in this man. This man was a stranger, with every feature cataloguing his lack of control from the bulging eyes to the cords of his neck standing to attention.

The fingers tightened further, the pressure beginning to cut off the oxygen and make it difficult to breathe. If he squeezed just that little bit harder, he was going to kill me. In a panic, I brought my hand up, fitting it over his and desperately trying to prize his fingers away, but it was like trying to detach the fangs of a snake. From somewhere, I managed to find my voice. "P...ple...ase...don't hurt me."

In the blink of an eye, his face changed. It was like a shutter coming down, the features relaxing until he looked like himself again; the murderous look gone so quickly I began to doubt whether it had ever been there. The fingers slackened and I could breathe again. He leaned closer, a faint look of confusion on his face. "Baby, I'd never hurt you. I love you."

I blinked up at him, the declaration of love so at odds with the behavior, and so bizarre, that I couldn't even begin to process it. I suddenly became aware that my hand was wet. Curious, I lifted it up, gasping at the sight of the shard of glass sticking out of the side of it. It must have happened when he'd shoved me into the table. Dripping blood accounted for the wetness I'd felt. "You already have."

His gaze swiveled slowly across to my hand, nothing but blankness reflecting in the blue eyes. "I didn't do that. You did it." The utter conviction in his words made me want to laugh. The sick son of a bitch actually believed that. He was nuts. Completely nuts.

Then Jack and David were there, the pair of them pulling Oliver away and delivering him into the arms of a muscly bouncer, who immediately wrapped him up in a bone-crushing hold. Jack's expression was a mixture of shock and concern as he moved closer to me. "Are you alright?"

I lifted my hand again, careful to avoid knocking the embedded glass. "Not really."

His face paled. "Fuck!"

Another bouncer floated into my eyeline. "The police are on their way."

David's displeasure in the statement was all too clear. "Never mind the police! He needs a doctor. Look at his hand...and look at his neck. He's got fucking fingermarks on it."

The bouncer held up his phone. "I'll sort it."

A wave of dizziness hit. Whether it was from shock or loss of blood, I wasn't sure. Maybe it was a combination of the two. I leaned my head back against the wall, cradling my injured hand to my chest and noticing the lack of music in the club for the first time. The DJ must have stopped playing when the commotion kicked off. Unfortunately, that meant that most of the people in the immediate vicinity had nothing better to do than stand around and watch the aftermath of the drama. It was funny that none of them had tried to intervene while he was strangling me.

Oliver was still being held by the bouncer, his struggles amounting to nothing in comparison to the bouncer's considerably larger build. As a result, his language was becoming more and more colorful by the minute with phrases like "Overgrown gorilla cunt" and "steroid-pumped fuck-face" being bandied about. When that didn't work, he tried pleading instead. "I just need to talk to my boyfriend."

"I'm not your boyfriend." I hadn't said the words loud enough for Oliver to hear, but it seemed important to say anyway. David squeezed my shoulder, the touch designed to offer a measure of silent comfort. I tried to force my mouth to curve up into a smile, but it refused to cooperate. I wondered where Harry had gone. He'd probably left. I would

have done the same if I was him. No hook-up was worth this amount of drama. It was a shame though. I 'd liked him. Jack stepped in closer to speak directly into my ear. "Police are here. Hopefully, they'll arrest the deluded maniac."

* * * *

"You can't charge him?" The young policewoman shook her head, the action dislodging even more wisps of hair from the bun that had no doubt started the day looking smart and elegant. It was the last thing I wanted to hear after hours spent waiting for someone to come and speak to me. It made me feel as if I was the criminal. All I'd done was go for a night out. Unless the criminal act was having awful taste in men.

I'd finally been asked to give a statement and now I was wondering why I'd even bothered. "What about assault?" I gestured toward my heavily bandaged hand, now containing six stitches after a painstakingly long process by the nurse to ensure she'd removed all of the fragments of glass during the trip to the hospital. It throbbed in time with my heartbeat, the painkillers they'd given me lessening the pain, but not removing it completely.

The policewoman pasted the most sympathetic smile she could manage on her face. "CCTV shows it was an accident."

"Which wouldn't have happened if he hadn't shoved me into a table full of people."

She fiddled with her hair, trying to push some of the stray strands back to where they belonged. "It still counts as an accident unfortunately. He didn't intend for you to cut yourself."

I let out a snort of laughter. Unbelievable! "I suppose he didn't intend to grab me around the neck either? Was that an accident as well?"

At least this time, she had the good grace to look slightly guilty. "The angle on the CCTV wasn't clear and you don't have any marks, so..."

"It's my word against his?"

She nodded.

"What about all the witnesses?"

"They can only say where he was holding you. They can't prove how much pressure he was using. If he'd left bruises, we might have had something, but without them..."

"So, it's my fault for not bruising easily." I laughed bitterly, almost wishing that he'd squeezed a bit harder. "Are you telling me that there's nothing I can do?"

She leaned forward. "Listen, you could pursue it. We can't stop you from doing that. But, my advice is, it would be a waste of time. Even if it got as far as court, without any physical evidence, the case will be dropped. He'll walk away with nothing more than a slap on the wrist."

"So, he just gets away with it? What about all the other stuff I told you about? The fact that he's been hanging around outside my house, even though I never told him where I lived. Doesn't that count for anything?" I sat back, sudden exhaustion creeping over me. It was hardly surprising. It was gone three in the morning. I wondered if Oliver was even still there, or whether he was already at home tucked up in his silk sheets. No doubt, he'd called some fancy lawyer, who'd had him released before my hand had even been stitched. "Nine times."

The policewoman's brow furrowed. "I'm sorry. I don't understand."

I rubbed at my face, making sure to use the hand that wasn't injured. "In three weeks, I only saw him nine times, and two of those he wasn't even invited. I didn't ask for this. Any of this."

Her face softened. It was obvious she wanted to help. "Did anyone else see him in any of these places? Friends? Family? You said he threatened you before when you ended your relationship? Were there any witnesses there that can back you up? Maybe if we could build a bigger picture, we might stand a better chance."

My shoulders slumped. "No, there was nobody. There were people I told. Friends. But, no one actually saw anything."

She didn't even have to say that that wasn't good enough, I could see from her face. I cast around for another solution. "What about a restraining order?" I'd read about them. I knew that it meant that Oliver wouldn't be allowed within fifty feet of me. That would be enough to stop him being outside my house, and if he arrived at a bar I was at, he'd have to leave. "Isn't there some sort of paperwork I can fill in to get that put in place?"

She shook her head. "It doesn't work like that. Unless it's a domestic violence situation, or a dispute between family members, then it has to go through the courts and therefore be accompanied by a criminal charge."

I looked down at my blood-stained clothes and contemplated the fact that I hadn't slept for close to twenty hours. I hoped that my parents had gone to bed early and weren't sat up worrying about my whereabouts. I wanted to go home but I wanted to go home with the knowledge that I'd be safe. Ignoring the exhaustion, I tried one last time. "There must be something."

She sighed. "I'm sorry. The only advice I can give you is to try and get more evidence if you notice the behavior continuing. If he's outside your house, take pictures and make sure that someone else has also noted the fact that he's there. If he approaches you again, make sure that there are witnesses around. If you can gather more evidence then we may be able to press charges in the future."

I sat back in the chair. "Great!"

"If it's any consolation, you'll probably find the fact that he's been arrested tonight will have been enough of a deterrent. He'll have been warned to stay away from you. In ninety-five percent of the cases that we deal with, that's sufficient."

I regarded her steadily. "What about the other five percent?"

She walked over to the door and held it open in a clear hint that I should leave. "Call us if there are any developments."

I levered myself out of the chair. "Sure."

Chapter Seventeen

Austin

Alex had been pushing food around his plate for the last twenty minutes. I'd counted less than four forkfuls that had gone into his mouth. It wasn't enough food to sustain a toddler, never mind a fully grown man. I studied him, trying to work out whether there was anything bothering him. His hands were steady. He wasn't twitchy. He didn't seem nervous. He just seemed like normal Alex.

"He disguises his body language." I shoved Mark's words out of my head, angry at myself for even recalling them. "How was the library?"

His head shot up as if the question had somehow surprised him. I didn't know why, I asked him about his work all the time. Even when he had hardly anything to say, I still persevered. It was only fair when I regularly regaled him with tales of burnt-out engines and awkward customers who expected their cars servicing in less time than it took for them to go and have lunch. His hesitation before answering stretched on far longer than it should and I wondered if the lack of appetite was due to someone upsetting him at work. That familiar surge of protectiveness welled up inside, the sheer power of it rendering me momentarily speechless as I waited for the response.

"It was okay."

Three words that told me nothing. Still unconvinced, I decided to dig further. "Anything exciting happen?"

A small smile played on his lips, as if I'd made a joke. "It's a library. What do you think might happen that could be classified as exciting?"

I shrugged. Just because I had a negative opinion about libraries, didn't necessarily make it true. "I don't know. New books?"

The smile grew wider, and I decided that if it had the effect of cheering him up, it was worth spending more time demonstrating my ignorance about libraries. "Record number of people that signed up? Someone returning a library book that they thought they'd lost? New shelving?"

He let out a little snort of air. It wasn't quite a laugh, but it was still like digging up the finest treasure known to man. "None of those things happened today. So, I guess it was an unexciting day." He pushed a potato over to the other side of his plate. That particular potato seemed to have spent time in every single position on the plate.

"Did someone upset you?"

There was the slightest pause in his movements before a piece of salmon was moved to the same place as the potato. "Who would have upset me?"

"I don't know. Someone you work with? You haven't told me much about your work colleagues."

"I don't really know them that well."

No surprise there. We'd been together five weeks. We had sex nearly every night. He was the first thing I saw when I woke up and the last thing I saw before I went to sleep. I spent the majority of my non-working hours with him and I was head over heels in love with him. But I didn't *know* him. Not really. I was honest enough to recognize the ridiculousness of it. How could I love someone I didn't even know? But, I did. Heart and soul. I hadn't told him yet, fearing it would somehow serve to shatter the fragile relationship we'd built so far.

I had a picture in my head. A day would come where he'd open up and talk about whatever horrible situation had affected the way he viewed the world. In return, I'd tell him that none of it mattered, that I loved him regardless. It would be the first day of the rest of our future. But, we weren't there yet. We still had some way to go.

Whatever it was, he'd buried it deep. I'd be lying if I said I hadn't given a lot of thought to what it could be. Rape or sexual assault seemed the most likely option. Something that had broken his trust and forced him into a position where he'd found it easier to be alone rather than to take the risk of letting people close. Maybe it had been perpetrated by a boyfriend? Or a member of his family? Perhaps it had been his word against theirs, and his family had taken the other person's side. That would explain his unwillingness to discuss family and his claim he didn't have one.

I was probably miles away from the truth. That was the problem with driving yourself crazy with trying to piece information together with very few clues to go on. Whatever it was, it made it all the more amazing that he was there with me now and willing to take a chance. I pulled his plate away from him. "You're obviously not hungry. Don't force yourself."

Relief flashed across his face. "Sorry. I feel bad that you cooked and I'm not eating it."

"It doesn't matter."

Without food to distract him, his head turned to the nearby window and he stared out of it. I needed to do something to snap him out of this strange mood. "Fancy going to the cinema?"

His head turned, his gaze meeting mine with a slight look of interest which gave me hope. "To see what?"

I pulled my phone out, bringing up a list of films showing at the local cinema. I scanned the information listed next to each, trying to find something that might appeal to Alex. "There's a courtroom drama. It stars — "

"No."

I frowned at his immediate and very definitive dismissal. "I thought you liked stuff like that...you know...from the books you were reading when I met you."

He shook his head. "What else is there?"

I went back to the list, still puzzling over why he'd be so happy to read books about the legal system, but not remotely interested in watching films on a similar subject. But then, it was Alex. He was a puzzle wrapped up in a mystery. I skimmed over a couple of definitely nots: Alex wasn't the slapstick comedy type. That was more Wilko's scene. Adrian and I frequently had to suffer as the recipients of some supposedly hilarious scene being acted out for us. "How do you feel about dinosaurs? We could watch *Jurassic World*?"

"That's fine."

"We can get popcorn."

"Sweet popcorn?"

I smiled. "Sure. Just for you. We'll get the biggest tub of *sweet* popcorn."

* * * *

Alexander

I felt guilty. There was no way of getting around it. I'd point blank lied to Austin when he'd asked me about work. I couldn't tell him the truth. If I admitted I'd quit my job at the library, he'd want to know where I'd spent the day and what my plans were for the future. It was better all round for him to believe that nothing had changed. Hard as it would be, I just needed to keep the charade going until the end of the trial and then nothing would matter anymore. It wouldn't be for long. The trial was expected to last no longer than a week. The only delay would be if the jury struggled to reach a unanimous verdict and that was an outcome I couldn't bear to think about. Then again, I'd rather it took longer and be the right verdict. I couldn't even contemplate the possibility of him being found not guilty. There was no room in my head or heart for that eventuality.

Therefore, the time I had left with Austin was probably down to a matter of mere days. The realization produced a sick feeling in my stomach, the popcorn I'd consumed lying heavy in my stomach. I was grateful for the darkness in the movie theater to hide my feelings.

As if sensing something, Austin reached across to squeeze my knee. I laced my fingers with his, refused the offer of more popcorn and tried to concentrate on the film, which just seemed to involve a lot of running about and being attacked. I managed it for about five minutes before Oliver Calthorpe's face floated back into my mind. I don't know what I'd hoped to see today. Maybe I'd hoped to see that prison had broken him. Would I have felt better, if a trembling, wreck of a man had climbed out of the van? Probably. The thing that really rankled though, was that he'd still held that same air of confidence. Even stood out on the street, cuffed, and faced with a barrage of media. He'd still looked like nothing could touch him. Did he think he could get away with it? What kind of bullshit must his defense lawyers have been feeding him?

In two days' time, I was scheduled to give evidence. I would have to stand in front of Oliver Calthorpe and every other person in that courtroom while they all stared. I'd have to say everything I'd avoided talking about for the last year. Was that where the confidence came from? Were they expecting me to crumble? To stand there and go to pieces? Well, they didn't know what I knew:

that my whole purpose for carrying on and surviving was for that exact moment. So, if that's what they were expecting, they were going to be disappointed.

Lips hovered near my ear, Austin's breath tickling my cheek. "Are you okay?"

I turned toward him, just able to pick out his facial features in the gloom of the theater. "Yes. Why?"

He lifted our still joined hands. "Because you've been gripping onto my hand for the last few minutes for dear life. I didn't think dinosaurs were that scary."

I relaxed my grip and resolved to put Oliver Calthorpe out of my mind. At least for tonight. He'd ruined everything else. He wasn't going to ruin the time I had left with Austin. "Sorry."

I didn't think about him once for the rest of the duration of the film, but it took a huge amount of effort.

Chapter Eighteen

Alexander

I sat on the wooden bench outside the courtroom, my gaze fixed on the floor tiles and my left leg jigging up and down despite my best efforts to keep it still.

"It should be any time now." I nodded at the smartly dressed woman in a suit who'd been tasked with babysitting me until I was called in to give evidence. She'd told me her name, but I couldn't remember it. I didn't know if having someone there was normal procedure, or whether the prosecution were concerned I might do a runner. If it was the latter, I supposed it was understandable: I'd been deliberately hard to trace up until the point it had been me who'd contacted them. I checked my watch again. Only two minutes had gone by. Time seemed to have come to a virtual standstill.

In a bid to keep my mind from going over and over what I'd need to do in a few minutes' time, I thought back to the previous evening with Austin. The man was an absolute angel, his every action and gesture demonstrating how much he cared. I had no idea where the infinite gentleness and patience came from, but I was incredibly grateful I'd gotten a chance to experience it. He'd continued to drop me off outside the library every morning, oblivious to the fact that I spent my days either in the park or in the coffee shop when I knew it was a time I wouldn't bump into Austin there. Then I'd make sure I was back in front of the library at least five minutes before he was due to pick me up. If he'd noticed my sudden ability to leave work on time, he hadn't commented on it. Maybe I should have kept working, but it had seemed so trivial, so meaningless while far more important things were happening in the courtroom.

"Alexander Philips."

My head shot up; my stomach suddenly dropping to somewhere in the region of my feet.

The woman in the suit offered a look of reassurance. "Are you ready?"

Was I? I had to be. I stood up, my legs shaking as if I'd just run a marathon. My mouth was dry and if my heart beat any faster, I was liable to have a heart attack. I managed a nod. She led me into the courtroom, an immediate hush falling across it at my entrance. I was the man who'd gone missing. The survivor. The witness that no one could track down. I'd never given a single interview to the media. Why would I?

I could imagine them sharpening their knives outside the courtroom, their excitement building at the knowledge that they finally knew where I was. That would be another obstacle to negotiate after giving evidence: the media crowds desperate to get some sort of comment. Well, they were going to be disappointed: I barely spoke to my own boyfriend so they were crazy if they seriously thought they were going to be able to get anything out of me.

I kept my eyes trained on the witness box I was being led toward, refusing to look left or right and relieved that my back was to the majority of the courtroom. But then I had no choice but to turn around and face it. I still didn't look up as I was sworn in, my clammy hand pressed to the surface of the bible as I repeated the words I needed to say with all the emotion of a robot. The longer I could put off looking in Oliver's direction, the better as far as I was concerned.

Then the barrister for the prosecution took her spot opposite me and I had no choice but to raise my head. Time stopped. There was no sound. There was nothing, but the face of the man directly in my eyeline who'd leaned forward to get a better look at me with a slight smirk on his face. I'd often wondered whether his obsession with me would have waned. It had to have, right? There'd been no contact between us for the last year. He'd had no way of tracking me down. No way of getting even the slightest bit of information about me. But now looking at the gleam in his eyes and the slight flush on his cheeks as his gaze swept every part of my body that was on view, I knew it was still there, still lurking below the surface; the year in jail having done nothing but let it fester.

I found myself trapped in his gaze, unable to tear myself away. My limbs felt like they were coated in cement, where even the slightest movement would take a superhuman effort. All I needed to do was turn my neck—just a few inches. Enough that I'd no longer be looking his way, but I couldn't. I didn't seem able to get the message through to my brain. Sweat broke out on my forehead, and the scar on my hand, caused by this very man when he'd thrown me against the table in the bar in a jealous rage, started to itch. A loud buzzing filled my head so I had no idea how many times my name had been repeated before it finally filtered through. Going by the note of urgency and concern, it must have been quite a few.

And just like that the spell was broken and I was able to turn my attention back to the prosecution lawyer. Susan Turner was her name. I'd met with her a couple of weeks ago, where she'd spent time running through what giving evidence would entail, including the types of questions the defense would be likely to ask while I was being cross-examined. She'd been professional but thorough, friendly enough to reassure me, but making it clear she knew exactly what she was doing. She aimed a tight smile in my direction. "Are you okay to carry on, Mr. Philips?"

"Do you need to take a five-minute break?" That was the judge, his face impassively blank. I shook my head, trying to get my quivering legs to hold me up straighter as I gripped on to the wooden edge of the witness box.

"No." The word came out faint, barely audible even in the subdued hush of the courtroom as every pair of eyes followed my every move. I swallowed and repeated it with more conviction. "No. I'm fine to carry on."

Susan Turner nodded. She cast a brief glance toward the jury at the side of the courtroom, probably checking that they'd noticed the heightened state of my emotions. "Mr. Philips, could you please describe the events of October fifteenth in your own words, giving as much detail as possible about everything you can remember."

I took more oxygen in, hoping it would help to combat the feeling of lightheadedness and making sure to keep my gaze firmly averted from Oliver. I started talking.

* * * *

"Shit!" I swore out loud as the familiar figure of Charlie the Shih-tzu bolted down the street and disappeared around the corner and out of sight. I knew he kept trying to escape, but seeing as everyone was aware of it, he'd never even come close to success. Until now anyway. I hesitated by the gate, contemplating the best course of action. I could go after him on my own and hopefully catch up with him before he'd managed to get too far, or I could drum up some family help first so that

between us we could cover more ground. I sighed. It was late. I was tired
and comfortably buzzed from the two beers I'd consumed while
celebrating my new job. I'd been hoping to go straight to bed, rather than
having to spend time scouring the streets for the dog incarnation of
Houdini.

The front door stood ajar. I was surprised no one had noticed the
dog's absence yet. I would have expected to see one of them hot on his
heels. And how had he gotten out anyway? One of them had to have been
on their way in or out for the door to be open. So, how had they managed
not to notice? Someone was seriously lacking in the observational skills
department. I shook my head. I'd left it too long now to go after him on
my own. Better to gather reinforcements.

I took the few steps down the path, placed my palm on the door and
gave it a push. The first thing that hit me was the silence. My parents'
house was never this still or this quiet, even at this time. They'd always
been night owls and it was rare they ever went to bed before midnight. If
it wasn't my father hammering away on his latest creation in the
basement, it would be my sister singing along to some song on the radio,
or my mum chatting to one of her friends on the phone. But, there was
none of that; you could have heard a pin drop. Then the smell filtered
into my nostrils. It was a strange smell, oddly metallic and one I
couldn't identify; the sheer wrongness of it sending my senses into
overdrive. Wet, muddy-looking pawprints covered the floor, leading right
up to the door where Charlie had made his escape. My mum wasn't
going to be happy about that.

"Mum?" No answer. I took a few steps forward, letting the front
door swing closed in my wake. The door to the basement was closest. I
stood by it for a few moments, listening out for the usual sounds floating
up the stairs. I would have even settled for the sound of my dad swearing
as something went wrong; his bad mood usually carrying on all the way
through dinner and the rest of us suffering as a result. Nothing. "Dad?"
Again, no response. My sense of unease grew.

I spun around as a quiet coughing sound came from the direction
of the kitchen. I headed in that direction, relief surging through my

veins. I'd only had a couple of beers. There was no reason for the overactive imagination. Shaking my head, I smiled at my own stupidity as I wrenched the kitchen door open.

The smile died on my face as I struggled to comprehend what I was seeing. Blood. So much blood. That's what the metallic, cloying smell had been. There was blood on the walls, blood splattered across the kitchen counter and puddles on the floor surrounding the prone bodies of my mother and sister. For a moment, I couldn't breathe, couldn't even begin to imagine that the sight in front of me could possibly have anything to do with reality. I'd fallen asleep. That was it. Maybe back in the bar. This was just a twisted nightmare. There was no way it could be true. Any moment now, I'd wake up. I'd joke about never eating cheese again. My mum would ruffle my hair while I ate breakfast and my sister would wind me up in the way that only siblings could.

I jumped, as one of the "bodies" moved slightly, the same coughing sound I'd heard previously escaping from their lungs. I rushed forward, dropping to my knees next to my mum and grabbing her hand as I tried my best not to look at the numerous puncture marks on her body oozing blood. "Mum, can you hear me?"

Her eyes opened so slowly that it was obvious that it was a struggle. "Al, is that you?"

I squeezed her hand. "Yeah, it's me. You're going to be fine."

"Your sister?"

I lifted my head, looking over at Victoria, her limbs were splayed unnaturally, her head slumped to one side and her glassy gaze stared right at me. I didn't need anyone to tell me she was dead. A hysterical sob threatened to escape. I pushed it down. Now wasn't the time to go to pieces. "She's..." I tried for a smile, but the corners of my mouth refused to lift. "She's going to be okay. You both are."

My mum coughed again, her body contorting in pain. "There's a man...in the house. I don't know who he is. He wouldn't say what he wanted. He just..."

I fumbled for my phone, my now blood-covered hands almost making it slip out of my grasp. With badly shaking hands, I somehow

146

managed to press the nine-button three times. The call seemed to take forever to connect. In reality it was probably no more than a few seconds.

"Hello, emergency services operator. What service do you require?"

I tried to clear the fuzz from my brain. The sooner I could get people there, the better. "Ambulance. I need an ambulance."

"I'll connect you now."

A calm voice answered and I quickly gave them the address and my phone number.

"Sir, can you tell me what's happened?"

Could I? I didn't even know. "My mum and my sister have been attacked. I think they've been stabbed. There's blood all over the floor. My sister, she's..." I couldn't say that. I'd assured my mum she was going to be okay. I looked down, wondering if she'd picked up on my hesitation. It was only then that it hit me. She'd let go of my hand while I'd been giving information to the voice on the other end of the phone. She was no longer breathing. She'd gone. "...oh God! My mum's dead! They're both dead!" There was no way I could stop the torrent of tears from cascading down my face. I barely registered anything else said to me by the disembodied voice on the other end of the line. I vaguely recalled promising I'd leave the house and wait for the police to get there. I stumbled to my feet, the knees of my jeans red with blood. Where was my dad? Had he gone out? Or would I find a similar scenario in the basement if I ventured down there?

It was then I heard it: the distinct wailing cry of a baby coming from upstairs. My nephew – Kieran. He was still alive. Alive and crying. Crying for his mum whose lifeless body lay on the kitchen floor and couldn't go to him ever again. No matter what I'd been ordered to do, there was no way I could just go outside and leave him. Doing my utmost to avoid thinking about the bodies of my mum and sister, I retraced my steps, the crying growing louder and more anguished the closer I got. Was he crying because he'd just woken up? Or was he crying for another reason?

With one foot on the first stair, there was no way I could fail to notice the bloody handprint on the wall; its position just at that height where someone would lean as they started their ascent up the stairs. Whoever had committed that atrocity in the kitchen, had gone up there. Could still be up there, for all I knew. The cries grew louder still, and I was filled with a cold resolve.

I looked around, searching for something that could be used as a weapon. I might be stupid enough to go up there, but I wasn't stupid enough to go without some sort of protection. There was nothing in the living room, apart from an umbrella propped up against the fake fireplace. I had two options: go down into the basement where my father kept his tools or go back into the kitchen. I chose the latter. At least I knew what I'd see. Not that the sight was any easier the second time around, especially when I was forced to step over my sister's lifeless body in order to extract a knife from the knife-block on the kitchen counter.

I hurried back the way I'd come, careful to avoid slipping in the puddle of blood which seemed to grow ever larger. Kieran was still crying, the sound offering a twisted sort of comfort. At least while he was crying, he might be upset, but he was still alive. If the crying stopped, well, that's when I'd really panic.

There were more handprints decorating the wall on either side of the stairs. Almost, like the perpetrator had wanted to leave a trail. Halfway up the stairs, I paused, fighting the urge to flee in the opposite direction. What did I think I was doing? I wasn't trained in martial arts. I didn't have some sort of secret superpower. I just had one knife and a burning anger that someone could walk in there and do this to my family. Squaring my shoulders, I carried on.

At the top of the stairs, I walked as silently as I could toward the room my parents had turned into a temporary nursery. The door was open. I forced myself to walk inside, just in time to witness a man's back as he bent over to pluck Kieran from his crib, a blood-stained knife held in one hand, as he seized my nephew with the other.

"Leave him alone!" The words were out before I could stop them. It probably wasn't the wisest course of action to start making demands, as well as immediately alerting him to my presence but then I wasn't *exactly thinking clearly. The man turned slowly and I found myself staring at Oliver Calthorpe. Everything ground to a halt. If I'd thought he looked insane the night he'd attacked me in the bar, that was nothing in comparison to the way he looked now. His skin was flushed with what looked like excitement, or at least the parts I could see that weren't streaked with blood. It was everywhere. On his face. On his hands. And covering the front of what used to be a white shirt. Even as I stood there stunned, he wiped the back of the hand holding the knife across his forehead leaving another streak of bright-red blood. He looked like a demon, his crazed blue eyes shining like beacons in the shrouded darkness of the room.*

"Al! I wasn't expecting you home."

The bright greeting would have been sinister enough, even without the broad smile that accompanied it, and the insane glint in his eye. Anyone would have thought I'd interrupted him going about his daily business, rather than holding a knife to a screaming baby. "What do you think you're doing?" The question sounded stupid, like a gross understatement of fact. Like I was ignoring the horror scene slowly unraveling before my eyes. I should have been screaming at him or running across and plunging the knife into him.

If he'd been on his own, maybe I would have done, but my attention was firmly fixed on Kieran, his red screwed-up face demonstrating his distress at being held so unceremoniously by a complete stranger. If I tried anything, he'd be the one to suffer, so I stayed where I was, my hand tightening around the handle of the knife I held behind my back and biding my time.

Oliver took a couple of steps forward, waving the knife in my direction. I shrank back against the wall. His eyes followed the movement, a tiny furrow appearing on his brow. "What do you mean?"

Hysteria threatened to overwhelm me at the casual answer. Just like in the kitchen, I pushed it down. I needed to remember that he was far beyond being rational. Rational men didn't...I cut off the thought. If I was going to stay calm, I needed to concentrate on the here and now. If I was somehow going to manage to wrest my nephew away from him, I couldn't afford to slip into self-pity. I took a deep breath, trying to calm myself and modulate my voice, even though inside my whole body was quaking. "Why are you here, Oliver? In my parents' house?"

"To fix things." He moved over to the other side of the room, pulling the curtain back a few inches to look for something out of the window.

I kept my eyes on him, afraid to look away, like a zebra watching a lion that had wandered into his vicinity. "Fix what things?"

He swung back around to face me. There was that slight look of confusion again. "Us."

The word hit me like a hurricane. It was all I could do to remain standing. "I don't understand." He left his vigil by the window and walked toward me, agitation evident in the way he carried himself. He paused, a mere step away, Kieran now so close, that the temptation to reach out and take him was almost too much. "Why don't you let me hold him? He's upset. I can get him to stop crying." I lifted my arm, moving as slowly as I could manage and wishing I had both hands free. I reached across the space, my fingers grazing the edge of Kieran's powder blue Babygro. I just needed to get a firm grip on him and then Oliver wouldn't have any leverage.

Then, Oliver was turning, my fingers left grasping at thin air. He laughed and then shook his head. "No, he's the last one. I just need to do this one and then I'm done."

He lifted the knife, his intention clear. Sheer terror wrapped me in its clutches. I dived forward, stopping short of grabbing hold of Oliver, sensing that touching him would be a mistake. "Wait! Please wait."

To my surprise, Oliver did, his hand freezing as he lifted an eyebrow as if to say, "What can I do for you?"

"My mum? My sister? You did that?" It seemed a ridiculous question to ask, like there might have been two crazed knifemen loose in the house, but I needed to hear him say it.

Oliver nodded, almost too eagerly, his skin flushing again. "Got them in the kitchen." There was a note of pride in his voice, as if he was impressed with himself for bringing down two defenseless women. "They *were easy."*

I forced down the bile, working to keep my face impassively blank. "My dad? what about him?" I would have given anything at that moment for Oliver to say he hadn't been in the house. I clung to the faint hope as I watched the myriad of emotions cross the bastard's face as he considered my question.

Oliver began to pace, looking even more pleased with himself, Kieran hanging almost limply from his left hand. "Now that son of a bitch took a bit more effort." He swung around again, the eerie blue gaze finding mine. "Fucker tried to hit me with a hammer. Can you believe that?"

"So, he's dead?" It was amazing how flat my voice sounded. We may as well have been discussing a recent spell of hot weather rather than the cold-blooded murder of my entire family.

He chuckled. "I'd say so." He moved the knife in a stabbing motion, repeating the action at least seven or eight times before chuckling again and going back to pacing.

My knees threatened to buckle. I reached out, grabbing on to the edge of a chest of drawers to hold me up, while trying to make the movement look as natural as possible. "How did you get in?"

"Door was unlocked. I just walked right in." He delivered the statement in a sing-song voice. He tilted his head to one side, giving me a searching look. "Don't be sad, Al. There's nothing stopping us from being together now."

I shifted the words around in my brain, hoping that eventually they'd form themselves into an order that made logical sense. "How...how did my family keep us apart? They never...I don't..."

He wiped at his face, spreading the blood from his forehead down to his cheek, before pausing to stare at his blood-stained fingers as if he had no recollection of how it had gotten there. He shrugged, apparently unconcerned. "You don't have to pretend. All those times, Al, when you couldn't see me because of them...when you were babysitting" – he aimed a glare at the wriggling bundle held in one hand, the screaming having subsided to a quieter sob – "to have dinner with them...to help your dad

151

with something. They were never-ending. They monopolized your time. Time you should have been spending with me."

I'd told him all those things. But, they were nothing more than excuses to get out of spending time with him. He'd expected to see me every night, whereas two or three times a week had been more than enough for me. He came closer again, his fingers reaching out to touch my cheek. It took every inch of willpower I had to stay still and let him touch, rather than giving in to the natural instinct to wrench my head away. His fingers traced gently over my cheekbone and I had to push away the image of the bloody fingertips leaving an indelible mark: a psychological stain I'd never be rid of as long as I lived. But, still I stood there. I had to play along. At least until the police got there. How long had it been since I called them? Two minutes? Five? Longer? Blue eyes bored into mine. "I did it for us."

Us! There was that word again. He kept throwing it out. Did he not remember that I'd dumped him? Was there really no recollection of the fact that I'd had him arrested? Or did he remember, but somewhere in his sick, twisted brain, he'd found a way to ignore it. "I understand." They were two of the most difficult words I'd ever spoken.

His hand dropped from my cheek. "Do you? Do you really?"

"Of course." With most of my attention locked on Kieran, the lies were starting to roll off my tongue. "We had obstacles in our way. You did what you did..." My voice caught and I feigned a cough to cover it. "...to remove those obstacles."

"Exactly!" Oliver looked pleased, his enthusiastic head nod going on for a while. He returned to the window, pausing briefly before lifting the curtain aside again. "Did you call the police on me?"

I froze, blindsided by the question. Just because he was insane, didn't mean he was stupid. I didn't know what to say. There could be sirens any moment. If I said no, and he heard them, then God only knows what he'd do. But, if I said yes, things could go south just as quickly. I needed to pick my words very carefully. "I didn't call them on you. But, I did call them. I didn't know who'd done it, did I? If I'd known it was you, then I would have waited for you to explain...I would have known there was a good reason." I was babbling. I forced myself to slow down and think, trying to select the right words from the muddled mess of my brain. "We need to get out of here before they arrive. Both of us." I held my hand out, willing my fingers not to shake too badly. "What do you say? Just me and you." Oliver stared at my hand without speaking, making no move to take it. I tried harder. "What do you say, baby?"

He jerked his head toward Kieran. "What about him?"

My heart threatened to burst right out of my chest with the sheer effort of holding it together. "Leave him. He'll slow us down. He's no threat."

"No more babysitting?"

I could see the indecision on his face, the desire to believe me. I just needed to push that little bit more to convince him. "No more babysitting, I promise. Just you and me."

Oliver's look turned contemplative. "Where will we go? You know the police are going to be after me."

So, the sick fucker wasn't quite that far gone that he was completely out of touch with reality. "Anywhere you want. As long as we're together, that's all that matters. But, we have to go now. They'll be here soon. I don't want to see you get arrested." I didn't. That much was true. I wanted to see him die horribly. Preferably at my hands. Why should he get to keep breathing when my family would never have that same luxury?

He walked over to the crib and I held my breath. "My aunt has a house in the countryside. We could go there until we work out how we can leave the country?"

"Yeah! That sounds great!" The amount of enthusiasm I managed to force into my response was nothing short of nauseating, but he seemed to be buying it.

He lowered Kieran into the crib before straightening up. "How do I know you're not just stringing me along? Telling me what I want to hear?"

Fuck! My heart sank. I'd gotten him to put the baby down. Now, I just needed to get him out of the room. Where were the goddamn police?

Why was it taking them so long to get here? "I wouldn't do that."

"Prove it."

The words reverberated around my skull. "What?"

He lifted his head, a look of clear challenge present in the blue eyes. "I said, prove it."

"How?"

A slow smile spread across his face. "Coming over here and giving me a kiss would be a good start."

My stomach lurched violently. "But...the police —"

"Aren't here yet."

I nodded, forcing my legs to move a couple of steps in his direction. If I was going to pull off kissing this maniac, it needed to be the performance of a lifetime. I'd been good at drama at school. I'd even starred in two whole-school productions. The teachers had said I had a natural talent for it. I'd even considered going into acting before applying to do English at university, deciding I wanted to use my brain a bit more. I could do this. I had to do this. For Kieran's sake. Oliver's attention might have moved away from him at the moment, but if I didn't manage to keep him distracted, it could so easily switch back. I took another couple of steps, stopping right in front of Oliver, the knife still held behind my back, my fingers wrapped around it so tightly, they were starting to hurt. I couldn't take the risk of using it when he was still so close to Kieran. I needed to do whatever he wanted me to do. Say whatever he wanted me to say. If he asked me to get down on my knees and suck his cock, I would.

I leaned in, laying my lips over his and doing my best not to think about the blood on his face. I could taste it on his lips, the realization threatening to derail everything. I fought down the nausea and put everything I had into making the kiss convincing, meeting his tongue with my own as he responded to the kiss. I hated every moment. I wanted to bite his tongue off. I wanted to hurt him. But, I didn't. I thought of keeping Kieran alive and I kept going, figuring the longer it went on, the more convincing it would be. Finally, I pulled back, smiling into his face. "I love you, Oliver."

His face immediately brightened at my words. He gathered my fingers in his. There was no way he could fail to notice the tremble. He frowned. "Why are you so nervous?"

I wanted to laugh. Stood in a bedroom with a maniac, trying to keep my nephew alive, with my whole family slain downstairs and he really needed to ask. "I'm not nervous. I'm excited. We've got our whole future ahead of us. Aren't you excited?"

He nodded, his gaze never leaving mine.

I took the opportunity to tug on his hand, pulling him slowly and inexorably toward the door. "The police are going to arrive soon, Please...Oliver. Let's go."

This time he followed. Step by step, I navigated him backward, until we were finally out of the room and at the top of the stairs. There wasn't going to be a better time. Fingers gripping the handle of the knife, I pulled it out from behind my back and in one swift move, plunged it straight into his gut.

He sucked in air, his mouth widening into an "o" of surprise. He looked down, shock appearing on his face as he took in the sight of the knife handle protruding from his stomach. His eyes flew to my face as if he couldn't quite believe I'd do such a thing. I shoved him with my shoulder and he lost his balance, toppling over the bannister and tumbling down the stairs to lay prone at the bottom, his discarded knife hitting the wall and coming to rest a few feet away. Then, I was screaming abuse at him. I didn't care that he wasn't moving. I didn't care that he was probably unconscious and couldn't even hear me. All that mattered was that I had things I needed to say; a way to vent my grief and anger. My mum, dad, and sister couldn't speak. Would never speak again. So, I needed to do it for them.

I was still screaming abuse when uniformed police entered the house, two of them crouching over Oliver as they checked his vital signs while two more were up the stairs in a flash, unceremoniously forcing me to the floor and cuffing my hands behind my back. I sagged in their grasp, finally giving in to the despair tearing me apart.

Chapter Nineteen

Austin

The kitchenette at the back of the garage was too small at the best of times. It was for that reason that we normally staggered our breaks and took it in turns to be the one making the drinks for everyone. Therefore, I was completely mystified as to why Wilko had followed me in there. It was a good job I wasn't claustrophobic, or I'd have been begging for release by now. Raising an eyebrow, I gestured toward Wilko's mug. It was the huge one with *"Organized people are just too lazy to look for stuff"* emblazoned across the side. "Want one?"

Wilko nodded and proceeded to squeeze himself even further into the kitchenette. Now, the only way I could leave was to wait for him to back out first. Sighing, I spooned instant coffee into both mugs before adding boiling water. I'd much rather have paid a visit to the coffee shop, but on busy days like today, where everyone and their dog seemed to want their MOT done, it just wasn't an option and we had to make do with the instant stuff. "What do you want?"

"I just thought we could catch up?"

I eyed him over the rim of my coffee cup, recoiling when I

realized it was far too hot to drink. Of course it was, I'd only just poured it, and I didn't take milk unlike the man stood opposite who was currently pouring about half a carton of the stuff into his. "Catch up with what?"

Wilko raised one shoulder in a casual gesture, his eyes not quite meeting mine. "Stuff."

I leaned back against the kitchen counter and waited, my barely concealed irritation probably written all over my face. "Spit it out, mate. I've got to get the MOT finished on that Merc. The owner's coming back in an hour to pick it up."

Wilko crossed his arms over his chest. "I just wondered how things are going with...you know...you and Alex?"

"Fine."

"You never talk about him."

Didn't I? I supposed that was true. It wasn't as if we spent wild nights clubbing or did anything particularly exciting that was worth detailing. With previous boyfriends, it wasn't so much that I'd talked about *them*, it was more that I'd talked about the things we'd spent time doing. With Alex, it was different, we spent most of the time holed up together in the house, just happy to share the same space. With him, I didn't need excitement. I didn't need to go out and get drunk. I didn't need anything extra. He was more than enough. With no way of being able to convey that in words, I shrugged.

A frown crept slowly over Wilko's face. He reached down and began to fidget with the coffee jar, turning it round and round on the counter top. "I don't get it, that's all. All those other guys were nothing like him. They were muscly and loud. I thought that was your type? How do you wake up one morning and suddenly decide your...preferences have changed? It's like..." His gaze flicked briefly to mine before returning to the apparently fascinating coffee jar. "...one minute you liking girls and the next deciding you like men."

My snort of laughter at the strange analogy was out before I could stop it. "It's nothing like that! Alex is most definitely all man. I can assure you of that."

The coffee jar was turning even faster now, and it suddenly dawned on me. "Are we still talking about me? Or are we talking about you?"

The jar flew off the counter, hitting the floor with a *thud*. Luckily, it was plastic rather than glass so it stayed intact, bouncing rather than shattering. Wilko's head shot up, panic in his eyes. "What do you mean?"

I tried to pick my words delicately. It was obvious now that something had been bothering him for weeks. I'd been too wrapped up in my own life, too wrapped up in Alex to give it much thought. Some friend I was. I pushed the mug of coffee his way. "Don't push that off the counter. Listen, mate. I don't know what's going on with you at the moment...but you know...you can talk to me, right? About anything. I mean...let's just say...and I'm going to pick a random scenario out of thin air here. But, let's just say that something had happened between you and some guy..." The look of immediate alarm interspersed with a good dose of fear told me much more than words ever could that I was bang on the money with my theory. "...well, then you could talk to me about that." I held up a hand to stall the words of denial that were about to spill out of his mouth. I'd been there myself. Yes, I'd been a hell of a lot younger, but there was no set timeline for these sorts of things. I still remembered how confusing it had all been—and scary. I'd felt like there was no one else in the world who understood. "And if you aren't ready to discuss it yet...then that's fine and just know that I'm here...if and when you change your mind and do want to talk to someone. You can always call me. That's what friends are for, right?"

Wilko's curt nod didn't quite manage to disguise his look of relief. I wasn't sure whether it was because I wasn't pushing for details, or the fact I'd taken my head out of my ass long enough to offer support. Maybe it was both. "Thanks, man." He backed out of the small space, taking the mug of coffee with him, and I was left pondering what type of guy could possibly be Wilko's type. His girlfriends had all been the blonde artificial type: big boobs — usually with help from a surgeon — lots of make-up, and hair extensions down to their ass. It was hard to picture the male equivalent, unless he'd suddenly developed a penchant for drag queens. I laughed at the thought. Wouldn't that be a sight to see? Even Adrian might raise an eyebrow at that one.

It was similar to the situation with Alex though. I needed to give him space and when he was ready to open up, he would.

* * * *

Fuck! I swore out loud at the sight of my brother's name on the caller display of my phone, slamming the boot of the car down in an extra demonstration of my displeasure. I could ignore him. But I'd ignored the last three calls from him. In fact, I'd barely spoken to him since the night I'd gone for dinner and he'd forced his thoughts about Alex onto me. Only problem was, my mum's birthday was coming up in the next few weeks, so it was possible the reason he needed to speak to me was linked to that.

Reluctantly, I pressed the button to connect the call and answered with a grunt.

Mark's voice came over loud and clear. "You know what always impresses me about you, brother? Your sheer eloquence. Now, if you could just manage one or two words, I'd be reassured that I've gotten through to you. Because right now, I'm pondering the possibility that a stray gorilla might have picked up your phone."

"Fuck off!"

"Ah, there he is! It is you. The speech sounds are just ever so slightly too developed for a gorilla."

I made my way outside of the garage. Adrian wouldn't mind. I'd worked solidly throughout the day, only taken ten minutes for lunch and my only break had been the one I'd spent with Wilko earlier. "What do you want? Or did you just call to insult me?"

Mark laughed. "That's just a bonus. I called about Mum's birthday..." I relaxed slightly, glad I'd been right about his reason for calling. "...I was thinking about booking that restaurant we went to a few years ago...the Caribbean one. Mum really liked it. Do you remember?"

"Yeah I remember it. Fine by me." It was. Especially if he organized it all, and all I had to do was turn up and eat.

"I need to know how many I'm booking for?"

I scuffed at a stone with my shoe. "You need help with your counting? I thought your fancy degrees might have given you enough qualifications to manage that on your own." The silence on the other end was deafening, and I finally got what he was driving at. "You want to know if Alex will be coming or not?"

Mark made a noise of agreement. "I don't expect you to let me know now. I presume you'll need to talk to him first and find out if he'll feel comfortable enough to come along. Just let me know as soon as you can, so I can get it sorted."

It rankled that after one brief meeting, Mark felt like he knew my boyfriend well enough to tell me what I needed to do. It was on the tip of my tongue to tell him that of course Alex would be there. Only thing was, annoyingly he was right, and I couldn't make that sort of decision for Alex without talking to him first. The last thing I wanted was to stress him out. "Sure."

"How is he...anyway?"

And there it was...the conversation I'd been trying to avoid. "He's fine." There was no way I was going to mention the panic attack he'd suffered that had scared the life out of me, or the fact that he'd started having nightmares. I didn't buy Alex's attempts at brushing them off as nothing, especially when he disappeared off into the bathroom for anywhere up to thirty minutes, leaving me feeling completely useless while I paced the bedroom and waited for him to come back to bed. I wanted to help, but I didn't know how, and he'd made it pretty clear he wanted to be alone.

"Really?" The disbelief in Mark's voice was evident.

"Yes. Really?"

"Where does he work?"

At least this was safer territory. "At the library."

"That's good."

"Is it?" I couldn't stop the comment from coming out as unnecessarily sharp.

"Yeah. He needs to be around people. He—"

I interrupted. "Listen, I need to go. There's a customer waiting to speak to me." There wasn't. Save the clearing up and catching up on some paperwork, I was about done for the day, but he didn't need to know that.

"Austin—"

"Gotta go, Mark. Speak to you later." I ended the call with Mark's protests still ringing in my ears. I didn't need him digging for information to add to his off-the-cuff diagnosis of my boyfriend. He probably had a clipboard next to the phone to take notes. I headed back into the garage, finding Adrian stretching his fatigued muscles. "A bit sore, old man?"

He gave me the finger. It was a running joke between the two of us. In reality, he was only about four or five years older than I was. He gestured at the tools I'd left lying all over the floor. "I'm clocking off early. We've got parents' evening to suffer through. Wilko's already gone because he came in for seven this morning. You alright to lock up when you leave?"

"Sure."

He made a beeline for the door, turning back just before he

went through it. "Oh, I almost forgot to tell you. I saw your boyfriend yesterday in the park. I waved, but he seemed pretty deep in thought. I don't think he saw me."

"When did you see him?" It didn't make sense. I'd dropped him off for work in the morning at the library and picked him up from there as well, and then we'd spent the whole evening together. So, unless he'd gone there in his lunch break, it wasn't possible.

Adrian thought for a moment. "Think it was about three. It was just after I'd picked up those parts for the Range Rover, so had to be around that time. I was back here by four."

I shook my head. "It couldn't have been him. He was at work. He never goes for lunch that late."

Adrian's forehead creased. "Huh! Sure, looked like him. He must have a doppelganger." He raised a hand in farewell. "Later, old man."

I rolled my eyes and took a moment to ponder the case of mistaken identity. Adrian had only met Alex the once, so I supposed it was an easy enough mistake to have made. It wasn't as if he was the only dark-haired, slightly built man in the world. I checked my watch. Speaking of Alex, I needed to get a move on if I was going to get out of the garage in time to pick him up without keeping him standing around and waiting.

Chapter Twenty

Alexander

As I finished detailing the events of the night that had shattered my life into a million pieces, the silence that hung over the courtroom was an eerie sort of silence. The sort that comes from multiple people all holding themselves unnaturally still, so that there wasn't even the slightest rustle of clothing, or a cough to break it. I didn't know how long I'd spoken for. It had seemed like forever. Susan had done what she'd promised in the briefing beforehand: prompting me with questions, when I'd started to deviate too much, or became too lost in emotion, rather than simply stating facts.

It hadn't been easy. Apart from the statement to the police after it had happened, it was the first time I'd ever recalled the events. My cheeks were wet, tears having run constantly down my cheeks throughout my testimony. I refused to wipe them away. Let him see how much he'd ruined my life. I'd spent the whole confrontation with him in my parents' house pretending. Pretending I didn't care. Pretending I'd understood his actions. Pretending to be in love with the sick fucker who'd massacred my entire family. So, let him see how much it had cost me. He could think about it while he was rotting in a prison cell.

"No further questions, Your Honor." With a small smile of encouragement in my direction, Susan stepped away, leaving the floor open to the defense lawyer. He took his time, rifling slowly through the stack of papers on his table, before getting to his feet. It seemed like a deliberate timewasting tactic. Despite standing, he remained where he was, staring down at something on the piece of paper. I couldn't imagine that there was anything written there that he didn't already know inside out and back to front. He didn't strike me as the type. I kept my eyes on him, refusing to let them stray to the man next to him. I didn't want to see what effect my testimony and tears had had on him, if any. There was nothing to be gained from it.

He took another moment to straighten a tie which didn't need straightening before strolling to the space recently vacated by the prosecution. I wondered what kind of person you had to be to spend your days defending hardened criminals who were clearly guilty of heinous crimes. No doubt, he was quite happy living in his huge house and driving an expensive car around from the proceeds. I bet the man slept far better than I did at night.

As well as filling me in on the types of questions I was going to be asked, Susan had given me a bit of background on this man. Grant Meyer-Smith was his name and he came from a long line of lawyers. She hadn't pulled any punches, making it clear, he wouldn't hold back. The man's job was to somehow try and devalue my testimony: to make the jury doubt that I was telling the truth, or to at least put doubt into their mind about what had really happened and the circumstances behind it.

I glanced in their direction. Some of them looked visibly shaken. I felt guilty for spoiling their nice break from the day job by dragging them into the horror of my life. I hoped it wouldn't take them too long to get over it once the trial was over and done with.

"Do you need a break, Mr. Philips?" The same offer Susan had made. With her, it had come across as genuine concern. With this man, it was like he was already probing for weaknesses. I shook my head, turning the offer down. I'd waited a year for today, for the chance to play my crucial part in bringing down Oliver Calthorpe. It was the only reason I was still alive. The thing that had kept me going through the despair, loneliness, self-recrimination, and nightmares, so if Grant Meyer-Smith thought his intense stare and smarmy false charm was enough to make me fall at the last hurdle, then he was in for a surprise. I stood up straighter, finally using the back of my hand to wipe away the remains of the tears that hadn't already dried on my face and then I met his gaze head on.

He pasted a deliberate frown on his face. "I just have a few questions for you, Mr. Philips. A few things that don't add up and need some elaboration, if you don't mind. I'd like to start by clarifying a few things about the nature of your relationship with my client." He smiled. It was just as fake as the frown had been. I didn't think it was possible to hate anyone to the extent I hated Oliver. But, this man, who'd probably spent hours laughing and joking with Oliver while he plotted a way to help him escape justice, was forcing me to revise that opinion.

"You instigated the relationship. Is that correct?"

I froze, my brain working overtime to try and work out what he was insinuating. Susan had told me to answer the questions honestly, but to always try and add more information if I felt he was trying to lead me in a direction I didn't want to go. This was only the first question and already I felt lost. "I approached him first, if that's what you mean? But, not for a relationship. I never wanted a relationship with him."

He cocked his head to one side. "So, just sex then? That's all you wanted from him?" It was obviously a rhetorical question as

165

he didn't bother to wait for an answer. "And did you share this knowledge with my client...that you simply required him to act as a" — he gave a small laugh, making sure his body was partly turned toward the jury so they couldn't fail to hear the words clearly — "a...what...shall we call it...for want of a better word...a glorified sex toy."

"No, of course not. It wasn't like that. I—"

"So, you can understand my client...you can understand *Oliver* having the wrong idea about your relationship then? Because you weren't clear with him?" The frown appeared again. "I'll also admit to being incredibly confused why...if you didn't want a relationship with him, you continued to see him for weeks. That is not the actions of someone who doesn't want a relationship, Mr. Philips. How could my client be anything but confused?"

"I tried to break up with him. He—"

Like a shark seizing on a juicy leg being waved in front of them, he jumped on the word I'd provided with obvious relish. "Ah, you tried to *break up*? So, you admit you *were* in a relationship with him?"

He was making my head spin. I'd expected questions based around what happened in the house, not about things that weren't relevant before then. I glanced toward Susan. She deliberately scratched her head. It was a pre-arranged signal that meant I needed to slow down and think. She'd warned me that one of the lawyer's well-known strategies was to spit out questions so fast that witnesses often slipped up under the pressure of being rushed. I took a deep breath. "I said I didn't *want* a relationship. However, due to his pushiness, manipulation, and refusal to listen, I couldn't get rid of him."

"So, why did you see him again after the first night?"

I wondered if there were going to be any questions about Oliver's actions on the night he'd murdered my family, or whether he was simply going to concentrate on trying to drum up some sympathy for him. I guessed that it was hard to get around the sheer amount of forensic evidence that was piled up against him. The man had even left bloody fingerprints on the wall. The tactic appeared to be to try and make the jury feel sorry for him. Poor Oliver strung along by the evil English student, treated so callously that he'd felt he had no choice but to commit multiple homicides and threaten a baby. "He took my phone and forced me to give him my number and then he kept messaging me."

He let out another of those condescending little laughs. "He *forced* you, Mr. Philips! What did he do? Hold you down? Tie you up?"

"No. But he emotionally blackmailed me. Made me feel guilty. I felt like I had no choice if I wanted my phone back. I don't even know how he'd gotten hold of it." I did. I had no doubt in my mind with the advantage of hindsight that the moment my back was turned, he'd been across the room in a flash to extract it from my jeans pocket. The minute I'd approached him in the bar, my fate had been sealed, and I'd been paying for it ever since.

"And what did these messages say? Were they..." He paused dramatically. "...nasty? Was he emotionally blackmailing you then?" I opened my mouth to answer, but he held up a hand to stall me. "Hang on! I have a transcript of the messages. Let's see." He gestured for his assistant to hand him a piece of paper. I continued staring straight ahead, unable to take the risk of my eyes straying back to Oliver. Grant began to pace the length of the courtroom as he read from the list. "*Thank you for a great night. Hope we can do it again soon? I'm so glad I met you the other night. When can I see you again? I was thinking about you today. Let me know when you're next free and we can do something together.* Perfectly normal messages, Mr. Philips, and no more than three in a day. Not too pushy. Just a man who's met someone he likes. And I would say very easy for you to respond with a 'thanks but no,

thanks,' yet you didn't. You simply ignored the messages until" —
he made a point of staring more closely at the paper — "August
eleventh, a week after you had spent the night with him, where
you requested that he should take you to dinner in Paris. Isn't that
right?"

"I didn't write that?"

"No? Who did?"

"My friend. He'd taken my phone. He wrote it."

Grant walked slowly to place the piece of paper back on the
desk before turning back around. "Another person who *took* your
phone. How convenient. So, you deny that the real reason you
saw my client again was because of his money? You were an
unemployed student, Mr. Philips. It must have been nice to have
had a rich boyfriend at your beck and call, until you got bored
that is, and even the money wasn't enough to keep you
interested."

"It wasn't like that."

"I think it was. I think you thought you could just use and
discard my client and he would just accept that."

White-hot fury blossomed inside me. I'd stood and bared
my soul less than ten minutes before; talked about the most
painful part of my life. A night which had changed me forever
and left me scared of getting close to anyone else, of trusting
anyone else. I'd locked myself away ever since, scared of my own
shadow, letting creeps like my next-door neighbor intimidate me
and convincing myself that I must give off some sort of vibe that
made me a born victim. I knew that what happened that night
was my fault. I had to live with the guilt of knowing that if I'd
never approached Oliver Calthorpe in the first place then none of
it would ever have happened. I'd put my family in that situation.
I'd put them in the firing line, and I started off each morning
knowing that and went to bed at night, still living with that
knowledge. That's why once this trial was over, I didn't deserve to

be around any longer when they couldn't be. But, I was damned if I was taking all of that guilt. I may have lit the fuse, but Oliver Calthorpe was still responsible. He was the murderer, not me. He deserved everything that was coming to him.

So, how dare this man stand there and try and push it all on to me, making out like I'd forced Oliver into it? The notion was ridiculous. For some reason, an image of Austin floated into my head; the way he'd smiled at me over breakfast. Well, he'd eaten breakfast, I'd taken a few bites, just enough to stop him worrying too much or at least I hoped so. He was the only good thing that had happened to me since that fateful night. Just thinking about him gave me an extra boost of belief in myself.

I lifted my head, speaking slowly and clearly. "Even if I did lead him on and let him believe at any point that our relationship was more serious than it was, that does not mean that I deserved to get attacked by him in a club. I did not deserve to be followed around by him, and I certainly didn't deserve for him to murder my entire family. There is no acceptable excuse for that, no matter how badly I supposedly treated him, which for the record wasn't very badly at all...it was just like any normal relationship where one of the people is not as invested emotionally as the other. He murdered three people. Three people he'd never even met before. And it would have been four if I hadn't stopped him. The fourth being a poor defenseless baby who hadn't even started walking. I've broken up with boyfriends before and I assure you that none of them ever considered murdering anyone."

By the end of my outburst, I was breathing hard, but it was worth it for the look of annoyance on Grant's face. He hadn't liked what I'd said at all. Susan, however, was nodding at me. I took that as an indication that I hadn't gone too far. I braced myself, for the onslaught of more questions. Instead he turned to address the judge. "No further questions, Your Honor."

I sagged with relief. Was that it? Was it over? The clock said it was four fifteen. I'd waited a year for what had amounted to no more than thirty minutes.

Chapter Twenty-one

Austin

Alex looked like a strong gust of wind would be enough to blow him over. Actually, strike that, it wouldn't even take a strong one, a light breeze would probably do the trick, given how pale and vulnerable he looked. It made me want to wrap him in my arms, hold him close, and never let go.

It had been an hour since I'd picked him up from outside the library and he'd barely said two words. Even more worrying, was the fact he didn't even seem to have the energy to keep up the pretense of playing with his food. It just sat in front of him; the simple concoction of pasta and tomato sauce completely untouched. "Alex, you need to eat."

He jumped at the sound of my voice, as if he'd forgotten I was even there. Like clockwork, his head dipped, hiding his expression. "Sorry. I'm just not hungry today. Thank you for cooking though. It was very sweet of you, but...sorry."

"But, you didn't eat breakfast either." I couldn't keep the note of pleading from my voice. "You can't live on fresh air. What did you have for lunch?"

The hesitation before he answered was just that beat too

long. That meant the information I was about to be given was more than likely a lie. "A sandwich...and there were biscuits in the staffroom at work...chocolate digestives."

I stared at him, wishing there was some way I could see inside his head and figure out what was going on in there. If I was right and he was lying, then he hadn't eaten all day. But then, what was I supposed to do? It wasn't as if I could force him to eat. He was an adult. Not a child I could encourage and cajole into taking a few bites. Still, I found I couldn't let it go completely. Not eating *enough* was one thing, but not eating at all was another thing entirely. "Are you ill? Is that why you don't have an appetite?"

There was an even longer pause before he finally gave a jerky nod of his head. "Sorry."

"You don't need to apologize for being ill. Why didn't you say something?"

"I should have gone home. I don't know why I didn't really." He gave a wan smile. "I *should* go home."

My arm shot across the table, grabbing a tight hold of his hand. "No!" I couldn't explain my fear, but it felt like if he left now, I'd never see him again. Like he'd cease to exist if I let him out of my sight. I knew it was a crazy overreaction and completely irrational, but I just couldn't shake it. He went still, his hand lying in mine like a rock, before visibly relaxing. I wrapped my fingers around his, gripping more tightly as I struggled to convince my brain that I was being stupid and needed to back off. "Your hands are cold. You must be ill." They were. They were like ice. I used both hands to rub the one I held, trying to force some warmth back into it.

His eyes slowly lifted to mine, his gaze traveling over every part of my face. It was like he'd never really looked at me before. The way he was scrutinizing me did nothing to calm the unease still trickling through my veins. His sigh was nothing more than a whisper on the breeze. "I'm sorry, Austin."

I was convinced he was apologizing for a deeper reason than simply being ill, or not eating, or for barely speaking. I just didn't know what that reason was. I found myself transfixed by the long-lashed brown eyes. Struck, not for the first time, by how pretty they were. I desperately searched for the right thing to say, the right question to ask. It felt like if I could just find the key, I'd be able to unlock him and all his secrets would come tumbling out.

He looked away, and the spell was broken, the moment gone. I let go of his hand and sat back in the chair. Did he really want to go home to his bare apartment? If it was what he wanted, I needed to stop taking his choices away. Sometimes, it was all too easy to forget that he went along with things. I didn't want to be the person who treated him like a possession under the pretense of protecting him. That wasn't a healthy relationship for either of us. "If you want, I can drive you home? Or...you can go for a lie-down here? I won't be offended. I'll..." I cast around for something I could do rather than following him around like a lost puppy, worrying about him. "...wash up and then watch *Top Gear*. Maybe go for a walk or something."

I held my breath while he considered my offer. "A lie-down sounds good. Thank you." He rose from the table, walking around it to drop a kiss on my cheek before disappearing up the stairs toward the bedroom. I fought down the sense of relief at him choosing to stay and pondered how even his lips had felt cold against my cheek.

Eighty-two minutes. That's how long I lasted before filling a glass with water and using it as an excuse to go and check on him. I entered the bedroom as quietly as I could—almost tiptoeing—in case he was asleep. He was curled beneath the covers, facing the window. It wasn't until I drew closer that I could see that his eyes were open. It took him a moment to register my presence, his gaze

173

shifting from staring into space to find mine. I smiled and held up the glass of water before placing it down on the nightstand next to him. "I thought you might be thirsty."

"Thanks."

The word was whispered so quietly, I barely heard it. On his side in a fetal position, hand tucked beneath his face on the pillow, he looked even more fragile, and I had that peculiar feeling again like he was slipping away and there was nothing I could do to stop it. I gave myself a mental shake. He was ill, that was all. I didn't need to start reading anything more dramatic into it. I pulled a chair next to the bed, easing myself into it so I could be more on a level with him. "If you still feel like this tomorrow, then maybe we should make an appointment to see a doctor. Check that everything's alright."

He shook his head vigorously. It was the most animated he'd been all evening. "I don't need to see a doctor. It's just a bug or something."

"But..."

He struggled up on to one elbow, an unreadable but intense expression on his face. "I'll be fine by the weekend."

I considered his words. It was Wednesday. The weekend was only a few days away. "Promise me, if you're no better by Saturday, you'll let me take you to see a doctor?"

"Saturday." The word was repeated as if it held great importance, without being either a question or a statement. It was like he knew something I didn't. Or maybe my brain was just working far too hard to give greater meaning to every look, word, and gesture I managed to force out of him. He was probably just echoing what I'd said. Still, it didn't escape my attention that he hadn't agreed.

"Alex, do you promise?"

He nodded as he lay back down. It was the best I was going to get from him. "Do you want to be left alone?"

He considered the question before giving a tiny shake of his head. "Can I ask you something, Austin?" He rolled on to his back, staring up at the ceiling.

"Of course. You can ask me anything. Anything at all."

"And you'll tell me the truth?"

My pulse sped up. I didn't know why. It wasn't like I had anything to hide. He could ask me anything and I'd tell him. In the unlikely event he wanted to know about old boyfriends, I'd even tell him that—warts and all. "Yes. Of course, I will."

"Have you ever hated anyone? Like really *hated* them?"

I was taken aback for a moment. It was such a strange question to come from the quiet and soft-spoken Alex. "Hate's a strong word."

"I know." His head rolled to the side so he was looking at me rather than the ceiling. "Have you?"

I thought about it, sifting through all the people that had passed through my life and had any sort of impact at all. "I don't think so. Disliked, then yes...I mean, my brother and I don't exactly see eye to eye about a lot of things. Well, anything really, but I don't hate him." I thought back further. "There was a boy at school who used to put frogs in my lunch box, and I'm not just talking once. He must have done it at least ten times. I've no idea where he got all the frogs from. I think I probably hated him at the time, but thinking about him now, it's...well, it's faded, I guess. I don't hate him now."

Lost in musing over my past, it took longer than it normally would have to notice Alex's smile. It wasn't just a small smile. It was a great big, beaming smile, like he was trying not to laugh. "Oh, I see! I'm glad you find my childhood trauma so amusing." I reached forward, aiming a jab at the area where I estimated his ribs to be under the cover, and feeling absurdly pleased when he squirmed and let out a snort of laughter. "You try eating sandwiches that a frog's crawled all over. You've no idea how many times I had to go hungry because of bloody Geoffrey Hall and his damn frogs."

"Why did he do it?"

I shrugged. "No idea." I couldn't say I'd given it a lot of thought. It was one of those weird things that you'd simply accepted as a child. It was years since I'd even remembered it prior to this conversation.

"How old were you?"

"I was thirteen. He was in the year below me, so he'd have been twelve."

Alex's lips curled back into a smile, as if he knew a secret. "Bet I know why he did it."

I frowned. "Why?"

"He probably had a thing for you. He was trying to get your attention."

I pulled a face. "Well, it didn't work. I stayed as far away from the loon as I possibly could. So, don't go getting any ideas. Giving me frogs isn't the way to my heart."

We lapsed into silence until I remembered the whole reason Geoffrey Hall's name had come up in the first place. "What about you? Have *you* ever hated anyone?"

His face clouded over and I regretted bringing the mood down.

"Yes."

No consideration. No changing his mind or softening it once he'd said it. Just a definitive confirmation. "Who?" Even knowing that his answer wasn't going to lead to some nice, amusing story about a boy and his frogs, I couldn't stop myself from asking. Was this where he was finally going to open up, and I was going to start to learn the truth?

Alex's eyes closed. "His name was...is..." He paused and for a moment I thought he wasn't going to say anymore. He exhaled shakily. "...Oliver. His name is Oliver."

My fingernails dug into the palms of my hands and I leant forwards, my gaze never leaving his face. "What did he do?" I counted Alex's breaths as I waited...seven, eight, nine, ten, eleven. It was ironic considering I was holding my own. I wondered whether the fact his eyes were closed would help. Maybe he'd find he could talk with the mirage of nobody being able to see him. My hopes were shattered at the next words that came out of his mouth.

His face screwed up, almost like he was in pain. "I can't talk about him. Sorry."

I sat back, my breath escaping in a noisy exhale. "Okay." He may not have opened up, but at least it was something. I had a name for the man who'd destroyed Alex's trust. The rest would come eventually. I'd been patient this long. A little longer couldn't hurt. I don't know how long I sat there, turning the name over and over in my mind as if mere consideration of it might reveal more, but Alex was asleep before I left the room.

Chapter Twenty-two

Alexander

My wrists were sore. I assumed as a result of being manhandled by the police and then cuffed for an extended period of time. I couldn't have said how long it had been. Only that when they'd pushed me into a small, empty room and ushered me onto a wooden chair, they'd left them on. At least it was a room, not a cell. I didn't know whether that was a good sign or just standard procedure. I didn't know anything anymore. I'd stayed silent throughout the whole ordeal, knowing I should at least try and explain, but unable to muster the energy to do so. So, I sat and waited, shifting around in an effort to find a more comfortable position where the metal of the cuffs didn't bite into my skin.

Eventually, a uniformed police officer had entered the room. He hadn't spoken, simply removed the cuffs, and then left again. I had no idea what had prompted it. Maybe they'd worked out I'd been the one to call them. Either that or they'd somehow come to the realization that it had been my family inside the house. I didn't know. I was just tired. Tired and sore.

The next person that came in wasn't wearing a uniform. They asked if they could get me something to drink. I'd asked for water, and they'd returned a few minutes later holding a glass. I'd gulped down the contents before handing the glass back to them. They'd left, and I'd been alone ever since, only the ticking of the clock on the wall to keep me company, and to stop my mind from straying back to the evening's events. I concentrated on counting the ticks, the action providing a strange sort of reassurance.

I'd just reached a thousand when the door opened and a pair of officers walked in. The taller male one seemed to be in charge. I'd have put him somewhere in his early forties, unless the gray at his temples was premature. The shorter female officer was younger – probably only somewhere in her mid-twenties and seemed to be following the other one's lead. She carried an old-fashioned-looking recording device which she placed on the table. They took seats opposite, the female officer offering a reassuring smile as she clicked the button to start the recording for the interview.

The man steepled his fingers in front of him. "For the purposes of the tape, I'm Sergeant Dalton. Also, present in the room is Constable Fielding. Could you please confirm that your name is Alexander Philips?"

I nodded.

"We need you to state it aloud please, for the recording."

"Yes. My name is Alexander Philips." I zoned out as they began to detail the date and time of the interview, returning to counting the ticks of the clock instead. It was only when I realized my name was being said with some urgency that I reluctantly pulled my attention back to them. I'd reached one hundred and three that time. I decided I'd class it as a total of one thousand one hundred and three. That could be my aim: see what the total number of ticks I could reach on the clock could be.

The man started speaking. I'd already forgotten his name. "We need to ask you some questions about tonight. Is that okay, Alexander? Eventually, we'll need to take a statement, but at the moment, we're just hoping you can help us with some of the information that isn't very clear to us. Do you think you could do that for us?"

He had a nice voice: deep, with just the right amount of concern without tipping over into being too informal. I wondered if he was asked to carry out a lot of the witness interviews for that reason. Realizing I hadn't answered his question, I tried my best to recall what it had been. "What did you ask, sorry?"

Apparently, he was patient as well. If he was at all irritated, he didn't let it show on his face. "If you think you're up to answering some questions for us?"

"Is he dead?" I'd blurted the question out before I could stop it.

They exchanged a glance. It was the female officer who spoke first. "Who?"

"Oliver." I invested the name with as much venom as I could give it. "I stabbed him." A small voice in my head told me that perhaps it wasn't the best idea to openly state that on tape without having a lawyer present. Should I have a lawyer? Should I have requested one? My dad would know. He always knew stuff like that. But, I guessed he was no longer around to give me the information. Or any information ever again. A huge wave of sorrow hit me. I was just glad I hadn't gone down into the basement and seen his body. I knew that as long as I lived, I'd never be able to rid myself of the sight of my mum and sister sprawled across the kitchen floor, their blood soaking into the cracks. The floor that my mum had always kept fastidiously clean. She'd have hated to see it like that. Who was going to clean it now? At least with my dad, I'd be able to remember him the way he was.

"No, he's not dead. He'll recover quickly from the injury. It didn't hit anything crucial."

I should have felt relieved at the news. It meant I wasn't a killer. But, there was nothing but emptiness and the knowledge that my family's murderer would get to keep breathing and get to recall the things he'd done supposedly in the name of love. My gaze dropped down and I looked at my hands properly for the first time since they'd been uncuffed. They were covered in blood. Not just a bit, but completely covered; the dried blood starting to flake in places. Whose blood was it? Oliver's from when I'd stabbed him? My mum's? My sister's? I began to scratch at it, needing it off my skin, but it resisted any attempts to simply be wiped away. I scraped harder, trying to use the nails of my *other hand to dig into the skin and remove it. The pain didn't matter. Nothing mattered except the need for my hands to be clean.*

Then the female officer was next to me, grabbing at my hands and pulling them away. I lifted my head, absently noting the smell of her perfume as I stared up at her through the tears in my eyes. It was the same one my dad had bought my mum for Christmas. The one she'd said was far too expensive and had hardly ever worn apart from on special occasions. I wondered where the perfume was. Was it still in the house? I supposed it must be, sat there like nothing had happened.

I began to shake; my brain unable to regain any semblance of control over my body. I tried to focus back on the clock, hoping to restore the calm that counting the strokes of the seconds had given me before. But, it was like the numbers were jumbled in my brain. Then, I couldn't breathe. There was no oxygen left in the room. Over the sound of my own gasping breaths, I became vaguely aware of raised voices saying something about going into shock and needing a doctor urgently.

* * * *

Sat outside the courtroom, awaiting the call that the jury had reached a verdict, I stared down at my hands, almost expecting to see them covered in blood. Of course, they weren't, they were clean. Still, the memory was hard to shake. It had taken three days before the doctor had deemed my mental state to be good enough to give an official statement. Then hours of questioning had followed. Hours of rehashing every single thing I knew about Oliver and our "relationship." They'd announced that I wasn't going to be charged for my assault on Oliver. The stabbing had been deemed as self-defense despite the fact that I never pretended for one minute that the act had been anything other than what it was. Or maybe I had. They'd appointed a lawyer for me. I remembered words like "provocation" and "temporary breakdown" being bandied about. I didn't know any more. It was all so confusing.

They hadn't found Charlie. Apparently, they'd looked, or so

they claimed. I just hoped that wherever he'd run off to, he'd found himself a good home. As for my nephew, he was fine. No injuries. No signs of trauma. With no other relatives, my mum and dad had both been an only child and both sets of grandparents had passed away years before, he was currently staying with a foster family. I could see him whenever I was ready. They'd talked at me as if it were a done deal that I'd be providing a home for him. But, what did I know about babies? I was twenty-two and fresh out of university. He was better off in someone's care that had a clue what they were doing.

Behind my back, there was talk of more doctors, talk of organizing a psychiatric consultation for me, and keeping me monitored 24/7. I think they thought I wasn't listening. All I knew was, I didn't want that. I was done talking. I was done going over and over what had happened. I was just completely and utterly done. At the first opportunity where I wasn't supervised, I walked out of the police station. Nobody came after me. Either they hadn't noticed my absence or they didn't care now that they had my signed witness statement.

Stood out on the street, blinking in the sunlight, I'd almost changed my mind and gone back inside. At least in the police station or back at the hotel where they'd kept me in the evenings, there was structure: there were people bringing me food and drinks; telling me what I needed to do next, and how I should be feeling. Out there in the real world, there was nothing, apart from a house I couldn't go back to, and friends I didn't want to see because that would mean more talking.

"Jury have reached a verdict." My breath escaped in a rush. That had been much quicker than predicted. It had taken them less than an hour to reach a majority verdict. Assuming they'd found him guilty — and I couldn't even begin to consider any other outcome — then sentencing would follow straight away. I was almost done.

Those of us who'd chosen to take a break and leave, filed back into the courtroom taking our seats in the public gallery again. From the looks I was getting, there were obviously people who'd been there all week, fully aware of who I was and the importance of the verdict to me. I kept my gaze deliberately averted from them so that they couldn't catch my eye. I didn't need sympathy, or commiseration, or whatever else they might have felt the need to proffer to make themselves feel better. I just needed this over and done with. Once and for all.

There was still no sign of the jury, or Oliver for that matter. They must have taken him out while jury deliberations were ongoing. Unlike last time, I had every intention of looking at him. I wanted to see his face when the jury found him guilty and I wanted to note his every expression when the judge passed down the sentence.

As I waited I thought about Austin. He'd been incredible for the last few days while I'd kept up the facade, that he'd unwittingly provided for me, of being ill. Of course, I felt guilty. Every time I so much as looked at his handsome face, I felt guilty, both for being with him and for lying to him. But, there was no viable alternative. There was no way I could have dragged him into the horror story that made up my life. His life was about fixing cars, arguing with his brother, working out, and going for a beer with his mates, not blood and death and trauma. Nobody needed that in their life when it was avoidable.

Oliver was led back into the courtroom, his blue gaze unerringly finding mine straight away. I lifted my chin and despite the nausea that churned in my stomach at the mere sight of him, I refused to look away. He smiled, and I wanted to stab him all over again, and maybe twist the knife this time. I'd often wondered what would have happened if I'd done the job properly in the first place. Would I have gone to jail? Would I be the person stood there today waiting for my verdict?

The jury box filled up quickly, but I kept my gaze firmly trained on Oliver, the two of us taking part in a staring contest across the breadth of the courtroom. The foreman of the jury stood, most of what he said failing to register, only the word guilty filtering through. That's all I needed to hear. Then, it was my turn to smile, Oliver finally looking away as a muscle twitched in his cheek.

Sentencing brought an even bigger smile to my face, Oliver visibly flinching at the announcement of life imprisonment with a minimum term of forty years to be served before any chance of parole would even be considered. The monster was going to be behind bars until he was at least in his late sixties, and even then, it was unlikely they'd grant parole. The likelihood was that he'd die behind bars and in my opinion, no one deserved it more. With one last glance at an annoyed Oliver, deep in conversation with his defense lawyer, I got up and left the courtroom.

When I'd given evidence the other day, I'd been kept away from the press: both prosecution and defense were concerned that it might somehow affect their case. With the end of the trial, I had no such protection. I walked through them in a daze, blinking as camera bulbs flashed in my face and a barrage of questions — none of which I had any intention of answering — was thrown at me. *"Are you satisfied with the verdict? Do you wish we had the death penalty in this country? Why didn't anyone know of your whereabouts for the last year? Were you in hiding? Was it deliberate? Have you been living overseas? Is there anything you wish you could say to Oliver Calthorpe? Is it true you didn't bother to attend your parents' funerals? Why not?"*

The questions went on and on as I continued to weave my way through the throng and down the steps of the courthouse that led to the street. Most of them washed over me. The last one though hit a nerve. No, I hadn't attended my parents' funerals — or my sister's. I hadn't been in any mental state to cope with it. I regretted it now, wishing I'd found the strength to have dragged myself there and said goodbye properly.

I'd visited their graves numerous times since; the three plaques all in a row signifying where their ashes had been laid. A part of me always felt jealous that they were together. Even the organization of the funerals, I'd passed over to a company. It had taken nearly every penny of my parents' savings and life insurance. Maybe they'd ripped me off. At the time, I honestly didn't know — or care.

The house hadn't sold. Its grim history meaning that most people didn't want to touch it with a bargepole, no matter how cheap the asking price. You couldn't blame them. Who'd choose to live in a house where a triple murder had occurred? Eventually, the bank had repossessed it when the mortgage payments weren't met and after that I had no idea what had happened to it. I'd never gone back there — not even to collect my things. That was another thing to add to the long list of regrets. I didn't care about *my* things, but I couldn't help wondering what had happened to my parents' personal belongings — things like framed photos and photograph albums. Had the police taken them? Or had they just been thrown out like they were worthless?

I was only halfway down the steps and the questions were still coming thick and fast. *"Do you visit your nephew? How old is he now? Is he old enough to understand what happened? Does he ask you questions? What have you told him?"*

Despite my continued silence and refusal to answer, there was no sign of them letting up. *"Can we have a quote from you about how it felt to discover the bodies? I understand your mum was alive when you found her? That must have been tough. Can you tell us about that?"*

One particularly stubborn journalist attempted to block my path. *"Do you blame yourself for what happened?"* I all but shoved him out of the way, the street now mere meters away.

"Al?"

The shout, coupled with the use of the now unfamiliar name, sliced through the media frenzy. I stumbled to a stop, turning back, and searching the crowd of people to find out where it had come from. Two men stood at the top of the steps, their appearance not so different from the last time I'd seen them. Jack's hair was just that little bit longer, and David looked like he'd filled out a bit more. Whether that was from enjoying his food or upping his workout it was difficult to tell from a distance. The sight of them caused something in my chest to flare briefly to life.

They began to make their way down the steps with the obvious intent of catching up to me. I hadn't noticed them in the courtroom, but then all my attention had been firmly fixed on Oliver, and it hadn't even crossed my mind that someone I knew might attend the sentencing. Were they there because they'd wanted to know the outcome, or were they looking for me? Had they been there when I'd given evidence? Did *they* have to give evidence? The notion had never occurred to me before.

I'd thought about them over the past year. Of course, I had. I'd wondered how they were doing and whether they were still together. On a good day, I'd even considered contacting them. But, it had never gone any further than a thought. I remained frozen in place, the reporters surrounding me, almost buzzing with excitement as they misread my stillness as an intention to finally give them an interview. Their progress was slow; the media just as much in their way as they'd been in mine. It gave me valuable seconds to think. Did I want to speak to them? My heart said yes, but my head said no. It wouldn't be fair.

Tomorrow was Saturday: the day I'd promised Austin I'd see a doctor if everything wasn't better. Well, it wasn't going to get any better so I was out of excuses to explain away my increasingly erratic behavior. In my head, it was just another reason to keep to the plan I'd always had as soon as the trial ended. Therefore, was it really fair to appear back in their lives for nothing but a short, awkward conversation? Wouldn't that be a case of rubbing salt in the wounds? I spun on my heel, refusing to look back and see the disappointed looks on their faces as I pushed my way through the rest of the reporters and hurried away down the street.

Chapter Twenty-three

Austin

I placed the pint of lager down in front of Alex before swinging my leg over the wooden bench to retake the seat opposite him in the beer garden. He picked it up and took a large swallow. He was full of surprises today. You could have knocked me down with a feather when he'd suggested going for a drink, and now in the space of an hour, he was already on his third pint. It wasn't just that though. There was something different about him today. Something lighter. Like he'd lost the whole weight of the world on his shoulders. It wasn't a version of him I'd ever seen before and I had to admit I liked it. I liked it a lot. Rather than wasting time analyzing it, I resolved to simply enjoy it while it lasted.

I gestured at Alex's pint of lager, a third of it having disappeared already. "Are you getting drunk?"

Alex cocked his head to one side, his expression almost playful and the corners of his mouth curling up into a smile. The sort of smile that made my heart beat faster and my stomach do somersaults. "Maybe." He reached across, his fingers gently stroking the skin of my forearm. "Will you carry me home if I do?"

188

God, I loved this man! In a short space of time, he'd become everything to me. The fact he was referring to my place as home, sent a warm glow through my entire body. It may have been nothing more than the beer talking, but I allowed myself a moment of optimism anyway as I returned his smile. "Sure! I'd carry you anywhere."

Alex pretended to consider the notion. "What about as far as the coffee shop?"

I waggled my fingers in the air, faking a frown as I pretended to carry out a devilishly difficult calculation. "No further than a mile. Easy! You're not that heavy."

"Central London?"

I pulled an exaggerated thinking face, thoroughly enjoying the rare banter. "Bit harder. But, I reckon I could still manage it as long as you keep still."

Alex sat back with a pleased smile, his fingers still stroking the skin of my bare arm. I resisted the urge to lean in and kiss him, worried I'd get carried away, and then the only place I'd end up carrying him would be home to bed. It was nice to spend time with him outside of the house. I didn't want to bring it to a premature end. Who knew when the next time he'd feel this comfortable might be? He took another gulp of beer. "I wish..."

I waited for the end of the sentence, but it didn't come, his face clouding over with a look of sadness. It was so at odds with the rest of his demeanor that I was momentarily thrown. "What do you wish?" Whatever it was, if it was within my power, I'd move heaven and earth to be the one to give it to him.

His gaze dropped to the wooden surface of the table and like so many times before, I found myself staring at the top of his head. I knew from experience that the best thing to do was just to give him time. When he raised his head again, the smile was back, as if the sadness had never existed in the first place. "Nothing. I was going to say something stupid." He poked a finger at my pint, moving it a few inches across the table toward me. "Drink up. You're way behind me, lightweight."

"Lightweight!" I stared at him in amazement, the unexpected teasing managing to make me forget the swift alteration in mood. "Seriously! Mr. I-can-make-one-drink- last-all-night is calling *me* a lightweight?" Still, I obediently lifted the glass to my lips and took a long swallow, my gaze fixed on his.

* * * *

Back home, I reflected on the evening while I washed my hands in the bathroom. We'd stayed out for a couple of hours, Alex even suggesting that we should eat something. He'd ordered lasagna and chips, and to my surprise had eaten over half of what was on his plate. It was the most I'd ever seen him eat that didn't consist almost entirely of sugar. It reassured me that whatever had been ailing him this week had cleared up. Good! It meant we could do something more exciting over the weekend than visiting a doctor. Maybe I'd suggest a day out somewhere. Somewhere quiet that wouldn't be too stressful for him

When he'd started flagging, I'd suggested leaving. We'd walked home, the good-natured atmosphere of teasing between us still lingering on. I was looking forward to spending the rest of the evening with him cuddled up on the sofa watching a crappy movie. If I remembered rightly, I had some microwave popcorn tucked in the back of a cupboard somewhere. I could see whether I could get Alex to eat some, although that was probably pushing things too far. The poor guy had eaten a proper meal for once, and there I was still trying to force more food down him. It was never good form to stuff your boyfriend so full he was at risk of exploding.

Still smiling at the absurd thought of torturing Alex with popcorn, I did a double take on finding him hovering in the doorway of the bedroom rather than downstairs where I'd left him. "Are you okay?"

He nodded, gesturing that I should follow him in there.

Frowning and wondering what was going on, I did as he'd asked. "I was thinking we could watch a movie or something. There must be something on Netflix you want to watch. I'm not fussy. I'll watch pretty much anything."

Alex moved over to the window, drawing the curtains so that the bedroom became darker, the relatively early hour meaning there was still enough light shining through to prevent it being completely pitch-black. "I don't want to watch a movie."

It was rare for Alex to say no to something. I should have felt glad he felt he could, but it just left me confused. "Oh, okay. Well, I suppose we could..." *Could what?* We'd just been out. We'd just taken a walk on the way back from the pub. What did that leave for me to suggest?

Then Alex crossed the room, halting directly in front of me. Because of the difference in our heights, he was forced to look up. There was a strange expression on his face, one I'd never seen before. He lifted his hand and laid it flat on my chest, the heat of it warming my skin through the thin T-shirt.

Maybe I was stupid, or maybe it was the slowing effect of the beer I'd drunk but I didn't read his intention until the hand moved down, trailing over my stomach and creeping under the hem of the T-shirt, fingers inching back up over bare skin. Then, and only then, I got it. The look on his face was lust. Initiation of sex had always been left to me, and always in bed. I mean, we were only a few steps from it, but still, it was new. Despite my cock suddenly becoming incredibly interested in proceeding, I didn't want him to do anything he wasn't comfortable with. I grabbed his hand, stilling the movement of his fingertips over my skin. "Alex, you don't have to."

His brow furrowed, his head cocking to one side as if I'd said something incredibly strange. Rather than responding, he came up on tiptoes, his lips fitting themselves to mine and his tongue darting out to explore the seam of my lips. Still, I held myself rigid. Perhaps I was worried he was drunk, or perhaps I was still trying to get my head around this new version of Alex. I didn't know what it was, only that I was reticent to accept what he was clearly offering.

He pulled back, hurt plastered all over his face. It wasn't an expression I ever wanted to see, particularly not if I'd caused it. I reached out trying to communicate with touch alone that I wasn't rejecting him, would never reject him. He rubbed his face into my hand like a cat starved of affection. "I want you, Austin!"

My cock gave a twitch at the words. I normally struggled to get a yes or no out of him during sex. He'd certainly never expressed his desire so openly before. It did wonderful things to both my body and mind, making me dizzy with desire for him and filling me with optimism about the future. "I want you too."

The words seemed to be enough encouragement as he pushed me back against the wall, his hands moving to tug at the bottom of the T-shirt and pull it over my head. I lifted my arms obediently and then his mouth was on my chest; tongue and lips exploring every inch. I sagged against the wall, torn between closing my eyes and enjoying the physical sensations, or reveling in the visual feast of Alex touching me as the pale skin of his hands followed in the wake of his mouth, raising goosebumps across my skin. In the end, the desire to watch him, won out. I let out a strangled yelp as his teeth brushed my nipple. He smiled smugly before using his tongue to lap at the sensitive flesh. He repeated the action on the other nipple, laughing when even though I was expecting it, it produced exactly the same reaction.

When he put distance between us, I was convinced he'd come to his senses. I mentally prepared myself to assure him that it was okay, that we could watch a movie after all. Then he was stripping, leaving a pile of clothes next to him on the floor until he stood gloriously naked and completely at ease in front of me, his erect cock making it clear he was just as aroused as I was, despite the fact I hadn't even touched him yet.

I wanted to rectify that. I reached out, desperate to get my hands on the smooth, naked skin and itching to take the long, slim cock down my throat. He backed off, shaking his head, and leaving my hands grasping at thin air. The action was completely at odds with the teasing smile on his face. "My turn today, Austin." He closed the space between us again, dropping to his knees and unzipping my jeans until he could pull them down around my thighs. My cock strained at my underwear, his mouth mere inches away. He'd never sucked my cock. I hadn't asked and he'd never given any indication he wanted to.

"Alex?" We both knew what I was asking for. Slim hands made short work of pushing my underwear to the same point as my jeans, my cock immediately standing to attention. My thighs trembled as his mouth moved closer. So close, I could feel each breath feather across the sensitive glans. My cock throbbed with each beat of my heart. I curled my hands into fists, fighting against the temptation to sink my fingers into his hair and drag those delectable lips onto my cock.

As if sensing my struggle, his head tilted back until we made eye contact. "Don't hold back. Not tonight."

"Alex, I—"

"Promise me, Austin."

What could I do with a request like that, other than agree, especially given the amount of pleading in his eyes? I nodded, proving it by digging my fingers into the luxuriously thick hair and pulling him onto my cock until his mouth opened and his lips slid over the head, the tight suction causing my hips to buck up, pushing myself deeper into his mouth. I don't know what I'd expected from him. Maybe that he'd be cautious or unsure. Alex might not have sucked my cock in the time we'd been together.

But, one thing was for sure, he knew exactly what he was doing, his lips, tongue, and hand moving in perfect synchronized harmony to bring me close to orgasm in no time at all.

I let my head fall back against the wall, the weight of it on my neck way too heavy when all my blood seemed to be centered in my cock. Just when I thought his intention was to have me come in his mouth—a state of affairs I would have been more than happy to go along with—he pulled off, his lips leaving my cock with an obscene-sounding slurp. Breathing hard, I could do nothing but watch as he crossed the room, rifling in the nightstand drawer for a condom and lube before returning and pushing them into my hands.

Alex braced himself against the wall, his chest pressed against it as his ass tipped up invitingly. I took a moment to admire him, the sleek lines of his body only accentuated by the position. He looked back over his shoulder, the swollen mouth from sucking my cock completing the picture of complete and utter debauchery. It was hard to believe that he was the same man I'd had to coax out of his clothes in the darkness. Love and lust warred within me. Love wanted to peel him away from the wall, steer him over to the bed and treat him like a precious flower. Lust wanted to take what he was offering and fuck him hard against the wall.

Lust won. Condom on and lubed, I positioned myself behind him, one hand covering his against the wall, while the other positioned my cock against the tight hole that I was desperate to be inside. I paused for a moment, my brain not so fogged that I was prepared to hurt him. "Are you sure?" He spread his legs slightly, attempting to push his ass onto my cock. It still wasn't enough. I wasn't prepared to shatter everything we'd built up so far. "Alex, I need words."

He looked over his shoulder again, his eyes meeting mine, the desire in his eyes almost taking my breath away. "No holding back. Remember?"

"No holding back." I repeated the words as I eased myself inside him, inch by slow inch, my lips fastening on his neck, needing to taste the salt on his skin as I penetrated him. His body quivered under my hands, a low moan escaping from his lips as I bottomed out. Then he was wriggling back against me, and the control I'd fought so hard for, snapped. With one arm wrapped around his chest, I gave him exactly what he'd asked for and didn't hold back, the soft moans escaping from Alex's mouth serving as reassurance that he was loving it every bit as much as I was.

Our bodies moved together. Our muscles strained. I wriggled my hand between him and the wall, wrapping my hand around the length of his cock and stroking him in time with my thrusts. He fucked my hand, the movement driving my cock even deeper inside him. Alex was wild. He was completely uninhibited, and I loved it. He came first, his body stiffening in my arms as he cried out, at the same time as his ass tightened on my cock. I gripped on to his hips, so close I could almost taste the orgasm. It only took a few more thrusts and then I was burying myself deep, my body shaking as I spilled into the condom.

I wrapped my arms around him, both of us leaning against the wall. It was only when the sweat began to cool and I felt a slight shiver pass through Alex that I withdrew, disposing of the condom on the way to maneuvering both of us over to the bed and beneath the covers.

Normally after sex, I fell into a relaxed stupor. But, my head was buzzing, my body singing like a live wire with all the possibilities of the future flashing before my eyes. Whatever switch had been flipped in Alex's head, made the future look a lot rosier. It wasn't just the sex. It was his whole demeanor. It couldn't all be put down to recovering from illness. That wouldn't produce such a rapid change. It was more likely he'd finally reached the point in our relationship where he felt like he could truly be himself. He had to be feeling the same, right? I leaned up on one elbow, looking over and expecting to see the same optimism and joy reflected back at me.

He wasn't looking my way. Just like I'd seen so many times before, his gaze was firmly fixed on the ceiling. I nudged him. His gaze didn't waver. "Alex?" Still no response. I nudged him again. This time, his head slowly rolled to the side until our eyes met. He managed a smile, but it was weak at best. I leaned in, brushing my lips against his cheek. He was tired. That was all. I should probably let him sleep.

I couldn't though. I'd been waiting to ask him a question for the last few days. After a perfect evening, and the barriers we'd just broken through, it seemed like a perfect time to cement our relationship into something more permanent so I went for it. "I've been thinking...and you can say no...but, you're here all the time anyway...so it's kind of already happening." At the look of confusion on his face, I slowed down, trying to dampen down the sudden attack of nerves at moving our relationship to the next level and ensure the words coming out made a bit more sense. "Moving in...that's what I'm trying to say. You moving in here. If you want? Like I said, you're here most of the time. So, it's just making it official, really...and moving your stuff in here as well. And you didn't seem to have that much so that probably won't take long. If you're worried about, you know, me paying all the bills, well then don't be...we can sort that out. It'll be cheaper for both of us." I paused to take a breath, backtracking when I realized my words could easily be misconstrued. "That's got absolutely nothing to do with why I'm asking you. I do okay at the garage. Honest. I just want us to be together." I finished my rambling speech with a smile, only then realizing how silent he'd been. No questions. No comments. Nothing. There wasn't so much as a flicker of emotion present on his face. Finally, he spoke.

"Austin, that's a lovely offer."

"But?"

He shrugged, one thin shoulder moving under the sheet. "Can we talk about it tomorrow? I don't want to talk about it now."

Disappointment sliced through me. Despite not being a no, it still felt like I was being fobbed off. I lay back down, wishing, not for the first time, that I could read him better. "I thought we were getting on well?"

"We do. It's just... Tomorrow, Austin. Please."

I tried to convince myself not to take it too much to heart. After all, it didn't mean anything would change. It just meant he wasn't ready to make that sort of commitment yet. I needed to wait. Give him more time. It had only been a few weeks. I was getting ahead of myself and trying to rush him. "Sorry. Tomorrow. Sure. No problem."

Alex rolled onto his side so that he faced me. I did my best to school my emotions, but I wasn't a master at hiding them like he was, and going by the look of guilt that blossomed on his face, I'd failed miserably. "I'm sorry, Austin...I can't...not tonight."

I forced a smile. I felt like an asshole. The evening had been going so well and I'd had to go and ruin it. "I'm fine."

He reached out, his fingertips grazing my cheek before his hand settled, warm and comforting on my neck. "I would never deliberately hurt you, Austin. I need you to know that. Remember that please."

I opened my mouth to speak, but a tiny shake of his head signaled he hadn't finished. I closed it again without so much as a sound escaping.

"These last few weeks you've been..." Alex's gaze drifted to somewhere just over my right shoulder as if the words were floating in the air and he needed to select the right ones. "...kind...and patient and understanding. Far more than I deserved. I know I've not been an easy person to be with. I'd built a wall, and somehow" — his lips curled into a smile — "you managed to find a crack in that wall and break through it. I don't think there's anyone else who could have done that. If I was going to move in with anyone, it would be you. I guess what I'm trying to say is...thank you. For everything."

I lay there stunned. It wasn't so much the words, although some of them did put my mind at rest, it was more the fact that the man I could sometimes barely get two words out of had delivered a speech. Emotion bubbled up inside to such a degree that I couldn't bear to keep it to myself any longer. "Alex, I lo..."

His hand moved from my neck to cover my mouth at a speed that would have given a striking cobra cause for jealousy. An emotion akin to panic or fear sparked in his eyes. "Please don't say it."

With his hand still plastered over my mouth, it was left to my eyes to ask the question. He removed his hand slowly, as if he was scared the words would leak out through the gaps in his fingers. Free to speak, I still had to ask. "Why?"

He shook his head. "Not tonight." He rolled over, presenting his back to me. If it hadn't been for the fact he dragged my arm over his body, fitting himself back against my chest, it would have felt like a stinging rejection.

I snuggled closer, loving the feel of his bare skin against mine. My lips found a natural resting place at the back of his neck. Unable to let the subject drop all together, I had to ask the question. "Is that another tomorrow conversation?"

I felt the exhalation reverberate through his body. "Yeah, tomorrow. We'll talk tomorrow. About everything." His voice sounded strangely flat. "Now sleep, Austin."

I held him even tighter, my eyes closing as I listened to his breathing gradually slow. Tomorrow was going to be an interesting day. I was going to put all my cards on the table and I just hoped he'd do the same.

* * * *

Two things were immediately apparent on waking. It was far too bright, which meant I'd slept in, and there was a distinct absence of Alex in the bed. Still struggling to full consciousness, I stared at the indentation on the pillow next to me, smiling at the sight of the single dark hair which lay there. Christ! I was completely smitten if that was enough to make me soppy.

It was rare, but it wasn't the first time I'd woken up alone so it wasn't a cause for alarm. I'd usually find him pottering in the kitchen, or on the sofa reading. I sat up, listening for the familiar telltale sounds of movement downstairs. There was nothing except silence. Definitely reading then. I swung my legs out of bed, grabbing a fresh pair of boxer shorts and stepping into them before making my way down the stairs.

There was no Alex on the sofa. No sign that he'd been there either: the cushions arranged perfectly, the same way I'd left them before going to bed; a habit I'd picked up from my mum. A cursory search of the rest of the rooms produced exactly the same result. The bathroom door had been open when I passed so I already knew he wasn't in there. The only explanation was that he'd gone out. That was unusual, but it was doubtful he'd gone far.

Chapter Twenty-four

Alexander

The advantage of catching the train so early on a Saturday morning was that it wasn't busy. I headed for the emptiest-looking carriage I could find and found a seat by the window, praying that the one next to me would remain empty. I didn't need someone trying to make conversation, no matter how well-meaning they might be. I just wanted to be alone.

I kept my eyes fixed on the moving scenery as the train chugged slowly away from London and headed for the coast, each mile covered bringing me closer to my date with destiny. This was the day I'd been promising myself for a year and it was hard to get my head around the fact that it had finally arrived. It was difficult to describe my emotions. I didn't feel happy. I didn't feel sad. Just a strange sort of peace in the knowledge that all of the pain was coming to an end. A detachment, where everything around me seemed more akin to a dream than reality.

Closing my eyes, I allowed my mind to drift back to earlier that morning. I'd hardly slept, waking nearly every hour in anticipation of rising as soon as the first strains of daylight showed themselves. Paranoid about waking the sleeping Austin,

I'd inched myself slowly out of the bed, barely daring to breathe
in case he stirred. I needn't have worried, there wasn't so much as
a flicker from him. Then, stood at the side of the bed, I'd allowed
myself a few moments of indulgence. A few moments to take one
last look at the man I was leaving behind. The man who was as
beautiful on the inside as he was on the outside.

I'd wondered whether when it came down to it if I'd be hit
by self-doubt, or at least a desire to wait. After all, I'd waited a
year. What would a few more days matter? Or even a week? The
longer I'd looked at Austin though, the more convinced I was that
he'd be better off without me. He deserved a man capable of
returning the love I'd refused to let him voice aloud, not a broken
shell of a man who made him step on eggshells so that he didn't
upset them or risk triggering a panic attack. I'd been dragging him
down for weeks. He barely went out any more. He ferried me
around like a taxi driver. He put my needs before his. And what
did I give back in return? Nothing. I knew he'd be hurt in the
short term, but in the long term he'd understand. Perhaps in some
way there might even be a measure of relief there. Eventually,
he'd find someone else. Maybe another mechanic. Someone with
who he shared far more in common. Someone who'd hopefully
shower him with all the love and affection he needed.

I hoped with the benefit of hindsight, he'd realize what the
previous night had been about. I hadn't been able to say goodbye
in words, but I'd done my best to say it with my body, managing
to drag Al back from the recesses of my mind and use the benefits
of his sexual confidence and expertise to make love to Austin the
way he deserved. At least he'd have one experience to remember
which was more than poor repressed Alex simply lying there
while he did all the work.

I'd tried to leave a note, laying the piece of paper out on the
kitchen table, and clutching the pen while I thought about what I
wanted to say. And then I'd stood there, staring at it, with no

words appearing on the page. What was I supposed to write? How was I meant to explain that the die had been cast long before I'd ever met Austin? I could tell him the truth, tell him everything, but that didn't seem fair to write it down rather than tell him to his face, and I couldn't risk that. Even if I could manage to somehow force the words out, I couldn't run the risk of him being able to read my intentions of killing myself. He'd try and stop me. Probably have me sectioned and then I'd never be free. I'd be trapped in a world of medication and psychologists, all wanting me to talk incessantly about Oliver and my family. I'd wanted to write something. Anything. But the clock had been ticking: I'd had a train to catch and the ever-increasing likelihood of Austin waking up. In the end, the crumpled paper had gone in the bin with nothing more than Austin's name scrawled on it. It was better to write nothing than a few meaningless words that may as well have been nothing.

Then I'd left, taking nothing but the clothes on my back and my wallet. I didn't go back to my apartment. It would serve no purpose. There was nothing I needed from there, and I had no wish to bump into Richard Simpkins one last time.

The train stopped at a station and a few more people piled on. To my relief, none of them chose to take the vacant seat. I still had an hour of the journey left before I'd arrive in Eastbourne. I began to run through the next few stages once I arrived at the station. There was a short walk from the town center to reach the sea front and from there a much longer walk of a few miles to reach Beachy Head.

If I wanted to, I could get a cab from the station. Hell, I could have gotten a cab all the way from London to Eastbourne. There was still money left in my account. It wasn't as if I was going to have any need for it after today. I should have found some way of giving it to Austin without giving the game away. It was too late now. I wondered what would happen to it. I didn't have a will. Making one had seemed pointless. Apart from the money which amounted to little more than six hundred pounds, I didn't own anything else of worth.

I had no intention of getting a cab though. Ironic as it might seem, I didn't feel there was any need to rush. It was a lovely day, the sun shining with barely a cloud in the sky; the temperature already creeping into the mid-twenties despite the fact it wasn't even nine yet. It couldn't have been any more different to the cold and rainy weather on the last day I'd made the same journey. On that day, even after arriving back in London, it had taken hours before I'd managed to feel warm again, the cold and damp having seeped right into my bones. It felt right that I should take my time, enjoy those last few hours of breathing in scenery, and feeling the heat of the sun on my skin.

I wondered if Austin was awake yet. I knew from experience he often slept later on a weekend, sometimes not opening his eyes until after ten, so it was possible he was still asleep. Would he find it strange that I wasn't there? Or would he just assume I'd be back soon? How much time would pass before he realized I wasn't coming back? An hour? Half a day? Longer? I told myself to stop thinking about it before it drove me crazy. Okay — crazier. It was done now. I'd had my chance to leave a note and I hadn't. A sudden desire to hear his voice one last time, swirled in my gut, and the wisp of an idea surfaced. I could call him. I didn't need to speak, or if I did, he didn't need to know where I was. I could lie to him. What was one more lie added to all the previous ones I'd already told?

I lifted my hip from the seat and fumbled in my pocket, my heart sinking as my hand came up empty. I'd left the phone behind in Austin's bedroom. In Eastbourne, there'd be phone boxes I could use, or I could ask to borrow someone's phone, but I didn't know Austin's number. I'd never bothered to learn it. So that was that. No note and no last conversation either.

I blinked back the tears that were threatening to fall, hoping no one was looking my way. *Should I have told Austin I loved him?* Or would that just have been cruel once he discovered what I'd done. It would be like saying I love you, just not enough to live.

I kept my eyes closed the rest of the way, trying to focus on nothing but the reassuring darkness behind my eyelids, only the movements of the train and the quiet murmur of voices as people chatted or got on or off filtering through. Then the train was slowing as it pulled into the last station on its route, and my legs were carrying me out into the open, past the ticket barrier and the assortment of snack kiosks to the busy street beyond. I blinked in the sunlight, momentarily blinded and wishing I'd brought sunglasses before crossing the road and following the path past the tennis courts and onto the sea front.

Ten minutes later, I leaned against the railings separating the promenade from the beach and stared out at the sea view stretching in front of me. Gulls squawked as they swooped and dived, searching for tasty titbits of food dropped by passersby. I made my way down the steps and onto the beach, the sound of the pebbles crunching underneath my feet, stirring up a childhood memory.

For the last year, I'd avoided remembering. Memories were painful. They just served to remind me of everything I'd lost and would never get back. But, today was different; I wasn't going to hide. I was going to embrace the pain. I started with the first time we'd visited. Five-year-old me, staring open-mouthed as my eight-year-old sister had rushed onto the beach, a bucket and spade clutched in her hand and immediately burst into tears at the sight of all the stones where she'd expected sand.

I sank down on the beach as I recalled the scene. There'd been no consoling her. Why my parents hadn't thought to warn her, I had no idea. It was only when the tide had gone out revealing a few patches of sand further down the beach that she'd stopped crying. Five-year-old me hadn't given a damn about sandcastles. He just wanted to find crabs in rockpools and swim in the sea under the watchful eye of my dad, his brawny hand plucking me out of the water numerous times when my head had disappeared beneath the surface.

I grabbed a handful of the pebbles, enjoying the smoothness as they trickled through the gaps in my fingers. The last time we'd visited as a family, I'd been thirteen. Moody teenage me, had outgrown swimming in the sea and seemed to think he'd also outgrown being made to visit anywhere in the company of his parents. I'd walked around sullenly, kicking at pebbles, and constantly asking when we could leave. Meanwhile, my sister's ear had been glued to her phone the whole time. It was little wonder then, that they'd never brought us back after that. That memory was particularly painful, given the fact I'd now sacrifice anything to spend five more minutes with them. Teenage me hadn't known how lucky he was.

I struggled to my feet, staying on the beach until the way was blocked, and I had to climb the steps back to the promenade. I took a moment to look around before I headed in the direction of the cliffs in the distance. Several places triggered further memories: the place where my dad had bought the kite and then taught me how to fly it on the beach; the cafe where my mum had always insisted on going for a sit-down and a cup of tea; the amusement arcade where my sister had flirted with teenage boys playing on the video games. I'd left her to it, concentrating on spending all my pocket money trying to win cuddly toys I didn't even want on the claw machine: the challenge more important than the prize. Any I'd won, I'd given to my mum, the smile on her face well worth the fact that I didn't even have enough money left for an ice cream. She'd either been genuinely overjoyed or a marvelous actress. Even now, I wasn't sure which one was the truth.

There was the hotel where we'd stayed when my mum had decided she wanted to spend a whole weekend in Eastbourne. The fact it had rained for at least forty of the forty-eight hours we were there, probably influencing the fact that they'd stuck to day trips after that. Then, I was walking away from the sea front and the steep gradient that led up to the cliffs lay in front of me. A walk of a couple of miles and I'd have reached my destination.

Chapter Twenty-five

Austin

Shaved, dressed, and making myself a cup of coffee, I was just pondering whether I should have made Alex one, when the knock at the door came. *Was that him?* I'd given him my spare key, but it was possible he'd forgotten to take it with him. That was one of the reasons his avoidance of the subject of moving in had hit so hard last night. It had already felt like a done deal. He stayed there every night; he rarely went home, and he already had a key. That's why it didn't make sense. Yes, it was commitment after a relatively short time, but it wasn't like I was asking him to marry me. My lips curved into a smile at the thought. He was the first boyfriend that I could actually see myself marrying. Not now. Not necessarily anytime soon. But one day I could definitely picture the two of us exchanging vows. I bet that Alex would look gorgeous in a suit. Hopefully, I'd get to find out.

I was only a few steps away from the door, when the knock sounded again — much louder this time, like someone was really pounding on it with their fist. Not Alex then. There was no way he'd be that impatient or that noisy. Grabbing the door handle, I flung it open, my face no doubt broadcasting my surprise at finding Wilko on my doorstep so early on a Saturday morning. I'd caught him just as he'd been about to go for a third knock, his hand pausing briefly in mid-air before dropping back to his side. *What is he doing here?* If he'd decided it was time to bare his soul, he hadn't picked the best time: I hadn't even had a cup of coffee yet. "Is Alex here?"

I leaned against the doorjamb regarding him steadily and trying to work out why he was asking. The only thing I could think of, was that he was hoping for a private conversation. I raised an eyebrow. "Well, good morning to you too. He's not here. I think he's gone out for breakfast or something, but he should be back soon."

Wilko nodded. The slight rustle of paper, bringing my attention to the fact that he had a newspaper clasped in his left hand. "Is he..."

When Wilko didn't finish his sentence, I prompted him. "Is he...what?"

His cheeks flushed slightly, as if he was embarrassed. "Is he okay?"

I should have been used to Wilko's strange behavior after knowing him for years, but even for him this was unusual. I shrugged. "Yeah, think so. I haven't seen him today yet. Did you just call round to ask after the welfare of my boyfriend? If so, that's...sweet, but you know...pretty damn weird as well."

Wilko didn't smile, or even acknowledge my attempt at humor. A flicker of unease tingled its way along my nerve endings. Something was wrong. I just couldn't work out what it was. He twisted the newspaper in his hands. "You *do* know though, don't you? You must know...I mean, I can understand you not talking about it...because it's your business and no one else's, but...it occurred to me that maybe you *don't* know."

I stared at him, trying to piece together some sense from the torrent of words he'd flung my way. When that didn't work, I studied his face for clues. Apart from looking worried, which did nothing to dispel the feeling of dread, there was nothing that gave away what he was thinking. "Mate, I'm sorry to break it to you, but I haven't even had caffeine yet, so you talking in code is way beyond me."

"Can I come in?"

I stepped back, holding the door wide open so he could come inside. Hopefully this, whatever *this* was, would be quick. I had no idea what Alex would make of Wilko being there when he got back, but the last thing I wanted was to start the weekend by freaking Alex out when he came back from wherever it was he'd disappeared off to.

I grabbed the mug of coffee from the kitchen before joining Wilko in the living room. He seemed even more agitated than he had on the doorstep, his lumbering frame shifting restlessly from foot to foot as he stood in the middle of the room. I took a large swallow of coffee, desperately needing the caffeine to start working its way through my system. I winced at the realization that it was far too hot, the burn working its way from my mouth and all the way down my esophagus. I had to stop doing that. Wilko was still silent. I sighed. "Listen, mate, whatever's wrong, spit it out. What is it? Girl trouble?" I hesitated. "Boy trouble?"

He exhaled slowly. "You obviously don't know. Shit! I shouldn't be the one to tell you, but..." He laid the newspaper on the table, inclining his head toward it in an obvious invitation to step closer and take a look.

It was open at a double-page spread; the story detailing a court case. I'd caught snippets of information about it, but hadn't paid it that much attention. It had been a horrific story back when it happened. Some poor guy's family had been murdered by his boyfriend, or his ex-boyfriend. I couldn't remember all the details. The case had taken ages to come to court, something to do with the defense constantly delaying. There'd been a lot of coverage of it, partly because of the nature of the crime, and partly because the media were obsessed with the whereabouts of the missing survivor. I remembered thinking that it was hardly surprising the guy had pulled a disappearing act. Who'd want to live with that kind of media scrutiny, day after day? The guy was probably fucked up enough as it was. I skim-read the article. The majority of it just rehashed what had happened, the tabloid newspaper doing their best to sensationalize it as much as possible.

The only new information it contained from what I could tell, was the sentencing: the murdering bastard, having been given a life sentence with little to no chance of parole. It was amazing he'd ever made it to trial. Surely, anyone that did what he'd done, had to be barking mad. But then, I wasn't exactly an expert.

It was a terrible tragedy, made even more terrible by the fact that it had happened locally, but I had no idea what possible relevance it had to either myself or Wilko. I lifted my head from the newspaper, not even trying to hide my frustration. "Much as I appreciate you bringing me some *cheery* reading material to go with my coffee, I'm struggling to work out why you want me to read this?"

Wilko stepped forward, his thick index finger making a beeline toward the newspaper and landing squarely on one of the photographs. "It's Alex."

I let out a snort of laughter at the ridiculous suggestion. "I don't think so. Why would he be in one of the pictures?" I'd barely spared any of the pictures a glance. I bent closer. The picture in question showed a man pushing his way through the assembled media circus on the courthouse steps. His head was turned away from the camera and partly obscured by another reporter who'd gotten in the way. In fact, all you could see of the intended target of the photograph, was their neck, and the part of the face that wasn't covered by the dark fall of their hair like they were using it for protection. My heart skipped a beat, my gaze dropping to the caption below the photograph to find out why the man had been photographed: *Survivor of mass family murder makes no comment as he leaves courthouse after sentencing.*

I shook my head. "It can't be him. He was at work. I dropped him off at the library and I picked him up from there." I sounded less positive by the end of the sentence than I had at the start, Adrian's words from earlier in the week coming back to haunt me: *I saw your boyfriend in the park.* "It's not him. It's just someone who looks a bit like him." I ran my finger over the photograph. "I mean...look...it could be anyone. You can't even see much of them."

A hand reached across taking my coffee mug out of my hand and stopping the steady drip of coffee on the carpet as I'd tipped the mug without realizing. I stared at the stain on the carpet before meeting Wilko's gaze, only to find him looking at me with sympathy. "Aust, it mentions his name."

"Where?" I found it before Austin could point it out, the name Alexander Philips in black and white, right there on the page, and named as the survivor. The room began to tip and I grabbed on to the edge of the table to keep myself upright, a million thoughts and memories assaulting my senses at the same time. *"He hides his body language." "Sometimes it can be even worse than it looks." "I don't have a family." "Have you ever hated anyone, Austin?" "His name is Oliver."*

I was suddenly aware of Wilko's strong hand on my shoulder. It pushed me gently toward the sofa, offering support and guidance. I sank onto it gratefully, relieved to be off my feet.

Wilko's knees appeared in my line of vision. "Where *is* Alex?"

I raised my head. "Why?" Given what I'd just discovered, the question sounded ridiculous even to my own ears.

The sofa dipped as Wilko seated himself beside me. I was shocked by the amount of empathy on his face. This was a whole new side of him I was seeing today. One thing he'd never been in all the years I'd known him was sensitive to others' feelings. But then I guessed that it wasn't exactly an everyday situation. His tone, when he spoke, was slow and carefully modulated, like he felt he had to treat me with kid gloves. "Because...no matter what you say, he can't be alright. Can he? What he's been through is awful...and then he's just gone through the court case, and if he didn't tell you...then who did he tell? Who's he been talking to? Who's he been leaning on?"

"No one." The words were out, before I even considered the question properly. But, I knew it was true. "He was happy last night though. We went to the pub and he had a few drinks...and he ate a proper meal, and then when we came back here, he was..." *Needy. Desperate. Not himself.* The way he'd made love to me was so far removed from all our previous sexual experiences, how could I not have realized there was something drastically different going on in his head. And after that, he'd been so sad. Everything had been about tomorrow. Well, tomorrow was now today, and he was God knows where.

I levered myself off the sofa reaching for my phone and calling the number of the cheap phone I'd given to Alex. A faint ringing came from above our heads, both of us automatically lifting our gaze to the ceiling where my bedroom was. He'd left the phone behind. "What if he's gone somewhere?"

"Where?"

I racked my brains. "He could have gone home. Or to the coffee shop. Or maybe the park. Adrian said he saw him there, earlier in the week."

Wilko thought for a moment. "You could call the coffee shop. They'll be able to tell you if he's there, or if he's been there. We can get the number from the internet."

"Good idea!" I was already on my way to the room that doubled up as a small office. I fidgeted restlessly as the computer started booting up. How was Alex going to react to me knowing about his past? If he'd wanted me to know, he would have told me. He'd obviously had his reasons to keep it from me. The password screen came up and I quickly typed it in.

"I didn't know whether I should say anything or not." Wilko's face was apologetic. "I almost didn't come around, thinking that you two might have stuff to sort out."

I smiled at him, genuinely moved by his concern. "I appreciate the fact you did."

"Yeah?" He looked relieved and I resolved to be a bit more patient with him in future and remind myself that although the delivery was quite often at fault, the intention was usually good.

I didn't immediately search for the number of the coffee shop, something making me click on the internet history instead. Knowing he didn't have his own, I'd always made it clear to Alex he could use my computer. He'd used it today, two sites coming up under the current date: Alex's e-mail and the National Rail website. Wilko leaned closer, peering over my shoulder to see what I was looking at. I clicked on the National Rail link. It opened, but didn't really tell me anything apart from the fact he'd been on the website this morning. *Why had he been looking at train times?* Pressing the second link took me to the login screen for his e-mail. Unless he'd saved his password to my computer, I wouldn't be able to get any further anyway. I hesitated as it automatically filled in the password box. I could access it, but it would be completely out of order, right?

Wilko nudged me. "What are you waiting for?"

I shot a glare at him, already forgetting my vow to demonstrate more patience. "I can't read his e-mail! It would be a complete invasion of his privacy."

He made a huffing sound. "Why has he been looking at train times?"

I sighed. "I don't know."

Another nudge. "Press return."

I shook my head. "I can't. I'm not reading his e-mail."

Wilko reached around me, pressing the button before I could stop him. "Fine. I'll do it. He can get pissed at me then, rather than you."

I averted my gaze from the computer screen, wanting to be honest when I told Alex I hadn't read it. Instead, I watched Wilko's face, trying to work out what might have prompted the frown he now wore. "What?"

He moved the mouse around, reading something as he scrolled down. "He booked a ticket to Eastbourne today. One way. Train left at"—he checked his watch—"seven thirty, so a couple of hours ago. What's in Eastbourne?"

I gave in, turning to the screen and reading the same information Wilko had just read, the news that Alex had apparently gotten on a train and traveled out of London undoing all my earlier good intentions. Wilko was right. The e-mail receipt made it clear. Alex had gotten up this morning and left without saying goodbye or leaving a note, and the one-way ticket seemed to suggest that he had no intention of coming back. He'd left his phone behind so I had no way of contacting him. *What was he playing at?*

Wilko was still staring expectantly at me, like I was supposed to have all the answers. "I don't know. He's never mentioned it." But then, that didn't mean much. I could probably fit the things he *had* mentioned on the back of a postage stamp. Bringing up the Wikipedia page for Eastbourne, I quickly scanned the information. "Beach. Pier. Older population...apparently. Clifftop walks. Beachy Head which is a popular...suicide spot." My voice trailed away, the implications of what I'd just said causing fear like none I'd ever felt before.

Wilko's look of horror reflected my own thoughts. "He wouldn't, would he? I mean you'd have noticed if he was suicidal? He probably just wanted to go to the beach, right? I mean, I've met him. He seemed fine, apart from being quiet. I know he's had a tough time, but...that's..."

I started to pace, trying to think clearly and logically in order to sift through all the information I had. I thought about all the things I'd done my best to block out and ignore over the last few weeks: catching Alex staring at a blank wall in the library, the fact that sometimes when I talked he barely seemed to be listening, and his reluctance to share any personal information. And then there were the nightmares and the panic attacks. If I added all of those things together, along with my brother's warnings, they didn't paint a pretty picture. But still, could he really be at the point where he didn't want to live anymore? "I need to go there."

"To Eastbourne?"

"Yeah." My voice cracked. I wanted to believe that the idea was completely ridiculous, but if it was a perfectly innocent trip, why hadn't he said anything, and why only buy a one-way ticket? And then there was the sex last night. I squeezed my eyes shut, the memory taking on new significance with the realization that there had been a strange sense of finality to it. Had that been Alex's way of saying goodbye?

"You shouldn't drive. My car's outside. I'll drive."

I nodded my agreement, managing to get my head together long enough to grab my keys, phone, and wallet before locking the door and getting into the passenger seat of Wilko's car. I needed to talk to someone who knew more about this sort of thing than I did. The problem was, the ideal person wasn't an easy person to ask for help. I swallowed my pride and made the call, Mark picking up on the third ring.

"Wow! Little brother *actually* calling me. Did I fall asleep for a few months? Is it Christmas already? Oh, hang on, what am I saying, you don't even call me at Christmas."

I pulled the phone away from my ear and took a moment to

remind myself that he was only talking the same way we usually spoke to each other in our twisted sibling relationship. He didn't know what was going on today or why I was calling him. After taking a deep breath, I pressed it back to my ear. "Mark, do you think just this once, we could skip the insults? I need your help. I need to talk to you." I could almost sense the resulting frown down the phone line. He was probably trying to recall the amount of times I'd ever asked him for help, which at my count, amounted to zero.

"About what?"

"Alex."

Just like that, it was like a switch had been flicked: Mark the brother was gone, and in his place was Mark, the doctor. Only this time I didn't mind. It was his professional opinion I needed. "What's happened?"

"I need to ask you something first."

"Go ahead."

"From what you saw, his...behavior...could he...is there any possibility that he could be..." The words were incredibly difficult to get out. "...suicidal?"

There was a long period of silence while I assumed Mark was giving the question the careful consideration it deserved. I'd have given anything for him to tell me not to be such a drama queen. "Tell me what's happened. I need background before I can answer that question. Tell me what's gotten you so worried."

I filled him in on everything that had happened that morning, including the discoveries I'd made about Alex's past. It felt wrong telling my brother all Alex's secrets when I wasn't even supposed to know them myself, but I felt the whole story was crucial in trying to gauge Alex's mental state. I ended by telling him we were on our way to Eastbourne.

"Have you left London yet?"

I eyed the queue of traffic in front of us, Wilko's fingers

tapping impatiently against the steering wheel. "No. Not yet."

"Come and pick me up. I'll go with you. Then we can talk properly on the way. I'm at *L'eau a La Bouche*. Do you know it?"

Yeah, I knew it. It was a pretentious — in my opinion — French deli, which suited my brother down to the ground. I turned to Wilko. "We need to make a brief stop on the way." He nodded and I told him where before addressing my brother again. "We'll be there in about ten minutes."

"I'll wait outside for you."

It only ended up taking us five, the traffic gods finally smiling on us and the traffic clearing. Despite that, as promised, Mark was waiting outside. Wilko pulled over and Mark slid into the back seat, looking anywhere but in the direction of the man driving the car. That was odd. What was even odder, was the fact Wilko looked equally uncomfortable. "Mark, this is — "

"We've met. How are you, Robert?"

Robert! No one called Wilko, Robert. He'd always been Wilko ever since the nickname had stuck at the age of seven.

Wilko's response was little more than a grunt as he put his foot on the accelerator to pull back into traffic. Mark immediately looked crushed, the hurt expression on his face making it all click into place. If I hadn't have been sat down, I would have probably fallen over. I'd known something had happened with Wilko and a guy. But, the guy was my bloody brother! No wonder Wilko hadn't wanted to go into details. Awkward didn't even begin to describe it. And as for Mark, I'd known he'd gone through a short, experimental teenage phase, but I'd always assumed that's all it was. Since then, he'd given the impression that he was more into girls. It was like straight and straighter getting together.

At any other time, I would have most likely demanded they stop the car and tell me what the hell was going on, but there were far more important issues at play, like working out where Alex was. He was the only thing I cared about. So, despite the fact you could cut the atmosphere in the car with a knife, unraveling the mysteries of my brother and my best friend's dalliance would have to wait.

Mark leaned forward, his head appearing between the space in the front seats. "Did you bring the newspaper article with you? Can I read it? And then we can talk about Alex once I've gotten a better picture of what's going on."

I nodded, throwing the newspaper into the back seat, and resigning myself to the longest car journey of my life.

Chapter Twenty-six

Austin

The atmosphere in the car was still decidedly strained. Besides the stilted greetings the two had shared, Wilko and my brother hadn't interacted in any way since. I got the distinct impression though, that if I hadn't been there, there'd have been a great deal of conversation between the two, with a high possibility that the majority wouldn't have been that civilized. The clue was in the way Wilko gripped onto the steering wheel, his knuckles almost white while a muscle ticked in his cheek. *What the hell had happened between them? Had they slept together? Do I really want to know?* Horrific as the idea was, at least it gave me a break from the thoughts that kept circling my brain about Alex. *Where was he? Was he alone? Could I have said or done something the previous night that would have stopped him from leaving?*

I swiveled in my seat to see what Mark was doing. Apart from a few comments while reading the newspaper article, he hadn't said a word since. He looked a damn sight more relaxed than Wilko though. So, it looked like whatever had happened between the two had left a lot more animosity on Wilko's side than on my brother's. Either that or he was just too wrapped up in whatever was so fascinating he couldn't take his eyes off his phone. "I thought you were meant to be giving me advice. You know...about my boyfriend, who may or may not be about to..." I couldn't get the words out. If I didn't say it, then it couldn't be true. Mark slowly lifted his gaze from the screen. "I will. I'm just finding out everything I can about what happened first."

"Oh!" It hadn't even occurred to me that what he was looking at could be connected. "Did you find anything useful?"

"He did a disappearing act after. Not just from the media. From everybody."

"Alex?"

Mark gave a terse nod. "Yeah. No one knew where he was until he turned up to give evidence. They weren't even a hundred percent sure he would turn up. I mean...this is written by the media, so you have to take it with a pinch of salt. He must have let the prosecution know where he was at some point to have known the court dates. It's not as if he just wandered in there. But, the fact he was gone so long, I would assume meant that he never got any help coping with the aftermath of what happened."

"He probably disappeared because he didn't want any help."

"Probably." Mark sighed. "Unfortunately, him not *wanting* help doesn't mean he didn't *need* it. And if you're right about what he's planning to do, then he definitely did."

My stomach felt like it was full of rocks. I could put it down to the lack of breakfast, but I knew it had more to do with confronting the truth.

Surprisingly, it was Wilko who stepped in to try and give a glimmer of hope, the first words he'd spoken in the last half an hour. "You're probably completely wrong. We're making these assumptions based on one train ticket. He's probably gone for a fucking peaceful day at the coast and we're turning it into a huge fucking drama."

God! I hoped he was right. But then, why buy a single

ticket? Why not tell me where he was going? He had to have known that I'd have been quite happy to go with him. Was that it? Did he just want a day alone? I wanted to believe it so badly it hurt.

"Two F-words in one sentence, Robert. I see your method of communicating is still the same." I turned in time to see the glower on Mark's face.

The muscle in Wilko's cheek ticked even faster. "Fucking right, it's fucking necessary. Do you have a fucking problem with it?"

Okay. So, maybe I should have appreciated the strained silence more. It was definitely preferable to outright antagonism. Mark opened his mouth, no doubt to spit out another withering put-down. I got in there first before World War Three erupted. "Mark, did you discover anything else?" I gestured to his phone when he looked confused. "Oh, right! Only that everyone was surprised that the case went to trial. They expected Oliver Calthorpe to plead insanity, but apparently he didn't want that, and all the tests they carried out couldn't prove he was anything but sane."

"What kind of sane person does what he did?"

Mark shook his head. "You'd be surprised. He's *legally* sane. It doesn't mean he doesn't have psychological issues. My guess is that he was smart enough to know what answers he needed to give to convince them he was sane."

"Were there any pictures of him?" There'd been a tiny one included in the newspaper article of him being led away after sentencing, but it hadn't been clear enough to get a proper idea of what he looked like. I wanted to see the face of the man who'd destroyed Alex's life.

Mark passed his phone over and I found myself looking at a picture of two smiling men. "Which one?"

"The one on the right."

The man was certainly good-looking. There was no denying that. It wasn't hard to see why Alex would have been attracted to him. There was a deadness behind the eyes though, or maybe I was just imagining it with the benefit of hindsight, knowing what he'd done. He reminded me a little of Alex's next-door neighbor. Was that why Alex had had such a visceral reaction to the man? None of this was making me feel any better about the distance that still lay between Alex and myself. "How much longer till we get there?"

Wilko checked the GPS. "Thirty minutes, as long as we don't get stuck in traffic anywhere."

I sat back in my seat, wishing we had a magic teleportation device that could transport us there immediately. "What if we're too late? What if he's already..."

None of us had an answer for the question that I'd been too afraid to voice completely. I stared out of the window, wishing I was more religious and could pray to a higher being because I'd have tried anything if I thought it might help.

Alexander

I came to a stop, my thighs aching from the uphill gradient I'd just climbed. And there it was, Beachy Head: the stretch of cliffs where numerous people had come to end their lives. My heart began to pound as I took it all in. I wasn't nervous. I didn't know how to describe the way I was feeling. Maybe a quiet sort of excitement that the time had finally come. I'd endured a year of living with the guilt of everything I'd caused. I'd managed to stand in front of Oliver Calthorpe without breaking down, and given evidence against him. I'd witnessed the look on his face when he'd realized that he was highly unlikely to ever see the outside of a prison again. I'd earned this.

My only regret was that he was still alive. He'd still get to breathe. He'd still get to work out, and do whatever else they did to pass the time in prison. Assuming he had visitors, he'd still get to chat and smile and laugh. I wished I could go back in time and do a better job of stabbing him, even if it did mean that I'd have gone to prison in his stead. It would still have been worth it. I'd been in a prison of sorts anyway for the last year.

I hoped he might meet a nasty end. I'd done my research. Prisons were dangerous places, especially for inmates who were no longer on remand. Prisoners apparently often made shanks from toothbrushes and razor blades. It pleased me to think that one day, Oliver might cross paths with one of those people. Maybe in the prison shower, or maybe he'd find himself sharing a cell with someone even madder than he was. The thought was enough to bring a smile to my face.

I picked up speed as I reached the part of the headland where the cliffs were at their highest, imagining the release almost within my grasp. *Should I feel scared? Should I be having doubts?* I didn't. I felt none of those things. *What about Austin?* I pushed down the unwanted whispers of my subconscious. *Poor Austin! Deserted without even a note, after everything he did for you.* "Austin will be fine." I said the words aloud, repeating them over and over again until I believed it. He would be fine. He had friends and family, a job to distract himself, and a body and face that would make lining up someone to replace me all too easy.

There were more people around than I'd expected. The last time I'd been there, it had been a cold, wet, and miserable day in February. There hadn't been a soul around for miles. It would have been the perfect time to jump. There were at least twenty people around today. I considered my options. I could make a run for it. It wasn't like anyone would realize my intention in time to stop me.

I took a deep breath, my muscles gathering in anticipation of the short sprint. It would be over in a matter of seconds. No more pain. No more pretending. No more closing my eyes and seeing blood, or the dead, staring eyes of my mother and sister as they lay on the kitchen floor. No more overreacting to sounds or smells that brought memories flooding back: my mum's perfume; the song that had been playing in the club the night Oliver had attacked me; the cologne he used to wear. That last one was a particularly violent trigger. One slight hint of it was enough to have me racing for the nearest toilet, throwing up anything that might happen to be in my stomach.

A child's laughter cut through the sound of the wind. There were two walking toward me, in the company of their parents. I turned, noticing another pair playing catch well away from the cliff edge. Then there was the lady pushing a baby in a pushchair. *Am I really going to end my life in front of children?* The baby would be too young to understand, or remember. But, what about the rest? Were they going to wake in the middle of the night, crying and asking their parents questions about the strange man who'd jumped off a cliff right in front of them? I couldn't subject them to that. I'd have to wait. There was a natural seat formed by the erosion of the cliff face a couple of meters away from the cliff edge. It was far enough away that I shouldn't arouse suspicion but close enough that when the time was right, I could be over the edge in a matter of seconds.

Chapter Twenty-seven

Austin

"Why are we stopping here?"

Wilko killed the engine before releasing his seatbelt, the car parked in a small car park, and car park was being generous, it was more a stretch of road. "It's the closest we can get in the car. We can't drive a car right up to the cliff edge."

I felt stupid. Of course we couldn't. At least one of us was thinking clearly. I climbed out, joining my brother on the grass verge, his hand immediately landing on my shoulder to give it a reassuring squeeze. Jesus! My brother offering comfort. To me, of all people. I really must look like shit. He leaned in. "We just listened to the local news. There was nothing on it. If anything had happened, it would have been mentioned." We had. It had been Mark's suggestion. The lack of dramatic news stories had managed to calm my nerves for a few moments but I still needed to get there. See with my own eyes that no one had jumped that day.

"Five minutes." Wilko answered the question, I hadn't even gotten around to asking.

It took longer than five minutes. Sure, it took only five

225

minutes to reach the cliff edge, but no one had told me that Beachy Head consisted of three miles of headland. I'd assumed it was one specific spot. That meant we had no choice but to start at one end and walk the length with all three of us looking out for any sign of Alex. Each additional minute without spotting him felt like a lifetime. *What if I never see him again?* We may have only been together for a short time, but I just couldn't imagine being with anyone else. If there was no Alex, then I'd rather be alone. It sounded melodramatic, but it was the way I felt. The things I'd discovered; everything he'd been through just made me all the more determined to keep him safe, and to spend every day trying my best to put a smile on his face.

As well as looking for Alex, we kept our eyes peeled for any signs of an earlier disturbance. There was always the possibility that something could have already happened and the local media just hadn't gotten wind of it yet. But, with each passing section of cliff with no sign of Alex, no sign of police, and no sign of the coastguard helicopter circling, I began to hope. *Maybe Alex isn't here? Maybe he's on the beach sunning himself and eating ice cream?*

I staggered back as Wilko's hand landed smack bang in the middle of my chest. "Look! Look! There!" Looking in the direction he'd pointed, I spotted the sight that had gotten him so excited, the familiar dark hair glinting in the sun of the lone figure sat on a shelf of rock far too close to the edge of the cliff. We were about the length of a football field away from him. Wilko's hand gripped a handful of my shirt. "That's him, right?"

I nodded, unable to form words as I was suddenly bombarded by a mixture of contrasting emotions. He was alive, so that was good. But, his presence in this place, especially so close to the cliff edge meant our assumptions must have been correct. *Why else would he be there?* There was no way it could just be a coincidence. You didn't endure what he had, and then just happen to visit a popular suicide spot the day after the trial ended without there being an ulterior motive. My limbs felt like lead, as if they were weighted down by the sheer terror of what Alex was planning to do.

Mark stepped forward. "I should be the one to talk to him. I'm the one with experience with this sort of thing."

"No!" I shook my head, my gaze locked on my brother's. At least his suggestion got my legs moving again as I stepped in front of him, my hand flat against his chest. "He won't talk to a stranger." *He might not even talk to me.* I didn't voice my doubts aloud. That was between me and Alex. All I knew was there was no way he'd take kindly to my brother attempting to do whatever it was that psychologists did. Mark looked less than convinced. I took a worried glance back over my shoulder. Alex hadn't moved, and we were too far away for him to have become aware of our presence. "I need to do this."

Mark sighed. "Will you at least let me give you some advice?"

My automatic response was to tell him I didn't need his help. Then, I remembered that I was the one that had asked for it earlier. He hadn't given me a hard time about it, and he'd dropped everything to come with us. I doubted his ideal Saturday plans had consisted of a long drive followed by a long walk. And he'd really tried. He'd been far less objectionable than he was usually. I'd swallowed my pride earlier. I could do it again and listen to him. After all, if I'd listened to him sooner, all of this might have been avoidable. "Go on." I took another glance in Alex's direction. "Just make it quick, please."

Mark's look of surprise at my willingness to listen wasn't lost on me. "Don't make this about you. He's not doing this to hurt you, or because you're not enough, or you've not done something or said something you should. Most people who plan to commit suicide, plan it well in advance. It's very rarely a spur-of-the-moment decision. The fact he's here the day after the trial ended probably means that was his intention all along. Just talk to him, and listen to him, and try and get through to him. Try and find something that will make him reconsider whether he's doing the right thing."

I nodded, my heart pounding so fast I could feel it in my throat. "Will you both wait here? I might be a while."

Mark smiled, a smile tinged with a distinct air of worry. "Of course. We'll be here." Wilko nodded, looking almost as sick as I felt. I took a calming breath and started walking quickly toward Alex.

Alexander

I didn't pay a lot of attention when the shadow fell across me, assuming it was just another one of the hikers continuing on their way. A few had already passed without sparing so much as a glance in my direction. To them, I was just another tourist taking a break and enjoying the sun as I took in the breathtaking view of the sea and the lighthouse. I did my best to look relaxed, not wanting to arouse suspicion. I'd heard there were patrols that took place in the area: people who walked the length of the headland, keeping their eyes and ears open for possible jumpers. The last thing I wanted was to alert anyone to my intention and run the risk that they could stop me.

It wasn't until the person lowered themselves to the chalky ground to sit next to me on the shelf of rock that all of my nerve endings went into overdrive. Somehow, without even looking their way and despite knowing that him being there made no sense at all, I knew who it was. Perhaps it was a slight trace of cologne, or maybe it was that thing he'd once said about our souls fitting together. Whatever it was, and as crazy as it seemed, I knew it was Austin.

I kept my eyes fixed on the sea, a lump forming in my throat as the possible ramifications of his presence started to circle in my brain. *Did he know what I intended to do? But, if he did, why was he just sitting there silently?* He hadn't said a word. *Shouldn't he be mad? Is he waiting for me to speak first? Does he think that just because I haven't looked his way, I don't know he's there?* My brain hurt from all the questions racing around it. And still he said nothing. We could have been two strangers just sharing the same space.

I cleared my throat, resigned to having to be the first to speak. I knew he was looking my way. I could feel his gaze like a hot brand on my skin. I couldn't bring myself to turn my head and return the favor. "How did you find me?"

"Long story."

"I've got time."

"Have you?"

I flinched, the tone of his voice and the fact he'd asked the question revealing the fact that he knew exactly why I was there. "Too many children." He didn't ask what I meant. Either he understood what I was saying, or he had more important things to think about. I wasn't sure. There was a long pause while I tried to think of something else to say. Finally, he broke the silence.

"I know, Alex."

I closed my eyes, wanting to shut the world out for a moment. Maybe when I opened them I'd discover there was no Austin. That he was just a figment of my deteriorating state of mind. I opened them. He was still there. "What do you know?"

He shuffled closer across the grass, his foot catching a piece of loose chalk and sending it hurtling over the cliff edge. His bare arm brushed mine, and my body reacted the way it always did to him: a desire to lean in and soak up the comfort and shelter it offered. "About what happened to you in your past?"

I felt sick, my heart starting to beat faster. "How?"

"You remember Wilko?"

I nodded. Of course, I remembered him. The gruff mountain

of a man who spoke first and thought later wasn't easy to forget. I'd liked him. Well, about as much as I'd been capable of liking anyone for the last year.

"He saw a newspaper article about the...sentencing. You were in one of the pictures. I didn't believe it was you at first, but it mentioned your name. He thought I knew. He came around to see how you were."

Tears pricked at my eyes, the thought of someone who barely knew me, caring about my wellbeing was sweet. "So now you know."

There was a long pause. Austin knowing all my secrets made it even harder to look at him. *What would I see reflected on his face? Pity? Disgust? Anger because I'd mislead him for weeks?* It was better not to know.

Austin shifted, his body language betraying his unease. "Yeah. I can't...I don't...shit! I don't know what I'm supposed to say."

The anguish in his voice finally broke through my barriers and I turned toward him. The expression on his face was nothing but pain as he struggled in vain to say the right thing. I patted his arm, wanting to provide some measure of comfort, no matter how inadequate it seemed. "You don't have to say *anything.* You don't need to say you're sorry or that you understand. It's fine to say nothing."

Austin's face turned pleading. "I just wish you'd told me. Why didn't you tell me?"

Well, that's the million-dollar question, isn't it? "I don't know."

"I could have been there for you, especially during the trial. I hate the thought of you going through that on your own. I thought you were at work. Christ! Adrian even told me he'd seen you in the park when you were supposed to be at the library. I thought he'd mistaken someone else for you. That it couldn't possibly be you. *Was* it you?"

"Probably." I hadn't seen him, but it was quite possible. I'd spent quite a lot of time in the park, reading and people watching. I'd had a lot of hours before giving evidence. "Do you" — the words caught in my throat — "hate me for lying to you?"

"No!" Austin didn't even hesitate. He twisted his body around so that he was facing me, his eyes softening. "No. I could never hate you, Alex."

"I didn't want to lie." Despite his assurances, I still felt I needed to do a better job of explaining myself. "I wanted to tell you! Some of it anyway, but every question I answered would only have led to more." I drew my knees in, hugging them to my chest, my head turned sideways to keep Austin in my eyeline. Now I'd forced myself to look at him, it was equally as hard to tear my gaze away. "I know how pathetic it sounds. Trust me, I do, and I'm sorry. I know it doesn't really make sense but nothing's made sense to me for a long time." We lapsed into silence for a few moments until something else suddenly occurred to me. "You still haven't told me how you knew I was here?"

Austin looked uncomfortable. *What was that about?* "After Wilko had told me the truth, I was worried that I didn't know where you were. We were going to look up the number of the coffee shop on the internet to call and ask if you'd been there. I clicked on the computer's history. You'd checked train times on there, and you'd saved your e-mail password. Wilko looked at it! Not me!" I stifled a smile at the look of guilt on Austin's face. So that's what had gotten him so worried. When I didn't comment, he carried on talking. "Once we knew you were headed to Eastbourne, well we put two and two together. I hoped I was wrong, but you're here..." His gaze drifted to the edge of the cliff, no more than two meters away from where our feet were. "...so, I wasn't. I — "

I cut in before he could directly address the thing that we'd both been skirting around. "Did you drive here?"

"Wilko did."

I turned around scanning the vicinity for Austin's friend. I spotted him almost immediately, a good hundred meters away, his bulk towering above the shorter man stood next to him. "Your brother's here?"

"Yeah. He thought—" Austin stopped abruptly, his face shadowing.

I finished the sentence for him. "He thought having someone around with a psychology degree would be useful."

Austin's gaze scoured my face as if he was trying to gauge whether that fact was going to upset me. "Yeah. Basically."

I took another glance over at the two men, noticing something I'd missed when I'd first looked over. "They don't look very happy with each other." They didn't. Their bodies were angled away from each other and both of their arms were crossed in a distinctly defensive posture.

Austin's mouth twisted. "Yeah. It seems they had, or are having...I'm not sure which...a thing."

My eyebrows shot up. "Wilko and your brother? I didn't know either of them were gay."

Austin's shrug was accentuated by the bewildered look on his face. "Gay enough to have pissed each other off it seems." He looked embarrassed for a moment. "Sorry. You don't need me ranting about this. It's my problem. Or their problem. I don't know which, really."

"It's fine." It was. It had obviously upset him and I found myself wanting to help in some small way. Perhaps it could be my parting gift to him. "It upsets you?"

"Of course, it upsets me! It's my best friend and my brother. What the hell were they thinking? And whose side am I meant to take? I mean I know my brother and I don't exactly get on, but he's family. But, Wilko...we've been friends since I was six years old."

It suddenly hit me. All those weeks when I'd been leaning on him, he'd been leaning on me too. Maybe not in such an obvious way, but I'd been there. I'd listened when he'd complained about a bad day at work and offered advice where I could. I'd been an outlet for his frustration; a salve for his exhaustion. *Who is he going to talk to when I'm gone?* I guess if anyone had asked me before this conversation, I'd have said Wilko, but he could hardly talk to Wilko *about* Wilko, could he? A tiny trickle of doubt started to inch its way down my spine. I shook it off. "Maybe you don't need to take sides. Stay out of it and let them sort their own shit out."

Austin sighed, a sad smile flickering across his face. Was he thinking the same thing I was? Was he wondering who he was going to talk to? "You're probably right."

Chapter Twenty-eight

Austin

I was so out of depth with the whole situation, it was scary. Initially, I'd taken solace from the fact Alex hadn't flipped out at my unexpected presence. Now, I was beginning to think that at least that would have been more of a natural reaction than his careful neutrality coupled with his refusal to even look at me for ages. I felt like I was dealing with it all wrong.

We were less than two meters away from the edge of the cliff he intended on jumping from, and what was I doing? I'd been talking to him about my brother and Wilko, which was hardly a priority in the grand scheme of things. Perhaps I'd made a mistake by refusing to let Mark be the one to talk to him; a serious error of judgement that could end up costing me everything. Mark had qualifications; he had training in this sort of thing. I was just feeling my way around blindly in the dark, and desperately hoping I didn't do or say anything that would make it worse.

I snuck a quick glance over at Alex. He looked so normal. *Weren't people who intended to kill themselves normally in a state of agitation?* Or had I just watched too many bad TV dramas? The calmness and composure, though, just didn't seem right. *Is it possible he'd changed his mind?* If only I could get him to move farther away from the edge, then at least I could stop panicking every time he so much as twitched, terrified that he was about to leap to his feet.

"Who did you call?"

"Huh!" I stared at him, trying to work out what he meant.

"About me. Who did you call? I don't know who it is usually. Is it the police? The coastguard? Or a psychiatrist?" He laughed drily, the sound containing very little actual humor in it. "I suppose you brought one of those with you, though." His face changed all of a sudden, something akin to panic settling on his features. "I won't be sectioned! I can't cope with that!"

Now he was agitated. I needed to be careful what I wished for. "I didn't call anyone. I wouldn't do that to you, and I'd never let you be sectioned. Never!" I was telling the truth. The thought of Alex locked away in some secure facility, possibly drugged up to the eyeballs on medication that was meant to help him, with people forcing him to talk, caused an actual physical pain in my gut. It wouldn't help him. It would do the opposite. It would make him wither away to nothing. He needed help. There was no denying that. But not that way. There had to be a better way. A way that would work for him. Large, brown eyes held mine without blinking. I leaned closer, projecting as much sincerity as I could. "Alex, I'm telling the truth. I've never lied to you and I'm not going to start now. The only people I brought were Mark and Wilko. We're the only ones who know you're here and what you're here to do. And they won't come any closer. It's just me and you. Nobody else."

He finally seemed to accept my answer, his chin dipping, and his gaze drifting back to the sea. "Why did you come here, Austin?"

"To see you. To talk to you. To—" I'd just told him I'd never lie to him. I could hardly say that and not be a hundred percent

235

honest. "—to stop you."

He was shaking his head even before I'd finished the sentence. "You shouldn't have come. It would have better to leave things as they were last night. That's what I wanted. That's what I *needed*. Why couldn't you have done that?"

"Better for you, maybe." I couldn't keep the note of bitterness out of my voice. I could tell he heard it too by the way his shoulders suddenly stiffened. I took a deep breath, remembering my brother's words of wisdom about ensuring I didn't make this about me, that I didn't start taking Alex's actions personally. He wasn't thinking straight. He wouldn't be intending to kill himself if he was. This was about Alex. I needed to remember that. "I'm sorry. I shouldn't have said that. The last thing I should be doing is having a go at you. I guess I'm just finding it difficult to understand."

He laughed bitterly, the sound almost lost in the wind which seemed to have picked up in the last few minutes. "What's not to understand? My life ended a year ago. I'm just going to make that official."

The words sliced through me like a dagger to the heart. "Don't say that! What happened to you was terrible. It was tragic. No one should have to go through that. But, you've been so brave—"

"Brave!" His head whipped around and he stared at me incredulously. "You don't get it do you?" He shook his head, his mouth settling into a firm line. "Of course, you don't. Why would you? You think I want to do this because I'm sad? Because I miss my family? That's nothing compared to the guilt, Austin. People lose people all the time. But they don't have to wake each day knowing it was their fault. I can't live with that any more. I deserve to die!"

"You think it was your fault?" I was amazed how calmly the words came out when I was shaking like a leaf. The only saving grace was that he was finally talking. He was sharing what was on his mind; the reasons that had driven him to this point. That, and the fact that, despite his words, he hadn't moved any closer to the edge.

"I don't *think* it was. I *know* it was."

I dug my fingernails into the palms of my hand, trying to keep my tone as emotionless as I could manage. "How do you work that one out?"

Alex shifted, his hands gesticulating wildly in an uncharacteristically animated state as he talked. "I thought you said you knew what happened. Oliver" — he said the name like the taste of it was something disgusting in his mouth — "was my boyfriend. Or sort of boyfriend. You see, Al was a bit of a slut. Al didn't really think about the consequences as long as he got a quick fuck. So, Al didn't usually think beyond, he's hot, let's proposition him. No getting to know anyone first for Al. He just got right in there for one-night stands a plenty. Maybe if Al had been just that bit more discerning, Al might have taken more notice of the fact that Oliver Calthorpe was ringing alarm bells even from the first night he met him. And then Al would have never even given him the chance to get obsessed with him."

I thought I knew who he was talking about but I sought clarification anyway. "Al?"

He shrugged. "That's what everyone called me back then."

"You talk about him like he's a completely different person?"

Alex's expression took on a faraway look. "He was. Al was nothing like me. Al was the life and soul of a party. He was confident. He was talkative. A bit slutty, like I already said but I guess that just meant you were in for a good time when you slept with Al."

"Was that Al last night?"

Alex laughed. "Sort of. Maybe Al lite. Al usually topped though, so you didn't get the full Al experience." His look turned wistful again. "You would have liked Al. Everybody did."

If I'd felt out of my depth earlier, that was nothing compared to the way I felt now, with Alex talking about himself as if he were two different people. "I like Alex. Al sounds a little bit too in-your-face for me."

Brown eyes studied me carefully as if he were searching for the truth beneath my skin. I forced myself to meet his gaze steadily. "Maybe." His scrutiny turned back to the sea. "Anyway, Al died in that house. Oliver murdered him too. Alex walked out, and Alex, well...you've seen him, Alex is a bit of a mess. Alex spent every day waiting to put Oliver behind bars and now he's succeeded, he's tired." He let out a long exhalation. "I'm tired, Austin. Surely, you've got to understand that?"

The defeat in his tone was palpable. I didn't know whether him switching back from third person to first person was a good sign. I didn't know anything, including whether I was supposed to agree or disagree with him. I felt like I was running out of time. There may as well have been an hourglass sat next to us, the sand slowly trickling through it. While I was still considering the best way to answer, Alex's body shifted, his neck turning to scan the area. *Is he checking that my brother and Wilko haven't come any closer?* I knew they wouldn't. I might not fully trust Mark, but Wilko was a man of his word, and I wouldn't put it past him to physically restrain Mark if he got any ideas about ignoring what I'd said. In fact, given the simmering antagonism between them, he probably wouldn't need that much encouragement.

"I need you to leave now."

My head shot around. Alex was back to refusing to look at me. "Why?"

"I don't want to do this with you here. You shouldn't have to see it."

My heart stopped, raw emotion clawing at my insides as the world slowed almost to a standstill. Alex hadn't been checking on my brother and Wilko. He'd been seeing how many people were still around. The same scan revealed an elderly couple and their Labrador only. No children. No walking-party. Nobody. "I can't leave."

"Okay."

Okay, what? He's not going to do it? Could it be that easy? Was that all I'd ever needed to do, just force myself on him as an unwanted witness? I let out a sigh of relief, my heart rate beginning to slow somewhat from the frantic pounding of a few moments ago. So, now I just needed to get him back to the car and then there'd be time to address some of the crazy ideas he had, and work out how to get him the help he needed.

Then Alex lurched to his feet, taking the three or four steps needed to reach the edge. Panic held me momentarily frozen in place—able to beg, but not to move—completely uncaring of how desperate I might sound. "Don't, Alex!"

"I have to. I'm sorry."

His voice sounded strangely flat. Like we were discussing something far more mundane than his imminent death. I finally got my limbs to move enough to stand. The higher vantage point revealing that he was even closer to the edge than I'd thought; his toes overhanging the edge. One slight lean forward or one strong gust of wind in the wrong direction and he was gone.

My phone buzzed in my pocket. I could guess who it was. Mark had watched me put it on silent. They'd have been able to see what was happening from where I'd left them and were no doubt just as concerned by the turn of events as I was. I held my hand up in what I hoped was a clear gesture for them not to come any closer, not daring to take my eyes off Alex even for one second. "You don't have to do this." I edged forward slightly, scared that if I moved too fast I'd spook him. "You've got it fixed in your head that there's no other choice. But there is. There always is."

No response. I took another step toward him, making the mistake of looking down, the sheer drop of hundreds of feet to the rocky beach below, making me dizzy, and I wasn't even as close to the edge as he was. I needed to keep talking. We were way beyond the stage where I could make it any worse. "What happened. It wasn't your fault. All you did, was what thousands of people do every day. You met someone attractive you wanted to sleep with. You had no way of knowing how that would turn out. You couldn't see into the future. And I don't think you're being fair on yourself, saying you were a slut. You were how old at the time?"

"Twenty-two."

At least the response proved he was listening. Was he only twenty-three now? I'd never asked his age. I'd always just assumed he was older. "Well, there you go, perfectly normal behavior for a twenty-two-year-old. You can't blame yourself. It was all down to Oliver and no one else. I bet your family wouldn't blame you." My heart broke as tears started to run down his face.

I took another step. It left me perilously close to the edge. One misstep and it wouldn't only be Alex tumbling to his doom. I put my arms out to the side for balance. "We can get through this together. We can get you the help you need. We can find someone for you to talk to. You'd get the final say though on the person. Nobody's going to force you to do anything. They'd have to go through me first." The words tumbled out of my mouth, none of them seeming to have any impact whatsoever. It was just like all of the other times when I'd felt like the correctly chosen words would be the key, only this time it was the difference between life and death. "Why does it have to be today?"

"What?"

"Why do you have to do this today? This place is not going anywhere. I'm not asking you not to jump. I'm asking you not to do it today. To try things my way for a while, and then if it doesn't work out, you can always come back. We can leave here together."

"You still want me?"

The question was so ridiculous I wanted to laugh. "Yes. I still want you. I love you, Alex. I know you don't want to hear that, but it's the truth." I was taking a risk, throwing the thing he'd been so adamant that I didn't say the previous night out there. Perhaps I was being selfish. Perhaps I needed to say it, whatever the outcome was going to be.

"You don't even know me. I don't even know who I am anymore."

"Then we'll find out together, and if you decide that whoever you are, doesn't want to be with me, then that's fine too. I'll still be your friend, Alex. I'll always be your friend, no matter what."

Tears were running even faster down his cheeks. "Do you promise?"

It was the easiest promise I'd ever had to make. "Yes. You just need to step back. Please!"

There was a moment where I felt like it could go either way, where all my senses were heightened: the constant drip of sweat down my back felt like a waterfall, the gusts of wind that had been blowing about our heads felt like a hurricane, and the pounding of my own heart sounded like an acoustic drum. Finally, Alex spoke, the words, the most beautiful words I'd ever heard. "Okay. You're right. I don't need to do this today. I'll step back."

Alex shifted his weight with the intention of doing exactly that. Chalk crumbled beneath his feet. He teetered for a moment, shock registering on his face. I reached out, grabbing onto his arm, and yanking him back with all of my might. We both toppled back onto the grass, my back taking all of the impact. I wrapped him in my arms, squeezing him tight and I cried like I'd never cried before. He cried too, and that was the way Mark and Wilko found us: wrapped in each other's arms, sobbing our hearts out.

Epilogue

Alexander

The view was the same, right down to it being a sunny day.
The sea was calm, just like it had been the last time when I'd stood
in this exact place.

"Ten, nine, eight..."

I peered over the edge at the rocky beach hundreds of feet
below, a tiny dot of a dog and its owner making their way along
it. Well, that was something different. They hadn't been there the
last time.

"Seven, six, five, four..."

There was a plant, growing from a crack between the chalky
rocks. Absurdly, I remembered that too. I remembered thinking
that it shouldn't have been able to grow where it was, that it
should have been scientifically impossible for it to thrive in its
current position. Yet, there it was, still surviving a year later. I
guess that plant and I had a lot in common.

"Three, two, one."

I stepped back, turning around and walking straight into
Austin's outstretched arms, my head finding that comfortable
place on his chest that I knew all too well. His heartbeat thudded

far too urgently beneath my cheek, giving away how nervous he'd been to see me standing so close to the edge again. I'd promised him I'd only stay there for ten seconds and I'd kept that promise. I could have done without him counting down though.

It had been my idea to return to Beachy Head to explore the feelings it evoked one year later. It wasn't just round about a year. It was exactly a year to the day, and what a year it had been.

It had been far from easy. There'd been tears. There'd been anger. There'd been multiple therapists until I'd finally found the one that was the right fit for me, something about her no-nonsense attitude and dry sense of humor finally striking a chord until a tentative bond had been formed. And all through it, there'd been Austin. My rock. My home. The man I loved more than anything else in the world. It was amazing how quickly he could flare up at Wilko, or his brother, or anyone else. Yet with me, he was the very model of patience and understanding.

Even on the worst day of our relationship, the day I'd told him I needed to be single, he'd accepted it stoically. Despite the fact that I could see that my decision was tearing him apart, he'd given me space. Even to the point of helping me look for a new place to live, the apartment next door to Richard Simpkins having been given up a long time before. I'd lasted two days before realizing I'd made a huge mistake. Austin had been just as ready to take me back with no recriminations, no questions asked, and no drama.

I had a new job, carrying out research for a local newspaper. It wasn't the journalistic career I'd once envisaged, but it was a step up from the library and I'd built a couple of tentative friendships with people that worked there. Speaking of friends, therapy had also led me to muster the courage to get back in touch with Jack and David. The three of us had met up in a cafe, Austin waiting outside in the car in case it was too much for me to handle. To say it ended up being a tearful reunion was an understatement. There was hardly a minute that went by where one of us hadn't been crying. It was the first time I realized the damage I'd done to others by removing myself from their lives.

It had been strangely nerve-racking when I'd finally introduced them to Austin. I needn't have worried, the three of them got along just fine and they were regular visitors to our home now.

Therapy had helped a lot, but it still had its issues. There was one major sticking point. My nephew. Everyone seemed to think I needed to be involved in his life and wouldn't listen to my arguments that he was better off not knowing anything about his early life. I'd caved slightly to the point of agreeing to meet his foster parents, more out of curiosity than anything else. They'd seemed like lovely people, with good jobs and enough money that Kieran wasn't going to lack for anything. They'd shown me photos of him — a chubby two-year-old riding around on his tricycle with a huge smile. It had made me cry: he looked so much like Victoria.

Far from changing my mind, it had only served to firm my resolve even more. He was happy. I didn't want to ruin that. Surely, it was better that he never knew that his life could have been very different? Despite my objections, his foster parents had made it clear that I was free to visit at any time. Maybe one day I'd get the urge to see him, but it hadn't happened yet.

I'd been scared for a while that therapy might involve being pressured to go and see the house where I'd grown up. I'd read somewhere that the healing process was about confronting your fears. Even the thought of going back there, dragged me back to some of the darkest points of my life. Patricia, my therapist, had reassured me that if it were ever going to happen, it was a long way in the future, and that it might be something I'd never be ready for. I guess if it told me anything, it told me that I still had an awfully long way to go, that years of therapy still lay ahead. Or perhaps it would be something I'd always need.

Austin shifted slightly. "Well?"

I knew what he was asking. It had taken a lot of convincing to persuade both him and Patricia to let me come back to Beachy Head, and even more convincing before Austin had even considered letting me go anywhere near the edge. "No. There was no urge to jump off." I'd needed to see how much I'd changed in a year. I'd needed to look this place in the eye and see whether I really was a different person from the one that had visited a year earlier.

His sigh of relief stirred the hair on my head. I leaned back so I could look up into the face I loved so much. "You really thought I might still want to?"

He gave a rueful smile. "Not really. But...I don't know...I thought you might get here, and..."

"The old urge might overtake me?"

He shrugged. "Something like that."

I buried my face back in his chest, breathing in the familiar scent. "Well, it didn't. I'm not saying it never will again, but I told you I felt differently. It's like the clouds have shifted, and I can finally see. Does that make sense?"

He nodded. "Perfect sense. Now how about that drink you promised me for coming all the way out here, and having to watch you stand there. Again."

I smiled, standing up on tiptoes to kiss the perpetually smiling mouth. "Sure. Lead the way."

Austin

I didn't mind admitting that I'd been petrified of coming back there. I'd requested a private meeting with Alex's therapist only for her to share the same concerns, which had done nothing to put my mind at rest. Alex, though, had been adamant that it was something he needed to do. He wouldn't let it drop. In the end, I'd decided that it was better to go along with it so that I could be with him, rather than run the risk of him coming alone. At least that way, I could control it to a certain degree. I could implement rules like him staying at least a meter from the edge and for no longer than ten seconds. Even that, had been hard to watch. Only now, with a positively euphoric Alex beside me as we walked hand in hand toward the Beachy Head pub, could I see the benefits.

Life hadn't been all sunshine and roses. Far from it. You don't reach the depths that Alex had and rise like a phoenix from the ashes after only a few months. But we'd faced every obstacle that came our way. There were still obstacles. One thing I did agree with Patricia about, was that Alex should be involved in his nephew's life. After all, it was his quick thinking that had saved the boy, but that was one area that Alex refused to budge on. He could be surprisingly stubborn at times. Like his insistence on coming back to Beachy Head. But I loved that about him. But then I loved everything about him. I loved him when he went back to being quiet. I loved him when the flashes of who he used to be shone through. I just loved him so much that at times it felt like my heart would burst.

He'd changed a lot physically as well. Eating proper meals meant that he was much closer to a healthy weight. His hair was shorter which meant he had nothing left to hide behind. The action was still there sometimes; old habits die hard. But then he'd realize and laugh at himself. The panic attacks weren't gone completely but it had been at least three months since the last one. It was the same with the nightmares. They'd become less and less frequent, and when he did have one, he no longer retreated to the bathroom. Instead, we'd talk about nonsense until he relaxed enough to fall back to sleep.

I carried the soft drinks back to the table, I was driving and Alex was taking a low dose anti-depressant which didn't mix well with alcohol. He smiled as I took the seat opposite him. No matter how frequent they were now, I never forgot how rare those smiles used to be. I still treasured each and every one. He leaned his chin on his hand, the smile still on his face. "Do you feel better now?"

I stared at him incredulously. "Do *I* feel better now? Shouldn't I be asking you that?"

He took a sip of his orange juice. "You were more worried about coming here than I was."

"Maybe."

He leaned across the table, dropping a lingering kiss on my lips. "Definitely."

I shrugged. There was no point in denying it. I thought I'd hidden it better during the drive to Eastbourne, but apparently, he'd seen straight through it. Sometimes, my gorgeous boyfriend was far too observant for his own good. I think he'd spent so long working on his own body language that he could pick up on someone else's in a heartbeat. I mirrored his posture, resting my own hand on my chin. "Can I give you something?"

His eyebrows furrowed. "Depends what it is, whether it's a good thing or a bad thing?"

I reached in my pocket, pulling the small box out and pushing it across the table. I hadn't planned to give it to him until we got home. In fact, I'd no idea why I'd even brought it with me. We were already engaged — just not officially. As in nobody but the two of us knew about it. I sat with bated breath while he opened the box and stared down at the platinum band inside it. "If you don't like it, then I can get it swapped and we can find something else. It — "

His head shot up, tears glistening in his eyes. "I love it!"

He picked the ring out of the box and I watched while he read the six words I'd had engraved on the inside: *"I'll always be there for you."* Tears spilled down his cheeks as he placed the ring on his finger. It wasn't a perfect fit, but it was easy enough to get altered. "You don't have to wear it yet. I just thought that it would be nice once we make it official, but there's no rush for that. This is not me pressuring you. I just saw it, and thought it was perfect, and it doesn't mean I expect one back. I—"

"Austin. Shut up." He dashed the tears away from his face. "A few things." He waited until I nodded to show I was listening. "Firstly, you were the one that suggested that we give it a few weeks before we made it official. I think because you seemed to think I'd change my mind. Which I won't. It's been a few weeks, so I think it's about time we let everyone know. We can tell your parents when we go for dinner on Sunday. Secondly, I *will* be getting you a ring. You just beat me to it." He smiled down at the ring, flexing his hand to get a proper view of it on his finger. "I can't promise it will be as beautiful as this one and I'm going to have to think hard now about what I get engraved on there. Thirdly, it's just an engagement. We both agreed that the wedding might be years from now. Fourthly..."

I raised my eyebrows when nothing was forthcoming.

He pulled a face. "No. That's it."

I sat back in the chair, smiling fondly at him. "Well, that's me told."

Alex looked sheepish for a moment. "Too much?"

Shaking my head, I grabbed his hand, lacing our fingers together, my index finger stroking gently over the ring as I admired the way it looked on his finger. "You could never be too much."

We stared besottedly into each other's eyes for a moment until we remembered where we were and broke apart laughing. I downed half of my Coke in one swallow. "Do you want to go straight back to London?"

Alex thought for a moment. "I thought we might head to the beach. Maybe take a walk down the pier."

"What about the memories?"

He looked momentarily sad. "I can face them if you're there. I can face anything with you by my side."

I tapped the ring and echoed the promise I'd made. The promise I'd keep until my dying breath. "I'll always be there for you."

Author's note

I took a couple of liberties with the legal information in this book. Sentences are rarely passed straight after the verdict. It is more usual for it to be five days to two weeks later. It is unlikely with most courthouses that Oliver would have been led in through the front, particularly through the assembled media. Most courthouses have more discrete entrances.

Thanks, from H.L Day

Thank you so much for choosing to read this book. You've made me really happy. How could you make me even happier? Well, you could leave a review. Then, I'd be ecstatic. :)

About H.L Day

H.L Day grew up in the North of England. As a child she was an avid reader, spending lots of time at the local library or escaping into the imaginary worlds created by the books she read. Her grandmother first introduced her to the genre of romance novels, as a teenager, and all the steamy sex they entailed. Naughty Grandma!

One day, H.L Day stumbled upon the world of m/m romance. She remained content to read other people's books for a while, before deciding to give it a go herself.

Now, she's a teacher by day and a writer by night. Actually, that's not quite true—she's a teacher by day, procrastinates about writing at night and writes in the school holidays, when she's not continuing to procrastinate. After all, there's books to read, places to go, people to see, exercise at the gym to do, films to watch. So many things to do—so few hours to do it in. Every now and again, she musters enough self-discipline to actually get some words onto paper—sometimes they even make sense and are in the right order.

Finding H.L Day

Where am I? I often ask myself the same question.

You can find me on Goodreads

You can find me on Twitter hlday100

You can find me on Instagram h.l.day101

You can find me on Facebook

Send me a friend request or come and join my group - Day's Den for the most up to date information and for the chance at receiving ARCs

Or you can sign up to my newsletter for new release updates.

More books from H.L Day

<u>A Temporary Situation</u>

Personal assistant Dominic is a consummate professional. Funny then, that he harbors such unprofessional feelings toward Tristan Maxwell, the CEO of the company. No, not in that way. The man may be the walking epitome of gorgeousness dressed up in a designer suit. But, Dominic's immune. Unlike most of the workforce, he can see through the pretty facade to the arrogant, self-entitled asshole below. It's lucky then, that the man's easy enough to avoid.

Disaster strikes when Dominic finds himself having to work in close proximity as Tristan's P.A. The man is infuriatingly unflappable, infuriatingly good-humored, and infuriatingly unorthodox. In short, just infuriating. A late-night rescue leading to a drunken pass only complicates matters further, especially with the discovery that Tristan is both straight and engaged.

Hatred turns to tolerance, tolerance to friendship, and friendship to mutual passion. One thing's for sure, if Tristan sets his sights on Dominic, there's no way Dominic has the necessary armor or willpower to keep a force of nature like Tristan at bay for long, no matter how unprofessional a relationship with the boss might be. He may just have to revise everything he previously thought and believed in for a chance at love.

<u>Coming Soon</u>

Catch up with Dominic and Tristan in my seasonal novella: A Christmas Situation.

Due out November 25th 2018

Time for a Change

What if the last thing you want, might be the very thing you need?

Stuffy and uptight accountant Michael's life is exactly the way he likes it: ordered, routine and risk-free. He doesn't need chaos and he doesn't need anything shaking it up and causing him anxiety. The only blot on the horizon is the small matter of getting his ex-boyfriend, Christian, back. That's exactly the type of man Michael goes for: cultured, suave and sophisticated.

Coffee shop employee Sam is none of those things. He's a ball of energy and happiness who thinks nothing of flaunting his half-naked muscular body and devastating smile in front of Michael when he's trying to work. He knows what he wants — and that's Michael. And no matter how much Michael tries to resist him, he's not going to take no for an answer.

Sam eventually chips through Michael's barriers and straight into his bed. But Michael's already made some questionable decisions that might just come back to haunt him. He's got some difficult choices to make if he's ever going to find love. And he might just find that he's too set in his ways to make the right ones quickly enough. If Michael's not careful, the best thing that's ever happened to him might just slip right through his fingers. Because even a patient man like Sam has his limits.

<u>Kept in the Dark</u>

Struggling actor Dean only escorts occasionally to pay the bills. So, his first instinct on being offered a job with a strange set of conditions is to turn it down. No date. Don't switch the lights on. Don't touch him. I mean, what's that all about? What's the man trying to hide? Dean certainly doesn't expect sex with a faceless stranger to spark so much passion inside him. It's just business though, right? He can put a stop to it whenever he wants.

When Dean meets Justin—a scarred, ex-army soldier unlucky in love. Dean's given a chance at a proper relationship. He can see past the scars to the man underneath. He's everything Dean could possibly wish for in a boyfriend: kind, caring and sweet. All Dean needs to do is be honest. Easy, right? But, Justin's holding back and Dean can't work out why. But whatever it is, it's enough to give him second thoughts.

They both have secrets which could shatter their fledgling relationship. After all, secrets have a nasty habit of coming out eventually. The question is when they do, will they be able to piece their relationship back together? Or will they be left with nothing but memories of bad decisions and the promise of the love they could have had, if only they'd both been honest and fought harder.

Refuge (Fight for Survival #1)

If you no longer recognise someone, how can you possibly be expected to trust them with your life?

Some might describe Blake Brannigan's life in the small Yorkshire village of Thwaite as bordering on mundane. His job in a café doesn't exactly set the world alight. But, he's got his own house, a boyfriend, and a close-knit group of good friends. For him, that's more than enough to lead a contented life.

Then in one fell swoop, everything's ripped away when he's forced to flee the village with only his boyfriend for company. He doesn't know why they're leaving. He hasn't got the faintest clue what's going on, and he's struggling to understand the actions and behaviour of a man he thought he knew. A man that it soon becomes clear knows far more about what's happening than he's letting on. A man hiding a multitude of secrets.

When the true extent of what's happening comes to light, Blake is rocked to the core. Peril lurks around every corner. The smallest decision suddenly spells the difference between life and death. If Blake's to have any chance of survival in this new and frightening world, he's going to have to unearth buried secrets, figure out whether love really can conquer all, and face emotional, physical, and mental challenges the likes of which he could never have imagined.

One thing's for sure, when life suddenly boils down to nothing more than the desperate need to find refuge, priorities change. Blake's certainly have.

Taking Love's Lead

Zachary Cole's new personal shopper is stunning in more ways than one. Gone is the staid, professional Jonathan. In his place is sexy, whirlwind Edgar, whose methods and lifestyle are less than orthodox. Still reeling from the experience, Zack can't get him out of his head. He needs to see him again. Even if it does involve dragging his heavily pregnant sister and her dalmatian into his cunning plan.

Sick of being dumped yet again, dog walker Edgar's pledged to stay single and put energy into finding a career more suited to an adult instead. Zack might be extremely tempting...and just happen to pop up wherever he goes, but that doesn't mean he's going to change his mind. He's got bigger priorities in life than a website designer who's after a brief walk on the wild side. Edgar's heart has taken enough of a bruising. He's not prepared to get dumped again.

Zack wants love. Edgar only wants friendship. Can the two men find common ground amid the chaos of Edgar's life? Or is Zack going to find that no matter what he does, there's no happy ending and he'll have to walk away?

Warning: This story contains dogs. Lots of dogs. Big ones. Small ones. Naughty ones. Ones that like ducks, squirrels, and lakes and ones that like to be carried. No dogs were harmed in the writing of this book.